It Ends Tonight

D0957565

A.M. Myers

It Ends Tonight
Bayou Devils MC
Book Four

A.M. Myers

A.M. Myers

It Ends Tonight

A.M. Myers

It Ends Tonight

Cover Design by Jay Aheer
Proofreading by Julie Deaton
Copyright © 2018 by A.M. Myers
First Edition

A.M. Myers

It Ends Tonight

Chapter One
Quinn

"No!"

The scream rips through the silence, yanking me from a restless sleep and I jerk forward in bed as a deep, painful sob racks my body, taking me by surprise. My gaze flies wildly around the four walls of my bedroom before I realize that the monster chasing me only exists in my mind.

Shit.

It was just another dream.

Drawing in a stuttered breath, I press my hand against my clammy skin as tears well up in my eyes and my heart thunders in my chest. I focus on that – the feeling of my pulse beating relentlessly against my palm and the feeling of my skin under my fingertips to pull myself back to the present as the memories get pushed further from my mind. They are so strong but I won't let them win. I can't.

With a sigh, I run my fingers through my hair and

fall back into the mattress. It cocoons me in its comfort and I let out another sigh, more stress seeping out of my system with each breath I draw in. Sunlight dances across the ceiling and birds chirp sweetly outside the window. It's so idyllic that you would never guess that we're in the heart of Baton Rouge right now but I suppose that's why Gram chose this house.

My phone rings on the bedside table next to my head and I turn to look at it before sitting up and scooping it off the table. Scrolling through my notifications, I smile when I see the text from Willa, my assistant.

Willa:
Don't forget.
Staff meeting at nine.

As I type out my reply, another message comes in and I laugh out loud.

Willa:
Don't be late.

Me:
You know I can't promise anything.

Grinning, I open my Spotify app and click on my country playlist while I wait for her reply. It comes as *Born to Fly* by Sara Evans begins playing.

Willa:

It Ends Tonight

Well, you're awake, at least. That's something.

My smile is wide as I shake my head and text her back, letting her know I'll be in on time for our "staff meeting". Staff meeting is a fancy way to describe our weekly rundown since it's only Willa and I working at EQA Events these days but she likes to call them something official so I let her. Maybe it makes her feel better to give it a title since we spend an hour each week just drinking coffee, binging on donuts, and gossiping. Whatever the reason, I'll let her call it anything she wants since she's saved my ass more times than I can count in the past year.

Resolving myself to the fact that I can't procrastinate anymore, I shove the comforter off my legs and stand up as the song changes to *Give It Away* by George Strait. I grin as I pull my tank top over my head and toss it toward the hamper on the other side of the room. There's nothing quite like the king of country to lift my spirits in the morning. Singing along, I shimmy out of my panties and grab my phone off the bed as I walk across the room to the attached bathroom. The sight of the old claw foot tub Gram installed in here catches my attention and I frown.

Too bad I don't have time for a soak this morning.

I imagine Willa's freak-out if she knew I was even thinking about taking a long bubble bath and I grin as I set my phone down on the counter and turn toward the shower. It rings again as I turn the water on and I just shake my head. No doubt it's one of the usual "you're going to be late" texts she sends me every morning. Willa is the perfect assistant for me because my weaknesses are her strengths - like showing up on time. My internal clock is always running about five minutes slower than Willa's but I just can't help it. No matter how much I try to be on time, I always seem to be just a little late. She even tried to set the clocks in my house fast once and I still showed up to work a couple minutes late. Watching her throw her hands up and scream, "That's it! I give up!" was one of the highlights of the week.

The song changes to *Guys Do It All The Time* by Mindy McCready and I grab my phone, turning it up before setting it back down and stepping into the shower. I hum along as I work the shampoo into my hair and dance in a little circle, careful not to fall on the wet tile. Once the conditioner is in my hair, I grab the loofa off of the hook under the shower head and start scrubbing my skin, my mood lifting more and more with each song that plays.

Modern Day Bonnie and Clyde by Travis Tritt echoes through the bathroom as my phone rings again and I whisper a curse. That'll be Willa with my thirty-minute text and I need to be out of the shower already if I have any hope of making it on time. Hurrying, I finish scrubbing my body and wash my face before rinsing everything and turning the water off. I grab my towel and wrap it around my chest as I step out and snatch my phone off the counter. Sure enough, I have two texts from Willa.

It Ends Tonight

I set my phone down and duck out of the bathroom before stopping in front of the closet and thumbing through the rack. When I finally find something I like, I toss it onto the bed and rush back into the bathroom to do my hair and makeup. As I dry my hair, I turn the volume on my phone up again, singing along to each new song that plays and by the time I'm done, I'm excited to tackle a new day - my rough start this morning forgotten.

Dr. Jeffers would be proud.

Tossing the towel in the hamper, I slip into a pair of panties and the matching bra before going back to the counter and curling my hair with big, bouncy curls. Satisfied, I return to the bedroom and grab the white tulle skirt and denim button up shirt I picked out earlier. My gaze flicks to the clock on the wall and I wrinkle my nose.

Shit.

Willa will be texting me any minute with my five-minute warning and I still need to grab my shoes and jewelry. Dashing back into the closet, I pick out my cream heels and a chunky necklace before walking back into the bedroom and sinking into the mattress. Sure enough, my phone rings as I slip my shoes on and I stand up, scanning the room as I fasten the clasp on my necklace. I can't shake the sense that I've forgotten something but I don't have time to look for it now. With my phone in hand, I walk downstairs, smiling when I hear the sweet cooing of the love of my life.

Hiding behind the wall to the kitchen, I peek around the corner and smile as I watch my daughter,

Brooklyn, squeal and smash banana between her fingers. She blows a raspberry and my sister, Alice, giggles so she does it again.

"Brooklyn," I call and her little head snaps up, her brows furrowing as she scans the room for me. Her little grunt when she can't find me draws another giggle out of Alice.

"Where's Momma, Brookie?" she asks her and Brooklyn scans the kitchen, frustration clear on her chubby little face. Placing a hand against my heart, I fight back the sadness rising up inside me. It seems like yesterday I was laying in a hospital bed, giving birth to her, but we just passed her first birthday and she's growing more and more every day. Watching her learn and discover new things is my greatest joy and greatest sadness.

"Brooklyn," I call again, stepping out from behind the wall and her gaze locks onto me almost immediately as she lets out another squeal.

"Mama!"

"Good morning, gorgeous girl. Are you being nice to your auntie?"

"Always," Alice answers, making a face at Brooklyn that she tries to copy. We both laugh and I sigh.

"Hey, thanks for getting up with her this morning." Alice is seven years younger than me and still in college but she didn't hesitate to move her schedule around to help me out when Brooklyn was born. Now, she takes her classes at night so she can watch Brooklyn during the day while I work. It's true what they say about it taking a village to raise a child and honestly, I don't know what I would do without her.

"No problem, you know that. I am going to have to drop her off at daycare around three today, though. I have to go meet with my advisor."

I nod. "That's fine. I should get out of work shortly after that."

My phone rings again and Alice starts laughing. "Willa's going to lose her mind sending you all those texts every morning."

"I think she automates them somehow but you're right, I should get going." I lean down and plant a kiss on top of Brooklyn's head. "Have a good day with Auntie Alice, baby girl. I'll see you later, okay?"

She reaches for me, chunks of smashed banana on her hands as she grunts. I take a step back, shaking my head.

"Mama."

"Sorry, sweet girl, you'll get Mommy all messy."

She starts to fuss and I back away. "I'll go before she gets really upset. Call me if you need anything today."

"Don't worry about us," Alice says as she scoops Brooklyn out of her high chair. "We'll be just fine."

I nod, turning toward the door and grabbing my purse. It doesn't matter how many times I've left Brooke, I still get a tiny little pang in my chest each time I have to walk away from her.

"Love you!" I call over my shoulder and Alice repeats it as I duck out the front door and dig the keys to my Maxima out of my purse. The dense heat practically chokes me as I make the short trek between the front door and the driveway and I say a little thank you to the good Lord for air conditioning. Seriously, I wouldn't survive without it - especially not down here in Louisiana.

As I back out of the driveway, I turn the radio on and flip it to the country station as I think about my day. *Bubba Shot the Jukebox* by Mark Chesnutt starts playing and I smile as I turn it up and pull out onto the street, singing along. The traffic is light as I pull onto the on-ramp and my phone rings, cutting off the music as Willa's name pops up on the screen.

"I'm on the interstate!" I yell as soon as I press the button and her laugh rings out through the car.

"Good. That means I don't have to yell at you today."

I shake my head. "You know, I thought owning my own company meant I could make my own schedule."

"Yeah, that's true, but then you hired me."

"Oh!" I exclaim dramatically. "I see where I went wrong now."

Playing along, she gasps. "That's fine, boss lady. See if I bring you any donuts today."

"Wait! I'm sorry!"

She laughs as I take my exit. "Any preference this morning?"

"What was the one you got me last time?" I ask, my mouth watering just thinking about the donut she brought to last week's staff meeting.

"Maple bacon."

"Mmm," I hum. "Yeah, get me a couple of those again."

"You got it. See you in a few." She hangs up as I turn onto the street that the office is located on.

"Yes," I hiss, spotting the open parking space right in front of our door. Pressing my foot down on the accelerator, I whip my car into the spot and turn it off before I grab my bag and step out. Downtown is bustling with folks headed into work and it invigorates me as I turn to look up at the sign hanging above our entrance.

EQA Events.

Growing up, I never really knew what I wanted to do with my life other than have a family and be a mother but when I started working here with my grandmother, I discovered such a passion for party and event planning that it only made sense for me to take over the business when Gram retired. With the help of Willa, I've managed to expand the business into newer, younger clientele since taking over and I'm proud of all the things I've accomplished in the last year.

"You just going to stand there looking at the front door all day?" a voice yells and I glance down the sidewalk, glaring as Willa grins and approaches me with her hands full of donuts and coffee.

"Need help?"

She nods. "Yes, please."

I take the drink tray from her and usher her into the building before following behind her. The office isn't all that big but it's enough for the two of us right now with a reception area and an office for me in the back. Willa flips the lights on and sets the donuts down on her desk.

"Come back when you're ready," I say as I pass her and step into my office with the coffee in my hand. A few moments later, she joins me and sets the small box of donuts down on my desk before opening it. The smell of sugar fills the room and I take a deep breath as I pull my coffee out of the tray and hand Willa her cup. When we're all settled in with our breakfast and coffee, she pulls out her planner and I pull my calendar up on my computer.

"Okay, go through it for me."

"First up, you have the final meeting with Jenna today to finalize plans for the children's hospital fundraiser."

I nod; double-checking that the time she rattles off matches my schedule as I take a bite of my donut.

"Speaking of, I'm going to need you there with me for the first part of the night, at least, but you should have the second half off if you want to bring a date," I say, passing her the ticket I had put aside for her.

"Oh, I might just do that. What about you? You have a hot date for the event?"

I shake my head, scoffing. "No, I'm going to be working."

"Not for the whole time. Besides, isn't it about time that you get back out there?"

"Uh, no. I don't think so." My heart twinges as I turn away from her. "What do we have coming up the rest of the week?"

She sighs and relief rushes through me as she starts going over the schedule again, letting it go. It isn't like Willa to let me avoid certain topics but this time, I'm glad she did. After my wake-up call this morning, the last thing I need to think about is my love life.

*   *   *   *

"Ma'am," the valet says as I step out of my car and hand my keys off to him with a smile. He waits for me to round the front of the car before he pulls out of the driveway to park it in the lot down the street and I walk into the historic hotel I secured for the charity event in two weeks.

"Miss Dawson," Ronald, the manager, calls from behind the front desk as I step through the door and I smile as I cross the lobby to the desk and shake his hand.

"Hello, Ronald. Is everything ready for me?"

He nods. "Just about, Ma'am. I can take you to the ballroom now and someone will direct your client there when she arrives."

"Lead the way." I gesture for him to step in front of me with my hand and he rounds the desk before leading me further into the hotel.

"How is your day so far, Ma'am?" he asks, glancing over his shoulder at me and I smile.

"Pretty good. Yours?"

Nodding, he turns down a hallway and I readjust the binder in my arms as I trail behind him. "Very good.

The sampler plates should be ready from the kitchen within the next ten minutes but as soon as I drop you off, I'll pop in and check on them."

"That would be perfect, Ronald. Thank you."

"Of course, Miss Dawson," he answers, stopping in front of two gorgeous cherry doors and pulling a set of keys out of his pocket. As he unlocks the door, I suck in a breath and take in the ornate beauty of the building. When I first started planning this charity gala a few months ago, I wasn't sure how well it was all going to come together since time was so short but we lucked out in a lot of ways and people have been eager to help the kids at the children's hospital.

"Here we are," Ronald says as the double doors swing open and the ballroom comes into view. It never fails to take my breath away. The room is extravagant without being gaudy and you can just feel the history of the hotel when you step into the room. It's one of the reasons I worked so hard to secure this venue.

My phone buzzes with a text and I unlock the screen.

Jenna Bueachamp:
Running ten minutes late.

"My client is running a little late so I'd love to check in on the kitchen with you if you don't mind, Ronald," I say as I look up at him and he nods.

"Of course, Miss Dawson. Follow me. I'll send my assistant to the front desk to wait for Miss Bueachamp."

I nod, setting my binder down on one of the tables filling the space. "Perfect. Let's go, then."

Ronald leads me back to the kitchen. There's a flurry of activity surrounding us as we make our way through the employees all rushing around to prepare the tasting menu for Jenna and I. When we reach the back office, Ronald knocks on the doorjamb.

"Chef, I have Miss Dawson for you."

Chef Thomas's head jerks up and he stands, rushing over to us with an outstretched hand. "Miss Dawson, lovely to see you again. Is there a problem?"

"No, not at all. I was just hoping to go over a few things with you."

He nods, motioning to the chair positioned in front of his desk. "Of course."

I sit down and pull up the notes app on my phone before asking him about his plan for the day of the event.

"I'm not sure I know what you mean, Miss Dawson."

"Are you planning on pre-cooking anything or will everything be cooked the day of? Do you have a plan to accommodate the thousand guests who have already RSVP'd yes?"

He nods and launches into his plan for the day of the event, explaining what things can be made early to save the kitchen some time and when he's finished, I stand and hold my hand out to him.

"That sounds good, Chef. I look forward to tasting the dishes you've come up with."

He shakes my hand and I check the time on my phone before turning back to Ronald.

"We should probably get back to the ballroom."

He nods. "Of course, Miss Dawson."

Ronald leads me back through the kitchen as my phone buzzes with another text from Jenna, letting me know that she just arrived at the hotel and I text her back to tell her that I'll meet her in the ballroom. As Ronald and I turn down the hallway to the room, Jenna emerges on the other side, being led by a young man who must be Ronald's assistant.

"Miss Bueachamp, how lovely to see you again," Ronald says as we all stop at the entrance to the ballroom and she smiles.

"Hello, Ronald." She turns to me. "Quinn."

"Hi, Jenna. Shall we get started?"

Her eyes light up and she turns to the ballroom. "Yes, please. I can't wait to see what you've come up."

Ronald leads the three of us into the ballroom and over to the table I left my binder on earlier. As Jenna and I sit down, Ronald and his assistant step back to let us talk in private and I grab the binder, flipping it open to the first page so she can see the two themes I've come up with for the event.

"Now, I know you said you wanted something different from the usual "stuffy" charity events you see so I've come up with two different ideas for you but I will need your choice today so I can get everything prepped in time."

She nods. "That won't be a problem. Let's see them."

"This is the first," I say, pointing to some reference photos I have for the roaring twenties theme I came up with.

"Ooh!" she exclaims. "I really like this."

"And this is the second idea." I flip the page to point to the photos for my second idea, a masquerade ball.

"Damn it, Quinn. You're going to make a liar out of me! I don't know how I'm ever going to choose."

I laugh as I flip the next page. "You don't have to decide quite yet. Just mull it over while we go over the rest of this."

"Okay."

"This," I say, pointing to the page in front of her, "is the artwork I've been able to secure for the charity auction. We have about twenty pieces right now."

"Oh my god. That's amazing."

I laugh, nodding. "Turns out, people are much more willing to help when you mention it's for children."

She laughs and I flip the page, pointing out each piece and its value before we go over the guest list. By the time we finish, the band I scheduled to audition walks in and Ronald leads them to the stage where they can set up.

"As for the music, we can either go with this band, The Renegades, or a DJ and I've got each coming to show you what they can do for you today."

She nods, gazing up at the band as they set up. "Perfect. I'm so impressed with all you've been able to accomplish, Quinn."

"I'm glad you're happy with everything," I tell her, pride welling up in my chest.

"Of course! Your reputation in this town is well

deserved and I'll be letting all my friends know about you. With any luck, you'll be booked for the next year straight."

I smile. "That would be amazing."

"Miss Dawson, Miss Bueachamp," Ronald says quietly as he approaches the table. "The band is ready."

"Let them know they can start."

Ronald nods and heads back toward the stage. He gives the band a thumbs up and the lead singer steps up to the microphone as a low beat pulses through the room. They start off with something a little more upbeat before transitioning into a slower song that will be perfect for slow dancing.

"What do you think?" I ask, turning to Jenna as she bobs her head along to the beat.

"They're good and there's just something about a live band, don't you think?"

I nod. "I couldn't agree more. We can even see if they would be willing to just do the instrumental bit if you didn't want everyone focused on the band all night long."

"Yeah," she agrees. "That sounds like a good idea."

I stand and hold my hand up to signal the band and the music slowly fades away. "Thank you for coming out today, y'all. Can we have a word with you over here?"

"Sure," the lead singer says into the microphone, flashing me a panty-melting grin as he takes a step back and unplugs his guitar. All four band members walk across the ballroom to our table.

"You guys sounded great," I tell them, ignoring the lingering gaze of the lead singer as it trails down my legs. "But we were wondering if you would be willing to just do instrumental versions of your songs and some covers on the night of the gala. This is a charity event for the children's hospital and as fantastic as you all are, we need to keep the focus on the kids."

Lead singer guy opens his mouth and I can tell from the pure disgust on his face that he's going to reject that idea but the drummer steps forward and thrusts out his hand.

"That won't be a problem at all."

I smile and shake his hand. "Perfect. We have one more person to audition but I should have an answer for you all by the end of the day."

"Thank you," he murmurs before they all turn and head back to the stage to pack up their things. My new admirer turns halfway across the room and winks at me before turning back to the stage and I sigh as I sink into my chair.

"Well, someone's certainly interested in you," Jenna comments, her gaze on the stage and I fight the urge to roll my eyes.

"He seems like the type that's interested in anything with a pair of tits." As soon as the words are out of my mouth, I regret them. A blush creeps up my cheeks as Jenna turns to me with her lips parted in an "O" before she starts laughing.

"Tell me how you really feel, Quinn," she sputters through her laughter and my blush deepens. God, it's been so long since I've had a girlfriend to talk to that I blurted out exactly what I was thinking before I could stop myself.

"I'm so sorry. That was so unprofessional."

She waves her hand through the air, dismissing my concern. "Don't worry about it. Besides, I think you might be right."

I glance up as the lead singer blows a kiss to one of the waitresses carrying trays of food across the room to our table.

Typical.

"And that, ladies and gentlemen, is one of the many reasons I'm single," I mutter and Jenna laughs again.

"Girl, I hear you!"

I smile as Ronald stops at the edge of the table with three waitresses, each holding a tray of food.

"Ladies, Chef Thomas has prepared three different meal options for you to choose from. Enjoy!"

He steps back and the first waitress sets her tray down on the table, revealing the two domes underneath before setting one in front of each of us. We work our way through each tray, discussing what Jenna likes and what she doesn't before we finally get the menu nailed down and move on to auditioning the DJ. Jenna and I agree that he's talented but ultimately she decides to go with the band and I make a note to have Willa call them. After going over the guest list and a rough schedule of events for the evening, I grab my binder and slap it closed.

"So, do you have an answer for me on the theme?"

She purses her lips, gazing around the room like she's trying to visualize the space. "I'm thinking with this venue, we have to go with the roaring twenties theme. It just fits this space so well."

"I absolutely agree."

"I'm going to have to throw another event so I can use that masquerade theme though," she replies, pointing her finger at me as she laughs. I nod with a wide grin on my face.

"Anytime."

She claps her hands together with a bright smile. "I'm so excited! I can't wait to see what you do with this event."

"I suppose that means I should get back to the office and start working," I answer as I stand up and grab my bag and binder. She joins me and Ronald approaches us.

"Ladies, can I escort you out?"

I nod. "Yes, please, Ronald. Thank you for all your help today."

"Don't mention it, ma'am. The two of you are always so pleasant to work with."

We follow him out of the ballroom and I frown at the sight of the band's lead singer leaning up against the wall, flicking through his phone. When we pass by him, he glances up and I turn away.

"Sweetheart," he calls, his deep voice like melted caramel. I turn to look at him with a lifted brow.

"Do you really think it's okay to call a woman you don't know "sweetheart"?" I ask and he shrugs as he pushes off the wall and approaches us.

"Don't know your name so what was I supposed to say to get your attention?"

Jenna scoffs next to me as I roll my eyes and take a step back from him. "Literally, anything else."

He takes a step toward me and the hair on my arms stands on end. He's too pushy and I don't like it. When he flashes me that cocky smile I'm sure has worked for him almost every other time in his life, I hold my hand up.

"Your band got the gig and my assistant will call you tomorrow with all the details. You'll need to make arrangements to come in and sign the contract but is there anything else I can do for you right now?"

He nods. "Yeah, how about your number?"

"Have a good evening, Mr…"

"You can just call me Nick, babe," he replies.

"Have a good evening, Nick, and I'll be in touch about the event," I reply, turning away from him and nodding to Ronald to lead the way. He casts a wary glance over my shoulder before he turns away with a determined expression, leading Jenna and I toward the exit.

"He was so hot," Jenna comments, fanning herself dramatically. "Why didn't you give him your number?"

Shaking my head, I suck in a breath. "The answer to that question is complicated."

"Isn't it always?"

We reach the lobby and Ronald turns to us with a smile. "This is where I bid you adieu, ladies."

"Thank you for all your help today, Ronald."

"Of course, Miss Dawson. I notified the valets we were coming so your cars should be out front." We shake hands with the promise to be in touch next week to go over details before Jenna and I walk out into the bright afternoon sunlight where our cars are waiting just as Ronald said. I check my phone and let out a sigh of relief when I see the time.

3:45 p.m.

Brooklyn's only been in daycare for about forty-five minutes and it eases my guilt over her being there at all. If I had it my way, she wouldn't ever leave my side no matter how unhealthy it is.

"Bye, Quinn," Jenna calls as she opens her car door and I wave as I open the door to the Maxima and climb inside. *The Night The Lights Went Out in Georgia* by Reba McEntire is playing as I start the car and I start singing along as I pull away from the hotel and turn toward Brooklyn's daycare, eager to see my baby girl again.

A.M. Myers

It Ends Tonight

Chapter Two
Lucas

Gasping for air, I jerk forward in bed as my eyes fly open and sweat trickles down my cheek. Images from years ago flick through my mind and I pull my knees to my chest, squeezing my eyes shut until I see white dots dancing behind my eyelids. I try to fight back the memories but I'm assaulted from all angles and no matter how hard I try, I can't forget. The smell of rain from that night is so strong that I would swear it was real if it wasn't for the sunlight streaming in through the window and warming my skin. My stomach turns as I remember the clap of thunder that shook the walls of my bedroom just seconds before my whole life changed and I suck in a breath.

Fuck.

I can't keep doing this.

Exhaling slowly, I let my legs fall back to the mattress and run a hand through my hair as I move to the edge of the bed and turn my focus to my phone on the bedside table. I grab it and pause when I notice the date in the corner.

Mom.

Gritting my teeth, I shake my head in an attempt to clear the memories and pain as I open my messages and let out a curse. The last three texts I sent my brother, Clay, remain unanswered and worry eats away at me as I grip the phone tighter and resist the urge to chuck it against the wall. Where the hell is he? My mind drifts to the last three places I've found him, each one worse than the one before and I wonder how long before I'll be getting the one call I have been dreading for years. Anger floods my system, mixing with the fear that's been a constant in my life lately and I toss my phone to the bed before dropping my head into my hands. My life is such a goddamn mess and I don't have a clue how to fix it.

Yelling from downstairs grabs my attention and my head jerks up. I stare at the closed door of my bedroom for a second before throwing the covers off my legs and grabbing my jeans off the floor. The silence that follows is eerie and it makes every hair on my arm stand on end as I pull a shirt over my head and grab my gun from the dresser, inspecting it.

I first joined the Bayou Devils MC ten years ago when it was a true outlaw club, running guns, drugs, and anything else that would make us money. Carrying a piece back then was life or death. Looking back, it's hard to believe that I used to be that guy but at the time, I didn't care about anything but making as much money as I could. After everything I'd been through, I wanted that security. About seven years back, the club fell into chaos. Our president, Blaze, was shot and our brother, Henn, was arrested for selling drugs and is still locked up to this day. Everything changed after that. Blaze wanted to take the club in a different direction and I think in some ways, a lot of us were relieved to go legitimate after so many years of risking it all. But it still feels weird to not have a gun on me at all times.

Tucking the gun into my waistband, I grab my phone off the bed and open the door, scanning the empty hallway before stepping out. Voices drift up from downstairs and I follow them down the steps, stopping when I see everyone gathered in the bar. Moose is off to one side, leaning up against the wall and I join him, nodding my hello.

"What's going on?" I whisper and he shakes his head before nodding to Detective Rodriguez as he sits in the middle of the room with his head in his hands.

"It's Laney."

The club first met Detective Rodriguez three years ago when he was a key player in a case we had a vested interest in and after some initial tension, we all realized that we could benefit from working together. We help him out when we can and he does the same for us when we need a little assistance. Most people balk at the idea of the police working with a group of bikers but with our new mission to help folks, it made sense to us and it's served both sides well ever since. A few months ago, he called on us to help him keep watch over a woman who was being stalked. We only found out later that Laney, the woman, was someone Rodriguez was in a relationship with but that didn't really matter to any of us. We helped her all the same and Rodriguez arrested her stalker only a month ago.

"What about her?"

Moose meets my eyes and from just a look, I know the news isn't good. "She's dead."

Fuck.

"How? What happened?"

He shakes his head. "Don't know. Rodriguez came home from work around eleven this morning and found her in a pool of blood in the kitchen."

"Did Owen make bail?" I ask, referencing the man Rodriguez just arrested for stalking her. Moose shakes his head.

"Naw. He's locked up tight."

I blow out a breath. "Fuck."

Moose nods in agreement and we both turn as Rodriguez stands and kicks his chair behind him. It falls with a crash but no one moves.

"It doesn't make sense! I got the guy. She should have been safe."

Blaze steps forward and slaps a hand on his shoulder as Rodriguez braces his hands on the table in front of him. "Are you sure you got the right guy?"

"Yes," Rodriguez snaps, meeting Blaze's eyes with rage lighting up his gaze. Blaze nods.

"Okay. We'll help you figure this out, Diego."

Rodriguez sinks into a different chair and releases a breath as his whole body seems to deflate. He and

Laney haven't been seeing each other all that long but he seems to have really cared about her. He pulls in a stuttered breath as he shakes his head.

"I promised her I would keep her safe and now she's gone."

Storm sits across from him. "You couldn't have known, man. This is just a fluke accident."

"Don't tell me you actually believe that," he growls, glancing up at Storm, who shrugs.

"If you're telling us that you are sure you've got the right guy locked up, what else am I supposed to think?"

Rodriguez shakes his head. "I don't know what the fuck to think."

"We're here for you," Chance adds, stepping forward in silent support. "But obsessing over it right now, when it's still so fresh, isn't going to do anyone any good."

"It can't wait," Rodriguez answers, his voice on the verge of breaking and I blow out a breath. Chance is right. I remember pain like that and there's no way Rodriguez is thinking clearly right now but I also know how that agony fuels the drive to find answers. It's enough to drive you crazy if you let it.

"Storm, grab a bottle from behind the bar," Blaze instructs and Storm stands as Blaze pulls another chair over to the table and sinks into it. "We'll work this out."

A few of the guys disperse as Storm and Fuzz gather around Rodriguez and throw back a shot in honor of Laney. Pushing off the wall, I check the time on my phone and shake my head. It's damn near three in the afternoon so if Clay went out last night, he should be waking up right about now and I need to go look for him. Blaze glances up as I approach the table and I nod to him.

"I've got to go look for Clay. Give me a call if you need me."

He nods. "We've got it covered for now, I think."

Nodding, I slap his shoulder before giving Rodriguez's a squeeze in support as he downs his second shot, not even sparing me a glance. That's all right. I understand all too well the hell he's going through right now. Leaving them to their drinking, I grab the keys to my truck out of my pocket and step outside, wincing at the bright sunlight beaming down on me.

Shit.

I really need to start keeping regular hours but with my job as a private investigator, that's almost impossible. While everyone else is out living their lives, I have to be working to capture it on film for our clients before coming back to the clubhouse and crashing in the early hours of the morning. Not to mention the jobs we have to do, sometimes at a moment's notice, to help out folks in need. None of it is really conducive to having a life.

Sighing, I slip behind the wheel of my electric blue '67 Chevy and start it up, smiling at the deep rumble she makes as the engine fires to life. Besides my bike, this truck is my pride and joy and I'm like a little kid every time I get behind the wheel.

Shifting my focus to my brother, I pull out of the parking lot and start heading toward one of his usual hangouts. If he's not there, then I'll have to check the next one and so on. It's the same thing I've been doing for the last week and I haven't been able to find him yet and even though he'll come around eventually, I can't just sit back and do nothing. Of course, I've also been doing this for six years and it hasn't made a bit of difference. As I pull up to a stoplight, I run my hand over my face and lean back in my seat, wondering if this whole situation is just hopeless. I hate to think it but some days, it really feels that way.

I glance up to check the light as a large red truck barrels through the intersection, smashing into a little black sedan who had the right away. A cloud of dirt billows into the air as fiberglass sprays everywhere and the car spins three times before coming to a stop just inches from my front bumper. One look at the mangled mess in front of me sends my heart racing. Throwing the truck in park, I open the door just as the red truck backs up, rights itself, and whips past me, fleeing the scene.

Jesus Christ.

"Piece of shit," I mutter as I slam the door and race around to the front of the truck, wedging myself between the two vehicles. "You okay?"

Ice blue eyes, full of fear, turn toward me as the little blonde behind the wheel gasps for air, clawing at her seat belt frantically. It's like one of the damn movies Iris always used to rent when I was a kid - everything seems to stand still as our gazes connect and something I can't quite describe smacks into me, knocking me off balance. It's like a punch to the gut and everything around me blurs because all I can see is the angel in front of me. Even through her fear and the haze of adrenaline, she's beautiful in a classic kind of way that makes me think of summer barbecues, white picket fences, and apple pie.

A car horn blares behind me and it snaps me out of my daze as I reach through the open window and grab one of her hands and give it a squeeze. Another punch to the gut as her skin meets mine and I suck in a breath, my heart racing.

Shit.

What is this?

She settles slightly at my touch and I offer her a reassuring smile.

"Are you okay?"

"Um…" she mutters, blinking and I rip my gaze away from her gorgeous eyes to check her head. It doesn't look like she hit it but she seems really disoriented and the thought that she could be more injured than I realize makes my stomach flip. "I think so."

"Does anything feel broken?" I ask and she tries to move in her seat before wincing and shaking her head.

"No, I don't think so."

I nod. "Okay. Just try to relax and don't move. I'm sure the ambulance will be here soon."

I didn't call them but we've gathered a bit of a crowd now and I see at least three people on their phones. She gasps, jerking my gaze back to her as she tries to move and hisses in pain.

"Whoa, take it easy, babe. Just wait for help to get here."

"My baby!" she exclaims, her worried gaze meeting mine and I glance in the back seat where a car seat sits. My stomach sinks.

Shit.

"I'll check, okay?"

She nods and releases my hand so I can move to the back seat and peer around the car seat. A little head pops forward and a little girl who looks just like her mama flashes me a toothy grin. Smiling, I move back to the front seat and grab her hand again, something settling inside me from her touch.

"I think she's okay."

A tear slips down her cheek. It guts me. "Really?"

"Well, she's grinnin' at me, so yeah, I think she's good," I answer with a nod. I'd do just about anything to ease her worry right now. She lets out a sigh of relief and relaxes back into the seat, closing her eyes. When she doesn't open them back up right away, my heart lurches in my chest and I give her hand a squeeze.

"Hey, darlin'. Stay with me."

She tries to move again and lets out a hiss of pain.

"Just hang on. I think I hear sirens in the distance."

"I need to get her," she forces out through clenched teeth and I shake my head and reach into the car with my free hand to gently turn her face to mine. Our eyes meet and it punches me right in the gut again.

"You won't do her any good if you're hurt. Just wait for the ambulance. I'll keep an eye on her."

She studies me for a second before nodding. "Okay."

"Okay," I repeat with what I hope is a reassuring grin. "I'm Lucas, by the way. What's your name?"

"Quinn." A shy smile sends my heart racing and I shake my head, trying to clear my thoughts. "And that's Brooklyn."

I glance in the back seat again, smiling at the baby girl staring at me in the little mirror secured to the back seat headrest.

"Sorry to be meeting you both like this," I answer and when Quinn doesn't reply, my gaze flicks back to her. She has a faraway look in her eyes and my stomach clenches as fear races through my veins. I squeeze her hand and force her gaze back to mine. "Stay with me, okay?"

"It hurts," she whispers and I nod.

"I know." The sound of sirens fill the air and I let out a breath. "They're almost here, though."

She nods. "How's Brooklyn?"

"Good. Pretty sure she's trying to flirt with me," I tell her, glancing back at the cooing baby again and she laughs before wincing. "Just a little bit longer, sweetheart."

Her eyes close as she nods weakly. "Okay."

"What were y'all up to today?" I ask, desperate to keep her talking so she doesn't pass out on me. Her eyes open and she meets my gaze but I can tell that she's struggling.

"Just got off work."

I wrap both my hands around her hands and rub. Hopefully, that will give her something to focus on so she doesn't lose consciousness. "Yeah? What do you do?"

"I'm an event planner."

"Sounds like a whole lot more fun than my job."

She snorts and lays her head back against the headrest. "And what do you do?"

"I'm a private investigator."

"You're right," she replies, wrinkling her nose as she fights back a grin. Goddamn, she's adorable. "That sounds terrible."

My mouth pops open. "Oh, I see how it is. This is what I get for being a nice guy, huh?"

"Sorry," she breathes as her face scrunches up in pain.

An ambulance and a fire truck stop behind her car and I breathe a sigh of relief as she squeezes my hand, drawing my gaze back to her. "Don't leave me."

The fear in her eyes and her pleading voice stab through me and I nod, squeezing her hand back. "I'm not going anywhere, darlin'."

Two paramedics race over to the car and I take a step back so they can get to her but make sure that she can see I'm still there the whole time as they check her over and the firefighters work to get her and Brooklyn out of the totaled car. Brooklyn comes out fairly easily since her side wasn't the one that was hit and one of the firefighters carries her over to the ambulance in her car seat.

"I think there's some internal bleeding." I hear one of the paramedics say and my heart clenches as I meet Quinn's gaze. She looks fucking terrified and something about it makes me want to rush over to her, knock the paramedics out of the way, and pull her into my arms. What the hell is going on with me?

They get her loaded up onto a gurney and as they pass by me, she grabs my hand again. The paramedics stop and look at me.

"Family only, man."

"I'm her husband," I reply without thinking. I promised her I wasn't leaving her and it's one promise I intend to keep. He studies me for a second before nodding,

"Let's go, then."

"Thank you," she whispers to me as they start pushing her toward the back of the ambulance. I glance down at her and nod.

"Promised you I wouldn't leave you and I meant it."

Her smile is weak but beautiful as she gives my hand another squeeze. I have to release her as the paramedics load her into the back of the ambulance but as soon as I climb in, she's reaching for me again and I can't stop myself from giving her anything she wants. The ambulance pulls away from the accident, racing toward the hospital and I can't tear my gaze away from her eyes.

Fuck, what is this girl doing to me?

It Ends Tonight

Chapter Three
Quinn

Knock!
Knock!

"Come on in," Alice calls as she bounces a sleepy Brooklyn in her lap. Bonnie, my nurse for the evening, opens the door and steps into the room, flashing me a warm smile. I try to reciprocate but I'm in too much pain to manage it.

"How are you feeling, sweetie?" she asks, turning toward the heart monitor on the wall above my head. I grimace.

"I'm in a little bit of pain."

That's a lie. My entire body aches and I fully understand what people mean when they say they feel like they've been hit by a truck.

"Oh, here." She reaches down on the side of the bed, pulls out a little clicker, and presses the button on top. "Just press this and you'll get a dose of morphine."

Relief washes through me as the medicine starts doing its job and I relax back into the bed with a sigh.

"Thank you."

"Of course. And don't be stingy with it either. You want to stay ahead of the pain and it's programmed so you can't give yourself too much."

I nod and she turns back to the monitor, jotting a few things down in her pocket-sized notebook before she turns to check my IV over.

"Now, I'm on for the next fifteen hours so if you need anything at all, you just press that button right there," she instructs, pointing to the call button on the side of the bed. I nod.

"Okay. How long do you think I'll have to stay here?"

"Hopefully, just tonight, Hun. You've got some minor internal bleeding that the doc wants to keep an eye on overnight."

Alice clears her throat and we both turn to look at her. Her face is pale and her hands are trembling as she clings to Brooklyn and it hits me how scary this must be for her after all the loved ones we've had to say good-bye to in our lives. "She's okay though, right?"

"Oh, I'm sure she'll be just fine, honey," Bonnie assures her. Alice's gaze flicks to me and I plaster a smile on my face despite how exhausted I am. "We just want to make sure the bleeding doesn't get any worse."

I didn't think it was possible but Alice's face pales even further and she meets my eyes as Brooklyn fusses and slaps her little hands against her aunt's chest. I understand her worry all too well and I wish I had the energy to reassure her right now but between the pain meds and my long day, I'm not going to make it much longer. Plus, the last thing I want to do is think about the accident right now.

My mind drifts to Lucas, the mysterious stranger who went above and beyond to not only make sure I was okay but to also keep me calm through the whole ordeal. I don't know what it was about him but despite never meeting him before, he made me feel completely safe in the chaos of the accident and I'm disappointed that I didn't even get a chance to thank him for everything he did for me. When we got to the hospital, they rushed me back into the emergency room and I lost him in the shuffle.

"What if it does get worse, though?" Alice asks, her shaky voice breaking through my thoughts.

Bonnie reaches over and pats her hand. "Why don't we just cross that bridge if and when we come to it, okay? I have faith that your sister will be just fine and back home tomorrow."

"Okay." Alice nods but she doesn't look all that convinced.

"All in all," Bonnie continues, turning back to me. "You are one lucky girl, Miss Dawson. I saw the photos from the accident and I'm convinced that you've got someone watching over you."

I smile, thinking of at least three angels I know are watching over me. "Yes, I think I do."

She grabs my hand and gives it a squeeze before backing away from the bed. "All right, now. I'll be back in an hour to check your vitals but try and get some sleep, okay?"

I nod and she turns to Alice.

"Visiting hours are almost over, honey."

"Okay," Alice sighs as Brooklyn yawns and lays her head on her shoulder. "I better get this little one home anyway."

Bonnie ducks out of the room as Alice stands and brings Brooklyn over to the side of my bed. She reaches for me and I take her from Alice's arms before gently folding her into mine, despite the pain it causes me. Her little head plops down on my chest and I bury my nose in her hair and close my eyes.

"Be a good girl for Auntie Alice," I whisper to her, tears welling up in my eyes. In her thirteen months of life, I've never once spent the night away from her and it's tearing me up to have to do it now. I didn't expect it to be this hard to say good-bye. Turning to Alice, I smile. "Thank you for all your help and I'm sorry. I know you'll probably have to skip your class again tomorrow night."

She rolls her eyes. "You were in a terrible car accident, Quinn, so everyone understands and if they didn't, fuck 'em."

"Fuck 'em?" I ask with a laugh. "If Gram were here, she'd pop your mouth for that one."

Her face falls and she sucks in a breath. "Don't you dare go dying on me, you hear?"

"I'm not going anywhere, Sis. You're stuck with me for life."

Tears well up in her eyes as she grabs my hand. "I'm holding you to that."

Before I can respond, a little snore from the baby on my chest interrupts us and we both start laughing.

"You'd better get her home and in her own bed or she'll be a bear tomorrow."

Alice nods. "Yeah, the girl does love her sleep. Wonder where she gets that from?"

"Dunno," I lie, making a face at her as she laughs. We gently maneuver Brooklyn from my arms to Alice's and she leans down to give me a hug.

"We'll come check on you in the morning, okay?"

I shake my head as she pulls away. "Just wait for me to call you. There is no sense in making two trips if they really do decide to discharge me."

"You sure?"

I nod my head. "Yeah. I'll be all right."

Her lips purse as she studies me for a moment before nodding. "Okay, but I want you to call me if you need anything. Oh, and you also need to tell your body to stop bleeding."

"You got it. I'll focus on healing my wounds with the power of my mind."

Fighting back a smile, she nods. "Perfect."

Alice leans down and kisses my cheek as I place a gentle kiss on the top of Brooklyn's head. She takes a step back and I can tell she's reluctant to leave me.

"I promise you I'll be fine, Alice. Go home and get some rest, okay?"

She stares at me for a moment before nodding and walking to the door to my room. "Love you," she calls over her shoulder.

"Love you more."

Once they're gone, I lie back on the bed and close

my eyes, slowly blowing out a breath. My eyes feel heavy but my mind is racing at a hundred miles an hour and random images from the crash keep popping into my mind. My hands start to shake as I piece it all together. I remember glancing over and the only thing I could see was the front grill of the truck just seconds before it slammed into the car. Then, the world was a blur as the car spun for what felt like forever and the blink of an eye all at the same time. And then he was there.

Sighing, I open my eyes and stare up at the florescent lights on the ceiling. Maybe the accident rattled me even more than I realized since I can't seem to shift my focus from Lucas, a man I don't even know. My love life in the last two years has been woefully lacking and no one has even caught my eye. God, I'm not even sure that I'm capable of being in a relationship anymore but something about Lucas cemented the inkling of a thought in my mind and it's not as if I'm planning our wedding after only one chance meeting but I am thinking – what-if?

"Quinn?"

Turning toward the door, I gasp at the sight of Lucas standing in the doorway. "What are you still doing here?"

He smiles and strolls into the room like I somehow conjured him up just by thinking of him as I try to get my racing heart under control. "I couldn't leave without making sure you were all right."

"Oh," I whisper, my cheeks heating. Who the heck is this guy and why does he have such an impact on me? "You've been waiting here this whole time?"

He nods. "Yes."

"Oh."

Our eyes meet across the room and butterflies dance around in my stomach as his blue eyes study me, almost like he can see right through me.

"So… are you? Okay, I mean…" he asks.

I shrug. "Um… I think so?"

"You sound really sure of yourself," he answers, chuckling as he moves further into the room and sits on the edge of the bed. Just the feeling of him sinking into the mattress, knowing he's that close to me, is driving me crazy. I think back to the way he held my hand at the accident and I wish he'd do it again.

"Well, they used very scary words like internal bleeding but no one seems all that concerned about it so I've decided to just go with it. Or maybe that's the morphine talking." I hold up the button Bonnie handed me and grin. He laughs, the kind of laugh that warms you all over and the hair on my arms stands on end.

"You're a lightweight," he teases and I nod.

"Oh, totally. I barely even drink." Reaching across the sheets, I grab his hand because I can't possibly resist anymore and he meets my gaze. Just like before, a spark of *something* races up my arm and my heart skips a beat. "Thank you, by the way. For coming to my rescue earlier and for waiting around all afternoon to make sure I was okay. I think you restored my faith in humanity."

He nods. "Of course. I couldn't just leave you there like that piece of shit did."

"I suppose I need to talk to the cops, huh?"

"Yeah," he answers. "I have a buddy on the force

and I would have asked him to handle this personally but he just lost someone close to him and he's not really in a good place."

"Oh, no. Please. You've already done so much for me."

He shrugs. "It's no big deal. I already talked to a detective and gave him my statement so they should catch the scumbag pretty fast."

"Thank you."

He grins and my insides turn to mush. God! He is so damn handsome. How the hell did I not notice that before? I mean, I know I'd just had my brain slightly scrambled but he's not the kind of man that blends into a crowd with his impressive build and armfuls of colorful tattoos. Not to mention his eyes, which remind of the deepest, bluest ocean. Something about them just draws you in and makes you feel at ease. Or maybe that's just me.

"You don't need to keep thanking me. I'm just glad I could help you and your daughter. Speaking of which, how is she?"

"Good. Not a scratch on her, in fact. She's home and sleeping soundly in her bed."

He flashes me that damn smile again. "Good."

"I'm sorry if we ruined any plans you had today," I say, thinking of the hours he's spent here. Shaking his head, he gives my hand a squeeze.

"Don't worry about it. I think this turned out way better than my other plans."

"Yeah?" I ask, fighting back a smile as he meets my eyes. "What were your other plans today?"

His face falls and I instantly regret asking the question. "I was going to look for my brother."

Before I can ask him anything else, Bonnie steps into the room. When she spots Lucas perched on the edge of my bed, she flashes him a stern expression.

"Visiting hours are over, young man."

He stands and gives my hand a squeeze like he regrets having to let go before he releases it. I feel weird without it and I'm just doped up enough to not care if I shouldn't be thinking things like that.

"I'm sorry, ma'am. I'll get out of your hair."

Turning back to me, he smiles and I feel like I'm melting into the bed. "I'll be back tomorrow to check on you."

"Oh, you don't have to do that."

He flashes me a look that makes it clear that he'll be back tomorrow come hell or high water and I have a love/hate relationship with the way it makes me feel.

"Get some rest, okay?"

I nod. "Okay."

He winks before turning and walking out of the room. Bonnie watches him leave before walking over to the bed and grinning at me.

"Girl, your man is fine as hell, no offense."

"None taken," I reply, shaking my head. "And he's not my man."

Her brow arches as she looks at the door. "You sure he knows that?"

"Yes. We just met today."

She hums as she takes my vitals. "Stranger things have happened, my dear."

Glancing back at the open doorway, I try not to give too much weight to her words but I'm already looking forward to seeing him again tomorrow.

Shit…

*   *   *   *

Alice:
Any news yet?

Smirking, I shake my head. She's so damn impatient that she's been texting me since six this morning but I know how she worries.

Me:
No, not yet.
How's Brooklyn?

Setting my phone down on the bed, I turn back to the TV and sigh. The only thing I've been able to find to hold my interest is HGTV and I'm getting a little tired of home renovation shows. The doctor came back this morning and they took me down for another scan but that was a while ago and I'm getting anxious to learn if things look better today. My entire body aches like nothing I've ever felt before and all I want to do is go home, take a nice long bath, and crawl into my own bed. My phone buzzes from the mattress and I scoop it up.

Alice:
Okay. She misses you, though.

Me:
Hopefully, I'll be home soon.

After I set my phone down again, I lie back on the bed and close my eyes, trying desperately to not think about the last time I was at this very hospital. It was one of the very worst nights of my life and it wasn't until I was alone last night that I realized where I was. The panic almost overwhelmed me but I was able to get a handle on things before they got out of hand. Now, I just want to get out of here and quite frankly, I'd be thrilled to never step foot in this place again. The memories from that night threaten to bury me and I focus on my breathing until I feel in control again, pushing the images from my mind temporarily.

Opening my eyes, my gaze drifts to the door and my heart sinks. Why do I keep checking the door for a man I don't know? Especially since he's already done so much for me. He owes me nothing but I'm eager to see him again. God, that's stupid. So what if he does interest me? It's not like I can do anything about it. Not right now, at least. I'm still a mess emotionally and even though I'm getting better each and every day, it's not a good idea to let someone in. Burying my face in my hands, I groan. I wish I could just figure him out. He's contradictory on every level and it's been driving me crazy since the moment his eyes met mine. Maybe he should have scared me with his arms full of tattoos and his large, muscular frame but something about him put me at ease immediately - like I already knew him. Despite my past, I felt safe with him and that's something I haven't been able to say in two long years. Then he flashed me that easy going smile and my heart rate slowed despite the fact that I'd just been hit by a truck. Laying my head back, I sigh.

I'm absolutely hopeless.

"Quinn?" His voice warms me like a cup of tea on a rainy afternoon and I suck in a breath as I glance up, fighting back a smile.

"Lucas. You came."

He walks into the room with a bouquet of flowers and that damn smile on his face as my heart beats a little faster. "I told you I was going to check in on you today."

"Yeah," I answer with a shrug. "But most people say a lot of things they don't mean and you've already been so kind."

"Well, let's just get one thing straight now. I'm not most people and I never say things I don't mean."

I tilt my head to the side as I study him. Usually, I would assume that a statement like that was just a line but there is something about the way he says it that makes me believe him. "That's refreshing."

"Here," he says, ignoring my comment as he hands the flowers to me. "These are for you."

I take the bouquet and smile at the bright cheery sunflowers wrapped up in brown paper before bringing them to my nose. When I meet his gaze again, I smile.

"Thank you. I love sunflowers."

He nods, sitting in the chair next to the bed. "You're welcome. I just wanted to get something to brighten your day. How are you feeling?"

"Sore and ready to go home."

"Have they given you an update yet?"

I shake my head. "No. They took me for a scan earlier but I haven't heard from anyone since then."

"Okay. Well, I'll keep you company until then."

"No," I blurt out, shaking my head. "You really don't have to do that. I don't want to intrude."

His brow arches and he leans forward, meeting my eyes with his intense blue gaze and I suck in a breath. "Didn't we go over this already? If I didn't want to be here, I wouldn't be. Besides," he continues as he leans away from me and lies back in the chair, "I have some news for you."

"Oh?"

He nods. "They caught the son of a bitch that hit you and he was still wasted when they arrested him last night."

"Wow," I whisper, lying back in the bed.

"You sound surprised."

I glance over at him and as soon as our eyes connect, I feel it rocking through my whole body. What the hell is going on here? "I guess I assumed he was going to get away with it."

"Hell, no. I wasn't letting that happen."

"You had something to do with this?" I ask, my brow arching.

"Well, I told you that my friend was unavailable

but I pulled some strings to make sure that bastard ended up behind bars."

Who is this man?

I see people everyday that can't even be bothered to hold a door for someone and offer up a smile in passing but he's been incredible since the moment we met.

"Why?"

His brows furrow. "Why what?"

"Why would you do all this for me? I mean, we don't even know each other."

He's quiet for a moment as different emotions flicker across his face and finally, he sighs. "I don't know why I'm doing it except that I feel compelled to. There's something different about you, Quinn, and there are other things I could be doing right now but all I want to do is sit here and talk to you some more."

"Well, I suppose I can do that," I whisper, my heart racing in my chest. It's scary and I have absolutely no idea what I'm doing but he echoed something inside me that I was barely able to admit to myself and I can't turn him away. At least not today.

"Miss Dawson?" Someone asks from the doorway and I pull my gaze from Lucas as the doctor walks into the room.

"Dr. Hudson, how do things look?"

He glances down at the chart in his hand as he nods. "Good. It looks like the bleeding has stopped."

"Does that mean I get to go home now?"

He laughs. "Yes. I have Bonnie getting your discharge paperwork ready right now. There are a few things that I want to go over, though."

"Okay."

He sits on the edge of the bed. "I'm willing to let you go home on a few conditions. You need to remember that you've been in a serious car accident, okay? I want you to stay in bed for the most part over the next few days and then you'll need to come back in for another scan to make sure things still look good."

"I can do that," I say even though the thought of being stuck in bed for days is unappealing.

"Good. I sent a prescription for pain meds down to the pharmacy and your friend can go pick them up whenever," he says, glancing over at Lucas, who stands.

"On it."

Before I can object, he leaves the room and Dr. Hudson flashes me a smile before making me promise to return for a follow-up scan in three days. Once he's gone, I lie back in bed and sigh. I'm excited to go home and see my baby girl and I know Alice will be relieved that I didn't need surgery. Grabbing my phone, I send her a text to let her know I'll be discharged soon but she doesn't reply right away so I toss it back down on the bed.

After a few minutes, Lucas comes back with a brown paper bag from the pharmacy and I smile at him as he sets it down on the table next to my bed and sits down in the chair again.

"Thank you for doing that."

"Not a problem. Has the nurse been by with the discharge paperwork yet?"

I shake my head. "No, not yet, and I can't get

ahold of my sister to come pick me up."

"I've got you covered, Darlin'."

I watch him for a moment but decide not to fight it since he'd probably just win anyway. As I nod, I grab my phone and text the new plan to Alice. She replies right away to tell me she'll have things ready for me.

"Thank you. Again."

He laughs, crossing his legs as he leans back in the chair. "You don't have to keep thanking me, Quinn. Like I said, I want to be here."

"Don't you have a boring job to get back to?" I ask, recalling a memory from the accident and he laughs again.

"Usually, yes, but things are slow at the moment."

"Oh, I see," I muse, fighting back a smile. "You're just bored."

His blue eyes sparkle as he nods. "Painfully. You're actually saving me here."

"I suppose I don't have anything else to do today."

He laughs, that deep, rich laugh that warms me to my very core and makes me feel all bubbly. Before he can respond, Bonnie walks in with a handful of paperwork.

"All right, Honey. Let's get you out of here."

I sit up as she pulls the table over to the bed and sets the forms down on top. She goes through everything the doctor already told me before having me sign in a few places and Lucas leaves to pull his truck up to the entrance as Bonnie helps me get dressed. Each movement hurts and I hiss and whine the whole time before blowing out a breath as I collapse into the wheelchair.

"So, I notice your not man is back again today," Bonnie muses as she pushes me out of my room and I laugh.

"Yes, you're very observant."

She playfully slaps my shoulder. "Don't sass me, young lady. You going to tell me the story behind the two of you?"

"He was there when the truck crashed into me yesterday and he sat with me until the ambulance got there and on the ride to the hospital."

"Hmm," she hums and I drop my head back to look up at her.

"What?"

She shakes her head and I look forward again. "Sounds like a mighty fine man to me. Those don't come along everyday, you know."

"I do know," I whisper, my mind flashing back to the last relationship I was in. God, I can't believe it's been just over two years since that relationship ended. Things were so different back then and sometimes, I wish I could go back to a time when my life was so much simpler but then I wouldn't have my baby girl and she's worth any hell I had to trudge through.

"You going to go out with him?" Bonnie asks, bringing me back to the present as we slowly make our way down the hallway to the entrance.

"Oh, I don't know," I blurt out before I get a chance to consider the option. "Besides, he hasn't even asked me."

"He will," she replies, sounding so certain and I laugh.

"How long have you been on shift, Bonnie? I think you might need some rest."

She scoffs but when I glance up, there's a hint of a smile on her face. "Girl, I could work seventy-two hours straight and I would still see the way that man looks at you. Besides, when you do what I do, you really start to understand people and I bet money that he asks you out."

"Don't you mean you *would* bet money that he'll ask me out?"

"Hell, no! I put fifty bucks on it with the other nurses so you have to come back and tell me when I win my money."

I laugh as she rolls me out into the bright sunlight and Lucas climbs out of his gorgeous blue truck before rounding the hood and opening the passenger door for me. Bonnie helps me stand and I wince as I walk the few steps to the truck and climb inside.

Damn, maybe I got more banged up than I realized.

Once I'm comfortable, Lucas leans into the car and grabs my seat belt, holding it up as he silently asks for permission to help me. I nod and he leans in further, securing it near my other hip and his scent surrounds me. He smells so damn good but it's subtle enough that I want to lean into him for a better sniff. I barely resist the urge and when he pulls back, I see Bonnie grinning behind him.

"You good?" he whispers, his face just inches in front of mine and I wonder how it would feel to lean in and kiss him. It's been so long since I've kissed anyone but then again, it's never been this tempting either.

"Yes."

Nodding, he drops his gaze to my lips before taking a step back and once he's gone, I suck in a breath. Clean air fills my lungs and my senses slowly return as I glance over at Bonnie. She winks at me as Lucas shuts the truck door and I roll my eyes. With a business to run and a daughter to raise, this is the last thing I need to be thinking about, but damn if he doesn't look good rounding the hood of the truck and slipping behind the wheel.

"Okay?" he asks as he puts the truck in gear and I nod, not willing to rip my gaze from his. He's the one to finally look away as we pull out of the hospital parking lot and slowly roll down the street. He hands me his phone and I scowl. "Go ahead and put your address in the GPS for me."

I nod and pull up the GPS on his phone before typing my address in the search bar. Once it's directing us, I hand the phone back to him. He glances over at me with a grin.

"Thanks."

I nod, peeking over at the speedometer. "You can go faster, you know."

He glances over at me. "You sure? I didn't want to hit a bump and hurt you."

"I think that's something I'm just going to have to deal with. Besides, I'd like to get home sometime this week."

"Okay," he says but he doesn't sound convinced. He speeds up a little and turns to me again. "You want to listen to music?"

I nod. "Yeah, that sounds good."

"Any preference?"

"Country," I reply and smile when he fights the urge to wrinkle his nose. He doesn't like it but he turns on the country station anyway and *The Shake* by Neal McCoy fills the cab. When he glances over at me, I smile.

"Thank you."

"Sure." He nods. "But let's just keep this our little secret."

I pretend to lock my lips and throw away the key. "My lips are sealed."

"Thank God. I don't think the club would let me live it down if they heard me listening to country music."

I scowl. "The club?"

"Oh, yeah. I'm a member of the Bayou Devils," he replies, glancing nervously at me and I flash him a reassuring smile. I've heard of the club before and I know they still fight against their old reputation in this town but I know differently.

"I've heard of you guys. You actually helped one of my brides a few years back."

He glances over at me, his brow furrowed. "Huh?"

"I just planned a wedding for a woman who y'all helped escape her abusive ex about four years back."

"No kidding?"

I shake my head. "Nope. Her name is Lucy Wilson and all she could talk about during the planning process was how she wouldn't even be here without y'all. Now, she's married to her soul mate and they have a baby on the way."

"Oh, yeah. I remember her. That's amazing," he says with a grin so genuine I have no choice but mimic the expression. "I'll have to fill the guys in when I get back to the clubhouse. They're going to love it."

"I was so inspired when she told me about you guys. It's really incredible what you're doing."

He shakes his head. "Naw, we're just doing what we can."

"And still so humble about it. How did you find yourself in the hero role?"

Laughing, he pulls into my driveway. "Well, that is a long, complicated story that I'll have to save for another time."

"I'm going to hold you to that," I tell him and he smiles. Reaching down at my side, I release the seat belt and reach for the door, already wincing. I can't wait to slide into my bathtub and melt these aches away.

"Hey, let me help you," he commands and jumps out of the truck before I can object. After jogging around the front of the truck, he opens my door and gently lifts me out of the seat before setting me back down on the ground. He grabs my bag and shuts the door before grabbing my hand and helping me up the front walk.

"I'm like a damn cripple," I grumble and he gives my hand a squeeze.

"Yeah, well, you got hit by a truck, remember?"

I shiver as the image of the truck's grill filling my window pops into my mind. "Believe me, I remember."

The front door opens and Alice steps out onto the front porch with Brooklyn in her arms as she studies Lucas. She meets my gaze and relaxes when I flash her a smile.

"Look who's here, Brookie," she calls and Brooklyn squeals, clapping her hands in front of her.

"Mama!"

"Someone missed you," Lucas says and I nod, my heart swelling at the sight of my little girl.

"I missed her, too."

When we get up the steps, I collapse into the swing and Alice hands Brooklyn over to me. I immediately kiss her forehead and hold her close, a sense of peace flowing through me now that she's back in my arms.

"Who are you?" Alice asks and I gasp, my head snapping up.

"Alice!"

Lucas laughs, holding his hands up. "No, it's okay. I'm Lucas. I was there when Quinn got in her accident yesterday."

"And why are you here today?" she asks.

"Oh my god, enough with the third degree. Alice, this is Lucas. Lucas, this is Alice, my baby sister."

She studies him for another moment before nodding. "Hurt my sister and I'll bury you in parts in the back garden."

"Jesus Christ, Alice!" I hiss as Lucas laughs, nodding his head.

"Noted."

She turns to me. "Do you need help getting up to your room?"

"I might be stuck on the couch for a few days," I admit. Just thinking about going up all those stairs is wiping me out. Alice takes Brooklyn from my arms and I slowly push myself off of the swing.

"I could carry you," Lucas suggests and I turn to him, unsure, but the thought of lying in my comfy bed wins out and I nod.

"Okay."

He leans down and scoops me up like I weigh nothing and it does crazy things to my insides. God, this little crush is turning into a big crush rather quickly.

Not good, Quinn.

Not good at all.

I wrap my arms around his neck and he follows Alice into the house as she points to the stairs. "Her room is up there. I just need to feed Brooklyn real quick."

Lucas turns toward the stairs with me in his arms and our eyes meet, our faces only inches away from each other.

"I'm still not sure why you're being so nice to me but thank you for everything you've done these past two days. I really do appreciate it."

He smiles and I just want to melt in his arms. "You're welcome, Quinn."

When we reach the top of the stairs, I pat his chest. "Okay, you can put me down now."

Nodding, he sets me down and grabs my hand again, helping me hobble along as we walk toward my bedroom. His hand feels so warm and strong in mine and for some reason it makes me feel safe in a way I haven't felt in almost two years. As soon as he lets go, he'll take that feeling with him and it's killing me to let it go. He makes me feel like the woman I was before everything fell apart and it's a little alarming how quickly I'm getting used to the feeling. What do I do when he leaves? How do I go back to this broken shell I've been lately?

Once in my bedroom, he helps me climb into bed and I pull the blankets up around me, sighing as my body relaxes back into the mattress.

"Can I see your phone?" he asks and I point to the bag he set on the floor next to the bed.

"In there."

Closing my eyes, I start to nod off when he places the phone in my hand. I open my eyes and meet his intense, enchanting gaze. "You have my number now and I want you to call me if you need absolutely anything, okay?"

"You've already done so much for me," I protest and he shakes his head.

"I'm serious. Call if you need anything and I'll be here."

My eyes feel heavy, the pain medicine dragging me to sleep again and I shake my head as I whisper, "Who are you?"

The last thing I feel before sleep claims me is his warm lips pressed against my forehead and for the first time in a long time, the nightmares don't plague my night.

It Ends Tonight

Chapter Four
Lucas

Sighing, I set my cup of coffee down on the bookshelf and sink into the lounge chair in the corner of my room before running my hand over my face and closing my eyes. I'm fucking exhausted and as much as I would love to sleep for the next thirty-six hours, I can't. Not until I find Clay. I spent most of last night hitting his usual hangouts again and even after two showers, I still feel fucking dirty. Each place was more run down and dirty than the one before it and I was accosted by numerous women looking to suck my cock in exchange for just a little bit of dope - anything to get their next fix. It's disgusting and looking back now, I can't believe I used to hang out in places just like that but back then, I didn't care about much.

I grab my coffee and take a sip before pulling my

phone out of my pocket and stare at it. I have one more person I can talk to before I have to start calling hospitals and morgues but I've been avoiding this conversation for six damn years and I don't know that I'm prepared for it. With a sigh, I set my coffee back down and dial her number.

"Hey, honey! How are you doing?" Iris asks and even through the phone, I can hear the cheery smile in her voice and a rock forms in my stomach. Iris is one of the only people that's ever given a damn about Clay and I know telling her the truth will disappoint her but I don't know what else to do anymore. I'm out of options.

"I'm good, Riz. How are you?"

There's a pause on the other end of the line and I turn to the window, my heart racing.

"You wanna tell me the truth this time?"

Shit.

I know better than to try and bullshit Iris. I've never been very good at hiding anything from her and she doesn't have the kind of personality that would let me get away with lying to her. I take another sip of coffee before setting it down on top of the bookshelf with a sigh.

"Uh... have you seen Clay at all lately?"

There is this nagging sensation, deep down in my gut, that's screaming at me to pay attention, to be on top of my game but I have no idea why. It's not like Clay hasn't disappeared for long stretches at a time before.

But this time feels different.

"No, I haven't. Is something wrong?"

I sigh and close my eyes. When Clay first started using, I thought I could handle all of this on my own but now, it's six years later and I'm no closer to managing my brother and his addiction than I was when it all started.

"Yeah, something is wrong, but it's not really a conversation we should be having over the phone."

"I see," she murmurs and my stomach rolls.

Shit.

I shouldn't have said anything.

"I'm sorry…"

"Don't you dare," she cuts me off. "Don't apologize for finally including me."

I nod despite the fact that she can't see me. "Okay."

"Why don't you come round for a meal in the next day or two and we'll talk?"

"Yeah," I answer. "I can do that."

The smile is back in her voice when she says, "Good. And I'll keep my eye out for your brother until then."

"Thank you, Iris."

"Oh, hush, boy. I think you know by now that I'd do just about anything for you boys. Y'all are family."

I smile, my thoughts drifting back to when Clay and I first met Iris years ago and I nod. Despite the fact that we're not related, Iris has been family to my brother and I since the moment she inserted herself into our lives.

"All right, I'm going to let you go."

"Okay, sweetie. I'll see you soon."

We hang up and I sigh as I lean back in the chair and grab my coffee, going over Clay's favorite hangouts in my mind. I fucking hate going there and searching for him but even worse is the feeling of my worry eating away at me when I don't find him. It's like one of those tapeworms you see on medical TV shows - the kind of thing that you never even realize is there until it sucks so much life out of you that you're barely hanging on. In the beginning, I worried about my brother but now, it's consuming me, devouring another piece of my soul each day and I worry that neither one of us is going to survive this mess. So many people have told me to cut ties but they don't understand - none of them do. Clay is all I've got left and who he is now, the chaos he's created in both of our lives - is all my fault.

Sighing, I throw my free arm over my eyes and try to clear my mind. A laugh bubbles out of me and I shake my head.

What a fucking joke.

My head is never clear... except recently when I'm around Quinn. My mind drifts to yesterday as I brought her home from the hospital and carried her up to her room. The thing is she felt so damn good in my arms in a way that I've never felt before and it was more than her lush curves or soft skin. When I'm with her, I feel free. Maybe she's just a pretty distraction, an easy way to redirect the toxic thoughts that are always spinning in my head but I don't know that I care anymore. I need to see her again because even after only spending a few hours with her, I'm clinging to that liberation. And then there's that little voice in my head that keeps screaming that she's different from all the other girls but there's too damn much going on in my life right now to even think about that.

My phone rings and I jerk up, glancing down at my phone as my arm falls from my face. A Baton Rouge number flashes on the screen and I scoop it up, praying it's not the morgue.

"Hello?"

"Hey. It's Diego."

My heart rate slows as I blow out a breath. "Hey, man. What's up?"

"You're going to want to get down to the station."

I jerk forward, spilling coffee on the floor. "Why? What's going on?"

"I've got your brother in a cell here."

"Jesus Christ," I hiss, shaking my head as I stand and set the half empty cup of coffee down on the bookshelf. "Do I need to bring bail?"

"Naw, you're good. They just kept him until he sobered up."

I nod. "Okay. I'll be there in fifteen."

We hang up and I chuck my phone across the room, irritated when it lands on the bed instead of smashing against the wall. Fuck this shit. Why am I jumping up to go bail him out of jail when he's just going to be right back there next week or the week after that? He's fucking using me but both of us know that I'll continue to let him.

Shoving myself up from the bed, I stomp across the room and grab my phone before going to the dresser and pulling the lockbox I keep in the underwear drawer out. I grab the chain from around my neck and pull it off before jamming the key into the lock and flipping the top open. Stacks of cash stare back at me and I grab one, thumbing through it before shoving the whole thing in my pocket. I know Rodriguez said he covered it but I have to pay him back for all the help he's given me. I couldn't even tell you how many times Rodriguez has kept my brother's issues under wraps after he's been arrested.

Once the lockbox is secure again, I shove it back in the drawer, slip the chain around my neck, and grab my bike keys off the dresser before yanking the door to my room open. I almost crash into Streak, the club's cyber expert, as I step out into the hallway. He holds his hands up in surrender

"Whoa, where's the fire?"

I shoot him a glare. "Clay's in jail again."

"Ah," he whispers, understanding crossing his face. "Well, good luck with that."

I nod and head for the stairs, leaving him behind me. The guys used to try and talk to me about my brother but they know by now it's a topic that's off limits. Especially since a lot of them just want me to cut him loose. I wish I could blame them but they have no idea the shit Clay and I have lived through together and even if I wanted to give up on him, I can't.

The bar is quiet when I reach the bottom of the stairs and I'm thankful that I can get out of here without having to explain the situation to anyone else. Shoving the door to the clubhouse open, bright sunlight blinds me and I slip my sunglasses on and jog over to my bike before swinging my leg over it and firing it up. It rumbles beneath me and my heart kicks against my rib cage as I race out of the parking lot and turn away from the clubhouse. Anger fuels me to go faster, whipping through the streets of Baton Rouge with no regard for my own personal safety. By the time I pull up in front of the police department, I'm panting and my anger has melted away to exhaustion.

Climbing off the bike, I make my way inside and stop in front of the desk as I wait for the receptionist to acknowledge me as she flips through a magazine.

"How can I help you?" she asks, not even bothering to meet my gaze.

"I'm here to see Detective Rodriguez."

She points to the waiting area. "Have a seat and he'll be with you shortly."

I take a seat in the waiting area and each minute that passes only pisses me off more as I wait for my brother. The worst thing is, I know he's going to act like this is no big deal. Just another day and I guess for us, it is. He keeps screwing up and I keep showing up to rescue him. In his mind, he can keep doing this forever because I will show up, I'll always come to bail him out - even if it's killing me.

"Smith."

I glance up and Rodriguez gestures me over. Damn, he looks like hell. He has dark circles under his eyes and his dark hair looks like he's been running his hands through it repeatedly.

"You look like shit, dude," I say when I reach him and he nods. "Why are you at work so soon?"

He leads me back to his desk and plops down in his chair with a sigh. "Because I can't be anywhere else. I have to figure out who killed Laney."

"We told you we'd help you out," I remind him as I sit in the chair next to his desk. He nods.

"I know and I appreciate it but this is my fight. It was my job to protect her and since I couldn't do that, I have to find this guy and make him pay."

I shake my head. "You need time, man. It's still too fresh and anyone can see that you're torturing yourself."

"Maybe it's what I deserve," he mutters as he stands. "Let me go get your brother."

"What did he do this time?"

Rodriguez rolls his eyes. "Got drunk and hit on the wrong dude's girl. He's got one hell of a shiner to go along with his hangover."

"He wasn't high?" I ask, stunned.

"Not when he was picked up."

I nod as he turns to leave and slip a stack of cash under some of the files on his desk with a sigh. He'd never take it if I offered it to him outright but it's the least I can do for all his help with my brother the past few years.

As I wait for them to come back, I rub my hand over my face. I'm not stupid enough to believe or even dare to hope that Clay being sober means anything more than they picked him up before he could shove a needle in his arm but it's certainly different from all the other times I've dragged my ass down to the station to bail him out. It's hard to remember a time when this wasn't my life. Clay's only been using for the past six years but it feels like forever and since I've built my life around trying to help him, I wouldn't even know what to do with myself if he ever got clean.

"Thanks for the hospitality," Clay says as he walks out of the back, followed by Rodriguez and I stand, rolling my eyes. Why the fuck does he always have to act like such a prick?

"I don't want to see you in here again."

Clay laughs. "Aw, but you'd miss me so much!"

"Hardly," Rodriguez grumbles and Clay's gaze meets mine.

"Shit, man. You called my brother?"

Rodriguez gives him a little shove, urging him forward. "Yeah, I called your damn brother. He's the only reason you're not behind bars on a permanent basis."

"What the fuck ever."

"Nice to see you, too, Clay," I say, narrowing a glare at him and he rolls his eyes. I turn to Rodriguez. "Thanks again, man."

He nods as he holds out a bag of Clay's belongings. "No problem."

I grab the bag out of his hand and grip Clay's arm, pulling him out of the station.

"Get your fucking hand off me," he growls as we step outside, ripping his arm out of my grasp and taking the bag. "What the hell is your problem?"

"My problem? My problem is that I had to bail you out of jail, yet again. What the hell are you doing with your life, Clay? You've got to stop doing this."

He scoffs, backing away from me. "You don't get to tell me what to do anymore. Remember what happened the last time you did that?"

"What the fuck is that supposed to mean?" I hiss, following him even though my bike is parked behind me.

"Never mind." He spins around and stalks away from me. "Why don't you just stay the hell out of my business?"

"Believe me, little brother, I'd love to but you can't stay out of trouble for more than a few weeks. You need to get your life together."

He sneers at me over his shoulder. "Aw, but then what would we talk about? We all know your favorite subject is what a fuck-up I am."

"I've never once said that and I'm just trying to help. I'm worried about you, Clay."

He stops and turns toward me. Track marks line his forearms and my stomach rolls just looking at them. "Well, don't be. I'm fine."

"We both know that's not true." My gaze drops to his arms and he crosses his arms over his chest.

"There's something I wanted to ask you," he murmurs after a moment, kicking at a pebble on the ground in front of him.

"What?"

"Tell me about that night."

I scowl. "That night?"

"You know," he urges with a nod and raised brows. "That night."

Memories from years ago flash through my mind and I shake my head as I back away from him. "No. You already know what happened. There's no use going over it all again and again."

"Maybe you were wrong. Maybe you misunderstood the situation."

"Misunderstood? No, there was no misunderstanding what I saw, Clay, and I'm not going to apologize for protecting you from seeing it, too."

"I was just a kid and you ruined my life."

"I ruined your life?" I whisper, looking around to make sure no one is listening to us. I can't believe he would even say that. "I saved you that night."

He throws his head back and laughs. "Oh, Saint Lucas, you're so full of shit. You know what... now that I think about it, maybe she's not even really dead."

"Jesus, how many drugs are you on right now?"

He throws himself on a park bench. "That's not an answer. We never should have left."

I shake my head and sit down next to him. "Clay. Leaving was our only option. Why is that so fucking hard for you to believe?"

"I am fucking done with this," he says as he stands. "Just leave me alone, Luke. I don't want to see you and I sure as hell don't need anymore of your help." He turns and walks away from me. I follow after him.

"Rodriguez called me this morning for you, asshole, and don't think for one goddamn second that I believe you won't call again the next time you're in trouble."

He turns toward me, walking backward with his hands up. "It was a mistake. Just forget about it."

"Clay!" I yell, stopping as he turns away from me and crosses the street without looking back. I sink onto the bench and drop my head into my hands. What the fuck is going on with him? He's always had questions about that night but to go as far as to say that I ruined his life when all I was trying to do was protect him... I don't know what to do with him anymore.

The door to the police station slams open and Rodriguez stomps down the stairs, his head down as he clutches a file to his chest. Fuck. He really shouldn't be back at work already and I worry he's going to lose it if he keeps obsessing over Laney's case. He needs to find her killer and we all understand that but this isn't healthy. Grabbing my phone, I dial Moose's number and press the phone to my ear as I watch Rodriguez throw himself behind the wheel of his car and beat his fists against the steering wheel.

"What's up, brother?"

"Hey. You doing anything today?"

There's a pause on the line. "I was gonna go watch some fireworks but I can change plans. What's up?"

"Are you fucking kidding me?" I hear a woman shriek in the background and I wince.

"Sorry, dude. I can call someone else."

"Naw, don't worry about her. It's not serious and she'll get over it the next time she wants some dick."

I laugh as I shake my head. "Yeah, okay. Listen,

you mind checking up on Rodriguez later today? I'm at the station to bail Clay out and he's not looking good."

"You got it, man. How's Clay?"

With a sigh, I run my hand over my face. "A pain in my goddamn ass."

"Sorry."

"Not your fault. Rodriguez is leaving the station now and I don't know if he's going back to the clubhouse or his place but I think someone needs to be with him."

"Don't worry about it. I'll find him."

We say good-bye and as I hang up the phone, I notice a text from Quinn.

Quinn:
Just wanted to say thank you
for all your help yesterday.

Me:
No problem. How are you feeling?

My knee shakes as I wait for her reply and I picture her as I carried her up to her bed last night as I fight back a smile. She's just what I need to turn this fucked up day around.

Chapter Five
Quinn

"I don't know," Alice muses as her gaze rakes over me, lying on the couch. I sigh and roll my eyes.

"Well, I do. Go out with your friends."

Her eyes flick to Brooklyn, who is sitting in the middle of the living room, smashing blocks together and laughing. "Are you sure?"

"Yes, Al. We'll be fine."

When she meets my eyes again, her teeth sink into her bottom lip and she looks even more unsure than she did just a second ago. "I really don't have to go. If you are feeling sore or you need to rest, I can stay and take care of Brooke."

"Alice, I love you so very much but you're turning into a stick in the mud. Go out and have fun with your friends, for Christ's sake. It's the Fourth of July, you shouldn't be cooped up with your injured sister and baby niece."

She walks over to the couch and checks the blanket over my legs. "Are you still in pain?"

"Will you stop?" I tsk, batting her hands away. "I am sore but in case you forgot, I was hit by a truck so that's normal."

"You know what, I'm just going to stay home with you guys. We can rent movies or something." She sits down next to me on the couch and tosses her purse to the other side. I swing my legs off the middle cushion and push myself off the couch as my body protests.

"Alice Ann Dawson," I mutter, limping over to the other end of the couch before grabbing her purse and putting it in her hands. "You are going to go have fun and I forbid you from coming home until, at least, midnight."

She sighs, staring up at me for a moment before she stands up and slings the strap of her purse over her shoulder. "Okay, but you call me if you need anything, you hear? I'll have my phone on the whole time and I'll text you to check in."

"Oh, my little worry wort," I sigh as I wrap her up in a hug. "Seriously, go have fun and don't worry about us. We'll be here when you get back."

"As you pointed out, you were just hit by a truck so excuse me for being concerned about you."

I release her with a smile. "I know but the doctor

gave me the all clear and between school and helping me with Brooklyn, I can't remember the last time you went out with your friends. You deserve a break and I don't want to hear anymore arguments."

She opens her mouth to protest and I cover her mouth with my hand.

"No. No arguments. Go have fun."

We move toward the door and she sighs. "All right but I am going to text you and if you don't answer me, I'm coming home."

"If I get even one text from you when you're supposed to be having fun like every other twenty-one-year-old on the planet, I'll change the alarm code on you and pretend to not know you when the police show up."

"Bitch," she teases through the grin on her face.

"Nag," I fire back and we both laugh.

"Fine. I'll be here at midnight, on the dot so don't be inviting any boys over."

I roll my eyes and give her a gentle shove toward the door. "Oh, yeah, cause you really need to worry about that."

"Go on," I urge her as Brooklyn babbles from the living room and I peek over my shoulder to check on her. When I turn back to Alice, she waves and steps out of the door as I release a breath. I honestly don't know how I'd do all this without her but my sister has paused her life enough for me. It's time that she gets out a little more and lives her life.

"What should we do tonight, Brooklyn?" I call as I turn toward the living room. She sees me and pushes herself to her feet, wavering a little before she plops back down on her butt. In the last week or so, she's shown signs of almost walking but she hasn't taken that first step just yet. Despite the accident, it's been amazing to be able to spend so much time with her since I'm usually working so much. Brooklyn babbles something as she stares up at me and I nod.

"Good idea, sweet girl! Beauty and the Beast, it is."

Before I can get to the couch, my phone buzzes and I hobble back to my seat and sink into the cushion before grabbing it.

Lucas:
Any big plans tonight?

Just seeing his message on the screen sends a flutter through my belly and I shake my head as a smile stretches across my face. When I texted him earlier to thank him for everything, I told myself that's all it was but the truth is, I want to see him again. As crazy as that is.

Me:
Yeah. Brooklyn and I have a date
planned with the DVD player.

Setting my phone down, I sigh. I would have loved to get a few little fireworks to set off for Brooklyn but with the accident, it just wasn't possible. It's not like she'll ever remember tonight but I was really looking forward to it. Brooklyn babbles and I glance over at her as she pushes herself to her feet again and wobbles.

"Come on, baby girl. You can do it. Walk to Mama," I encourage, holding my hands out in front of me. She meets my eyes and smiles before plopping down on her butt with a frustrated grunt as I laugh.

"It's okay. You'll figure it out soon enough."

A sweet little sigh slips past her lips as she reaches for her block again and I grin, my heart bursting with love as I watch her. A memory from when I first found out I was pregnant pops into my head and my stomach turns as I think about the fact that I almost didn't keep her. My life was such a mess back then and for a brief second, I considered terminating the pregnancy but all it took was one look at her on the sonogram machine and I knew I couldn't do it. Despite everything, she was mine and I wanted her. Honestly, I don't know where I'd be if it hadn't been for her. She gave me the strength and the drive to get my life back together. She saved me.

Sighing, I shake my head to clear those thoughts from my mind as I grab the remote and turn on Brooklyn and my favorite movie. As soon as the opening song starts playing, she stops playing with the block and stares up at the screen for a second before rolling to her hands and knees and crawling over to the couch. She pulls herself to her feet and I scoop her up, arranging her in my lap so she can watch the movie. With a sleepy sigh, she shoves her thumb into her mouth and starts sucking on it.

By the time Gaston starts singing in the pub, she is drifting off in my arms, her eyes getting heavier and heavier with each second that passes. The doorbell rings and she jerks up before looking at me with a pout and watery eyes.

"Shh, sweetheart. It's okay," I assure her, rubbing my finger along her cheek to calm her as I pause the movie and stand up. Climbing off the couch, I secure Brooklyn against my hip and walk over to the door, my body protesting with each step. When I reach the door, I yank it open and Lucas glances up, flashing me a gorgeous smile that takes my breath away.

"Hey," I whisper, my heart racing in my chest.

Stress lines his face but his smile is genuine as he holds up a plastic bag. "Hey. I hope you don't mind that I stopped by but I thought you might want some dinner."

"No. Not at all," I whisper, fighting back a big, cheesy grin. Brooklyn coos at him and when we glance down at her, she's smiling at Lucas around the thumb still in her mouth. He chuckles, reaching forward and nudging her cheek with his finger.

"Glad to know I have your approval as well, little lady."

She squeals, her grin firmly in place and I laugh as I turn to let him in. "Come on in. I was just putting her to bed."

"Oh, actually… before you do that, I brought a surprise for her."

I stop, turning to stare at him. "You did?"

With a smile on his face, he pulls a thin box of sparklers out of the bag before holding them out in front of me. My smile feels like it might crack my face.

"You brought her sparklers?"

"Of course, we couldn't skip Independence Day just because you're laid up."

My heart pounds against my rib cage and heat creeps up my cheeks. "This is really thoughtful, Lucas. Thank you."

"No need to thank me," he says, holding his hand out to me and I grab it, allowing him to lead Brooklyn and I out to the porch swing where he instructs me to sit.

"Do you need any help?"

He shakes his head as he holds his hands out for Brooklyn, who gladly reaches for him. "Nope. You just relax, sweetheart. I've got this."

With Brooklyn securely against his hip, he grabs the bag and carries her down the steps, into the yard. My pulse races watching him interact with her so effortlessly and for a brief second, I imagine what it would be like to have a real family with a mom and a dad for Brooklyn before pushing those thoughts from my mind. Even if I was ready for something like that, it's way too soon to be thinking that with a man I just met a few days ago.

Lucas sets Brooklyn on her feet in the grass and I

wince as she makes a face. She hates the feeling of the grass on her feet and she's going to start screaming any second. Before I can stand, Lucas scoops her back up and tickles her belly, distracting her. Oh, Jesus. If he keeps doing things like this, I'm doomed.

With Brooklyn still in his arms, he manages to maneuver one of the sparklers out of the box and lights it. Brooklyn's face lights up, transformed by wonder, as Lucas twirls the sparkler in front of them. She claps her hands, laughing as the sparks fly and my heart aches with happiness at the bright smile on her face. Lucas laughs along with her and my cheeks heat. I can't tear my eyes away from the two of them. He's so patient and loving that my mind has no problem drifting into territory that should be left alone.

The entire time I was pregnant, I knew this kind of thing wasn't in our future and it was my greatest regret - not because I'm incapable of taking care of Brooklyn by myself or because I need a man - but because my heart aches each time I think about the look on her face when she has her first daddy-daughter dance or every Father's Day when she has no one to celebrate. It's not her fault that everything worked out this way but she's the one who will bear the burden and that kills me. Watching them together now - it's the picture I always wanted but was too scared to dream of and truthfully, still am. It's the one thing I want most in this world and the one thing I'm terrified I'm never going to get.

They burn through two more sparklers before Brooklyn lays her head down on Lucas's shoulder and my eyes burn with unshed tears at just how beautiful it looks. I have no idea if we'll ever truly have a real family like I always dreamed of but this moment is pretty damn special.

"Are you ready for bed, Darlin'?" Lucas asks her so softly that I almost don't hear him as I stand up and walk over to the top step before leaning against the railing. A smile spreads across my face as I cross my arms over my chest.

"I think it's bedtime."

Lucas meets my gaze and I practically melt on the spot. "I think you're right."

He gathers up the sparklers and puts them back in the bag before carrying Brooklyn up to the porch. She's on her way to passing out and when I try to take her, he shakes his head.

"I've got her. Just lead the way."

Nodding, I turn toward the house and walk into the foyer before pointing up the stairs. "Her room is right next to mine. I'd show you but I'm only making it up there once tonight."

"Go relax on the couch, babe. I think we've got this handled," he assures me, rubbing his hand across Brooklyn's back as she sucks her thumb and sleepily looks at me. I nod with a smile on my face.

"Okay."

He hands me the bag of food before turning toward the stairs. When they disappear from my sight, I turn toward the living room and pull my phone out of my pocket, opening the app that connects to the baby monitors in Brooklyn's room. Lucas sits in the rocking chair in the corner of the room with Brooke lying on his chest, her thumb securely in her mouth as he begins rocking and telling her a story about a one-eyed dragon and a princess. He gets more animated as the story continues and a wide smile stretches across my face as Brooklyn giggles, her eyes getting heavy. After a few more minutes, the story comes to an end and Lucas stands carefully with a sleepy Brooklyn in his arms and gently lays her in her bed. He grabs her blanket and covers her before leaving the room. I tuck my phone back in my pocket as he comes down the steps.

"She's out like a light," he announces with a bright smile and I can't help but mirror the expression. The stress from earlier is gone and he looks so carefree and happy. It's infectious.

"Thank you. You're so good with her."

His warm smile washes over me as he sits down next to me. "No need to thank me and I'm only good with kids because I'm incredibly immature."

He flashes me a grin but it's obvious, to me at least, that it's covering up something deeper. As he leans forward to pull the food out of the bag, something flashes across his face and that same stressed look greets me when he hands me my food and forces a smile. I'm dying to ask him about what's wrong but the truth is, we still don't know each other all that well and I don't want to pry.

"You got anything to drink?" he asks and I nod, pointing to the kitchen behind me.

"Yeah, you're welcome to anything you'd like."

He leaves me on the couch to go to the kitchen and when he comes back, he has two bottles of water in his hands.

"I was gonna go for the wine but then I thought it wouldn't mix well with your meds."

I nod, taking the bottle from him. "You're probably right."

"Speaking of which," he starts, sinking back into the seat next to me. "Didn't the doctor tell you to stay your ass in bed?"

"Um… yes?"

"So why aren't you?"

Glancing down at my hands, I feel a blush creeping up my cheeks. Why do I care if he's upset that I didn't listen to the doctor? "I really tried but after a few hours I was bored to tears."

"Woman," he mutters, shaking his head. "I have half a mind to carry you back up there right now. Are you at least taking it easy?"

"I promise I am."

He nods with a sigh.

"You really don't have to keep taking care of me though."

He glances over at me and his eyes fall to my lips before he quickly looks away. "I couldn't walk away from you. Besides, you're not the hardest person to spend time with."

"Well, thank you for that glowing recommendation." I laugh and he grins. "You're a good man, Lucas. I… just wanted you to know that."

"Oh, I don't know about that," he says and although I know he is trying to make a joke, the pain on his face is too intense to ignore. Leaning forward, I reach up and run my thumb across the line on his forehead.

"Why do you always look like you're carrying the weight of the world on your shoulders?"

He shrugs. "I don't know. Maybe it's just my face."

"It's not."

He jerks back slightly as his eyes narrow and after a second, he sighs. "I've got a lot of shit in my life, Quinn, and the truth is, you're the only thing I've found that brings me any peace."

"You don't have to talk to me," I whisper even though I'm dying to dig deeper. "But I am a pretty good listener and I don't judge."

Setting his food on the coffee table, he sighs and turns to face me on the couch. "It's... uh, my brother, Clay. He's been using drugs for the last six years and if I'm not on a job for the club, I'm out searching for him and trying to get him clean."

"That's heavy," I whisper, watching as pain splays across his face. He nods.

"Yeah. I know it may seem pointless or stupid to keep trying when he doesn't even want my help but he's my brother and since we were kids, it's just been the two of us. He's all I have left."

I grab his hand and give it a squeeze. "You don't have to explain that to me. Alice is all Brooklyn and I have left, too, and I would do absolutely anything for her."

"You understand," he says like I'm the first to ever do so and I nod.

"Yeah, I do."

Clearing his throat, he smiles and my heart skips a

beat. It's terrifying but I have to admit that there is something about Lucas that gets to me. It would be so easy to fall for him if I allowed myself to but I don't know if that's something I could do.

"I'm really glad I met you, Lucas," I whisper, my heart racing and his smile is blinding as he reaches over and brushes his thumb over my cheek. A blush creeps up my own.

"You just read my mind, babe."

*   *   *   *

"Well, Quinn, car accident aside, you seem to be doing well. Have there been any more nightmares since we last spoke?" Dr. Jeffers asks from her chair across from me. She crosses her legs and sets her notebook down in her lap as she waits for my answer. I nod.

"Yes, a few."

"And how did you handle them?"

I think back to the last nightmare I had and smile. "Pretty well, I think. I was able to let it go and get my day started without too much trouble."

"Excellent!" she exclaims with a grin before her eyes narrow as she studies me. "There's something different about you since I saw you two weeks ago."

I twist my fingers in my lap, thinking about dinner with Lucas last night and the movie we watched together afterward. "I met someone."

"I see. More good news. How did you meet him?"

"He was there when I got in the accident and he sat with Brooklyn and I until the paramedics got there. He even rode with me to the hospital because I was so scared."

Her smile is soft as she jots something down in her notebook. Not knowing what she was saying used to drive me crazy but I've gotten used to it, for the most part. "Has he asked you out or are you just talking?"

"No, we're just talking. He also stopped by last night with sparklers for Brooklyn and dinner for me."

"Sounds like a good man."

I nod, twisting my fingers some more. "I think he is."

"But you're scared," she supplies, stating what I've been thinking for the past couple days. I nod.

"Yeah, I am. He seems like a really good man and my heart races anytime he's near me but there's just so much in my past and so much that would affect any relationship we could have."

She nods, jotting down some more notes. "This is an important step in your recovery, Quinn, and it's essential that you learn to move forward with love. After all you've been through, it would be so easy to close yourself off and spend the rest of your life alone but I know that's not what you want. Pushing yourself past this barrier won't be comfortable for you but I know you'll be happy once you're on the other side."

"Why don't you ever have any easy fixes?" I grumble and she laughs.

"Sorry. That's not how it works but I have faith in

you. You can do this."

I sigh, staring down at my fingers in my lap. "He hasn't even asked me out."

"Do you think he will?"

"I don't know."

She tsks disapprovingly. "Yes, you do. You just don't trust your instincts anymore. Don't overthink this."

"How could I not?"

"After what happened to you, I know you have this intense need to know what's around the next corner but life doesn't work like that, Quinn, and you're going to end up stalled out in the middle of the road for the rest of your life if you don't learn to swallow that fear."

"What if it goes terribly wrong?" I ask, meeting her gaze.

"The date? So what if it does? It's two hours of your life and in the end, it won't be that big of a deal. If you're referring to the relationship in general, I have good news for you."

I arch a brow. "What?"

"This is completely normal. These fears you have now are the same fears everyone has at the beginning of a relationship; they're not from the incident."

I nod, mulling over her words. "But what do I tell him about my past?"

"Whatever you're comfortable with, Quinn. The key here is baby steps. You don't have to unload everything all at once and if he's as good of a man as you think he is, he'll understand why you need to take things slow."

The timer on her desk goes off and I release a breath, feeling lighter than I did when I walked in the door.

Standing, I hold my hand out and smile. "Thank you."

She shakes my hand before going to her desk and flipping through her calendar. "Again in two weeks?"

I nod and after we have my next appointment scheduled, I go out to my car and turn toward home with a smile on my face. Dr. Jeffers is right - I can totally do this. I'm still scared to death but her comment about spending the rest of my life alone scares me more. Whether it's Lucas or someone else, I need to learn to move past this because I want a family someday - for Brooklyn and myself.

My phone rings as I pull into the driveway and I grin at Lucas's name on the screen.

"Hey, you," I answer.

"Hey, yourself. What are you up to tonight?"

I climb out of the car with keys and bag in one hand as I nudge the door shut with my knee. "Just getting home from a doctor's appointment and then probably just hanging out with Brooklyn. Why? What are you doing?"

"I'm stuck on this surveillance job and I'm bored."

I laugh as I step inside. "I'm so sorry about that."

"Don't be. You're the only thing getting me through."

Alice rushes past me with one shoe on her foot and the other in her hand as Brooklyn crawls along behind her, laughing. I bite my lip to contain my giggles.

"Hey, let me help Alice get to class and figure out dinner for Brooklyn and me and then I'll call you back, okay?"

He groans. "You're killin' me."

"I'm sorry. I'll call you back as soon as I can."

We say good-bye as Alice races back into the room, buttoning up her shirt. "Long day, Al?" I ask, laughing and she shoots me a glare.

"I fell asleep on the couch and woke up to Brooklyn screeching in my face."

Brooklyn plops her butt down next to me and reaches up. Laughing, I reach down and scoop her up, my body still aching something fierce.

"Did you scare your auntie?" I ask her and she screeches again, smashing her little hands against my chest.

"Little monster," Alice growls as her lips twitch with the smile she's barely holding back. Brooklyn blows a raspberry at her and we both laugh. "That girl is a ham."

"I think she gets it from her auntie," I muse and Alice shakes her head.

"Oh, no. I had nothing to do with that. This little girl," she says, tickling Brooklyn's belly, "is one hundred percent her mama."

Thank God.

The thought flits through my head without warning and my smile falls as I struggle with the memories threatening to resurface.

"Shit, Quinn…" Alice says and I shake my head, holding my hand up.

"No, I'm good."

My phone buzzes in my hand and I glance down, thankful for the distraction.

Lucas:
Don't worry about dinner.
Something is on the way.

Me:
Thank you.

I would tell him that it's really not necessary but I've already figured out that he wouldn't listen to me anyway. Besides, being taken care of for once actually feels pretty damn good.

"And who is putting that smile back on your face?" Alice asks, trying to peek at my phone. I lock the screen to hide it from her.

"No one."

"Mmhmm," she hums, walking to the door and grabbing her book bag before opening the door. "Tell Lucas hi for me."

"Go to class," I grumble, giving her a playful shove and she laughs as she steps outside and closes the door behind her. I turn to Brooklyn and make a face. "Your auntie is trouble, little girl."

She blows another raspberry and I laugh as I set my purse down and carry her into the living room. Once I have her set up with her toys, I sink into the couch and dial Lucas's number.

"Finally," he answers and I shake my head, giggling.

"I don't think that was even ten minutes. Thank you for dinner, by the way."

"You're welcome. It was entirely selfish, though since I wanted you to call me back sooner," he answers and I laugh again.

"Noted. How was your day, besides the boring stakeout?"

He sighs. "Okay, I guess. Went looking for Clay but didn't find him, which is pretty typical."

"When was the last time you saw him?"

"Yesterday. I had to bail him out of jail, then we got into it and he ran off."

My heart aches for him. "What did you fight about?"

"Uh…" he stutters before sighing. "My past is dark and complicated, Quinn, and I don't want to scare you off."

"I know a thing or two about dark and complicated," I whisper, tears welling up in my eyes. "In fact, I might have you beat."

"Now that, I doubt, but maybe you'd think about getting dinner with me and telling me about it?"

My heart skips a beat as butterflies race around in my belly. "Oh… I don't…"

"Don't give me an answer yet, okay? Just think about it and know that whatever is in your past, I can handle it."

Dr. Jeffers' comments from earlier pop into my mind and I suck in a breath. "I suppose I could think about it."

It's not a yes but it's not a no either and it feels like a monumental first step for me.

A.M. Myers

It Ends Tonight

Chapter Six
Quinn

My phone rings, rattling across the table top as I look over my binder for the children's fundraiser and I scoop it up, smiling when Willa's name flashes on the screen.

"Hey, what's up?"

"Hey, boss lady. How are you feeling?"

I lean back in my chair and sigh. "Oh, you know, like I got hit by a truck."

"Isn't that joke getting old?" she asks, barely holding back her laughter and I shake my head.

"No, never."

"We'll have to agree to disagree."

Laughing, I stand up and walk into the kitchen. "Oh, fine, ruin all my fun. So, what's up?"

"I'm just wondering if I'm going to see you in the office on Monday?"

"Yeah," I answer as I grab a bottle of water from the fridge. "I can't afford to take anymore time off with the hospital fundraiser so close."

"Did the doctor clear you?"

I roll my eyes. "Yeah, I saw him this morning."

"Good. Are you going to need a ride in the morning?"

Stopping in the middle of the kitchen, I breathe a curse and look toward the front door. "I totally forgot that I don't have a car anymore."

"So, is that a yes?"

"Um… I'm not sure yet. Let me think it over and get back to you."

It took the insurance company five minutes to total my Maxima and because I'd been ordered to take it easy, it never even occurred to me that I would need to go buy a new car.

"Have you gotten a check for the car yet?"

I sink into the chair as I shake my head. "No, not yet. They said it'd take a week or two but I may just go buy something today. I don't want to put you or Alice out."

"I really don't mind, Quinn."

"No," I mutter, my mind mulling over the options. "I might as well get it taken care of now. One less thing to worry about, you know?"

"Okay, well, let me know if you need any help."

I agree and we discuss a few things to go over on Monday before saying good-bye. When I hang up the phone, I set it down on the table and sigh. Shit. I guess I need to go buy a car today but Alice took Brooklyn and currently, our only vehicle, to the park to play. My teeth sink into my lip as my gaze drops to my phone. Lucas told me to call him if I needed anything but I don't want to bother him if he's busy. Tapping my fingernails against the table, I debate with myself for a few seconds before scooping the phone up and sending him a text.

Me:
Hey, you busy right now?

As I wait for his reply, I take one last look over the binder and make a list of the most urgent things I need to take care of before packing everything up. Just as I'm stacking it in the middle of the table, my phone buzzes and I grab it.

Lucas:
Nope. You okay?

Instead of texting him, I dial his number and press the phone to my ear.

"Everything okay?" he answers on the second ring and I smile, my heart beating a little faster at just the sound of his voice.

"Yeah, everything's good. I just need some assistance today if you're free."

"I'm always free for you."

A giggle spills out of me as I shake my head. "I'm not buying your lines."

"Are you sure?" The playful tone in his voice sends a blush creeping up my cheeks and I'm glad the house is empty so no one else can see how much he gets to me. Alice has been relentless since she came home on the Fourth and found us watching a movie together but I've been able to appease her without spilling too much information. That won't last long though.

"Yes, I'm sure."

He sighs. "Fine. What do you need help with?"

"Well, the insurance company totaled my car so I kind of need to go buy a new one and I was hoping you'd come with me."

"Absolutely," he answers without hesitation. "Give me ten minutes and I'll come pick you up."

Glancing at the clock, I nod. "Okay, I'll be ready. And thank you, Lucas."

"Happy to help, gorgeous."

We say good-bye and as soon as I hang up, I rush up the stairs as quickly as my sore body will allow and riffle through my closet before choosing a short white lace dress and my cowboy boots. I change and go into the bathroom to touch up my makeup as my belly does a little flip.

Oh, hell.

What am I doing?

I haven't agreed to his request for a date and even if I had, this is not one. He's just taking me to buy a damn car. I quickly change into a pair of jean shorts, a tank top, and a pair of flip-flops before ducking back into the bathroom. My hand shakes as I hold the lip-gloss wand in front of my face and I close my eyes as I suck in a breath.

"Baby steps," I whisper, reminding myself of my talk with Dr. Jeffers yesterday. Opening my eyes, I stare at my reflection in the mirror. My cheeks are pink and my eyes are alive in a way they haven't been in a really long time. If I close my eyes again, I can still remember the vacant look I've seen staring back at me for the last two years and I'm trying so hard to not get my hopes up but maybe I'm finally moving forward. Maybe the worst is really behind me. My lips stretch into a smile and I drop my gaze from the mirror as I shake my head. Who would have thought that getting hit by a truck would be just what I needed?

The doorbell rings, pulling my gaze to my bedroom door. "Shit."

I drop my lip-gloss into my purse and rush back downstairs before yanking the door open as I pant. Lucas's eyebrows shoot up and I bend over and brace my hands on my knees.

"You all right?"

I nod, sucking in air. "Yeah. I was just upstairs when the doorbell rang and apparently, getting in a car accident really takes it out of you."

"You sure we should be doing this today?" he asks as I straighten and I nod.

"Yeah. I saw the doctor this morning and he cleared me."

He watches me skeptically so I plaster a smile on my face and hope I don't look like a crazy person.

"If you're sure…"

I nod. "I am."

"Let's go buy a car, then," he answers with a smile as he holds his hand out to me. I hesitate for a second before grabbing it and letting him lace our fingers together. My heart races and I fight back a smile as we walk to his truck. It's been so damn long since someone's held my hand and maybe I'm not remembering things clearly but I swear, it never felt this good. There is something about Lucas that settles me and makes me feel safe - I first noticed it at the accident and at the time, I assumed it was the situation. Now, though, I know it's just him. No one else could have kept me calm the way he did.

"So," he says, drawing my gaze over to him as he climbs behind the wheel of the truck. "Do you know what you're looking for?"

I shake my head. "No idea. I liked my Maxima but I think I'm kind of wanting something new."

"Sounds good. I know a guy who brings a lot of work into the bike shop so I thought I'd take you over to his place. He'll take good care of you."

"Okay."

As we pull out of the driveway, he glances over at me. "Where's Brooklyn today?"

"With Alice. She took her to the park and I was going over work stuff for Monday when I realized that I'd need a new car."

He nods, turning back to the road. "If I had thought of it, I would have brought one over that you could borrow."

"Oh, no, it's really okay. It's something I need to take care of so I might as well do it today."

My phone buzzes with a text.

Willa:
Staff meeting Monday morning.
Don't forget.

"Oh, Lord," I mutter, rolling my eyes with a smile on my face. Like I could ever forget Willa's weekly staff meetings.

"Everything okay?"

I glance over at Lucas and nod. "Yeah. It's just my assistant, Willa, reminding me of our staff meeting on Monday."

"You have staff?" he asks, brows raised, and I laugh.

"Besides Willa and I... no. Hence, why it's so ridiculous but it helps her feel more organized so I roll with it."

He stares at me for a second before turning back to the road with a scowl. "How old are you?"

"Twenty-eight. Why?"

"I don't know. You just seem to have everything together and I still feel like I'm tripping through life."

Laughter bubbles out of me as I shake my head. "Oh, no. Trust me, I'm just as big of a mess as anyone else."

"Yeah, but you've got your own business, a great house, and a gorgeous kid. Looks like you're killing it from where I'm standing."

"Well, thank you," I reply, a blush rising to my cheeks. "But the business and the house were actually my grandmother's and she left them to me when she died a couple years ago."

"Oh, I'm sorry."

I shake my head, fighting back a few tears. "No, it's okay. She was an incredible woman and lived an amazing life, which is what I like to focus on, no matter how much I miss her."

"I know you said Alice is all you have left but what happened to your parents?"

Sucking in a breath, I twist my fingers together in my lap. "Wow. Going straight for the heavy stuff, huh?"

"Sorry. I'm just curious about you. You don't have to answer if you don't want to," he assures me but the sincerity and kindness on his face urges me to continue. Reaching across the cab, I grab his hand.

"When I was eight, they dropped Alice and I off at

Gram's house to have their weekly date night. Mom always wanted this special candy they didn't have at the theater so they stopped off at a gas station to pick some up and a man walked in with a gun. After he robbed the place, he shot the clerk and both of my parents."

"Jesus Christ," he breathes, giving my hand a squeeze as we pull into the dealership parking lot and he parks the car. "I'm so sorry, Quinn."

I shake my head. "You have nothing to be sorry for. It was hard and still is sometimes but Gram was there for us. She took us in after they died and she raised us all by herself."

"She sounds like an incredible woman."

Our eyes meet and I smile. "She was."

Time seems to stand still as the air around us grows heavy and he leans in, his gaze dropping to my lips. My body moves without any instruction from me, leaning into him as my skin prickles with anticipation and my heart pounds in my chest. Oh, god, what if I'm not ready for this? I want it so badly but there's a very real chance that the moment his lips touch mine, I'll lose it. My hand shakes and he gives it a squeeze, a soft smile stretching across his face and just when I think he's going to close the distance between us, a bang echoes through the cab and we both jump back.

"Luke, my boy! What are you doing here?"

"Hey, Calvin," he says, glancing out of the truck window as the round middle-aged man approaches the window. "I was hoping you'd help my girl find a new car."

My cheeks heat as he turns back to me and flashes me a grin that could melt butter.

"Absolutely," Calvin calls, excitement in his voice. "Nice to meet you, Darlin'. I'm Calvin."

"Hi, I'm Quinn," I call back with a wave. Calvin smacks Lucas's arm and lets out a whistle.

"She's fucking gorgeous."

"Watch it," Lucas growls. Calvin takes a step back with raised brows as I turn to look at Lucas. Maybe the edge to his voice should scare me but fear is the farthest thing from what I'm feeling. With him, from the very first moment we met, I've always felt safe and having him defend my honor, so to speak, stirs up feelings in me that I haven't felt in a long time. Feelings that will have me agreeing to his date and anything else he asks of me if I'm not careful.

"Well, should we find you a car, then?" Calvin asks, pulling me out of my thoughts and I smile as Lucas glances over at me, searching for approval with his blue gaze. I nod.

"Yeah, let's do this."

Lucas instructs me to wait for him before jumping down from the truck and rounding the front. When he opens my door, he holds his hand out and I grab him as he guides me safely to the ground. We meet Calvin around the front of the truck and Lucas wraps his arm around my shoulders. I can't help but feel like he's sending a clear sign to Calvin for his earlier comment but I kind of like it.

"Do you have a car in mind, Ma'am?"

I bite my lips to keep from laughing at his formal tone as I shake my head. "No, I'm not really sure what I want."

"Maybe you could just let us walk around for a bit," Lucas suggests, his tone indicating that it's really not a suggestion and Calvin nods.

"You got it. I'll be in the office so holler if you need me."

He practically scurries off and I turn to look at Lucas, barely holding back my grin.

"I think he's scared of you now."

He laughs and his whole face lights up, bringing back the carefree man I've been getting to know over the past few days. "Naw, I was just reminding him of his manners."

"Mmhmm," I murmur, glancing out across the lot as I cross my arms over my chest. "I'm pretty sure his shorts were wet."

He laughs again and it warms my entire body. "He is right about one thing, though."

"Yeah? What's that?"

"You're gorgeous," he whispers, taking a step toward me. I back up until my shoulders touch the truck but he keeps advancing until he's mere inches away from me.

Men have called me beautiful or gorgeous my entire life but somehow, when Lucas says it, it feels different - like he's looking at me as a person instead of just long blonde hair, blue eyes, and a decent figure. With him, it feels like he sees the real me when every other man I've ever met was only interested in having me as a trophy on his arm but I'm still so scared to take this leap.

"Lucas, I…"

"I keep trying to remind myself not to rush this because I think from the moment you looked my way amidst the chaos of that car accident, I knew you were special but that's so damn hard when all I want to do is kiss you every time you're near me."

"Oh, god," I breathe out, trying to focus on anything other than the thought of him leaning in right now and planting his lips on mine.

"Tell me you feel the same way," he urges, his breath fanning out across my face. "Tell me that I'm not losing my mind."

"It's complicated."

He shakes his head. "No, it isn't. This is the easy part so tell me, does your heart race just like mine every time we're in the same room?"

"Yes, but…"

My words are cut off by his lips pressing against my forehead and I close my eyes, just soaking it all in as my body trembles. When he pulls away, our gazes connect and he smiles.

"That's all I needed to know. Now, why don't we go find you a car?"

*　　*　　*　　*

"Congrats, Darlin'!" Calvin exclaims as I sign the paperwork for my new Toyota Camry. When I'm finished, I drop the pen on the desk and smile up at him.

"Thank you for all your help." We shake hands and he hands me the keys.

"You're mighty welcome. Make sure you bring her by for the first oil change in five months. I had one of the boys put a little sticker on the windshield to remind ya."

My smile is a little forced as I nod. Calvin seems like a nice enough man but I get the sense that he thinks I'm an airhead because of what's between my thighs and my patience is wearing thin.

"Thank you."

"Thanks, Calvin," Lucas adds, his arm securely around my waist as he leans forward to shake Calvin's hand. We all say good-bye before Lucas leads me outside where my new car waits for me and he holds his hand out.

"Let me get those keys, babe."

I arch a brow. "Why?"

"Because I'm gonna have one of the prospects swing by and drive the car to your house."

"I'm a big girl, Lucas. I can drive home," I protest, pulling away from him. He nods, grabbing my hand and pulling me close again.

"I know you can but I want to take you home myself."

"Oh," I mutter, studying him for a moment before I hand the keys over. He grins and leans in to kiss my forehead again. Since we started our shopping trip three hours ago, he's gotten more and more bold - grabbing my hand out of the blue and kissing my forehead anytime he pulls me close. I still have no idea what we're doing or if I'll even agree to a date but I can't deny that I'm quickly becoming addicted to the feel of his arms around me. He makes me feel like the girl I was before everything went to hell and that's a powerful drug.

Grabbing my hand again, he leads me over to his truck and opens the door for me before helping me up. Once I'm seated, he closes the door and rounds the front of the truck, texting someone and when he climbs behind the wheel, he glances across the truck at me.

"Someone is on their way to retrieve your new car."

"Thank you."

Turning back to the steering wheel, he starts the truck and leans over to turn the radio to the country station as I bite back a smile.

"So," I start as we pull out of the parking lot. "Do I get to hear about your family now?"

He steals a glance in my direction before shaking his head as he blows out a breath. "That's a heavy conversation that should probably be saved for later."

"Oh."

"I'm sorry… it's just…"

"Dark and complicated?" I supply, remembering our conversation from last night.

He nods. "Yeah."

Nothing I know about him would suggest that he is playing games with me but his unwillingness to tell me anything about his past doesn't sit well with me. But then again, how well do I really know him? It has only been four days since the accident. God, I'm officially losing my mind.

We spend the rest of the ride home in silence and by the time he pulls into the driveway, I'm practically scrambling out of the truck to escape the tension. He meets me around the front and wisely doesn't reach for my hand as we walk up to the front porch. At the door, I turn to him.

"Well, thank you for your help today."

He runs his fingers through his dirty blond hair and sighs. "Listen, I know things got weird back there but I'm really hoping that you'll still agree to that date we talked about."

"I don't…"

My words are cut off by the front door opening and Alice sticks her head out and grins at me. "Quinn, can I talk to you for a second?"

"Uh… Can it wait?"

She shakes her head and I peek over at Lucas before nodding.

"Just give me a second, okay?"

He nods and I duck inside with Alice. As soon as the door closes, my gaze roams over the hallway, searching for Brooklyn.

"Where's Brooke?"

"Sleeping."

I turn back to her and scowl. "So why did you call me in here?"

"Because you're about to turn down a date with that ridiculously hot man out there."

Sighing, I lean back against the door. "It's complicated, Alice."

"Because of…"

I cut her off by pressing my hand to her mouth, aware that she was able to hear my conversation with Lucas through the door.

"No," I whisper.

"Do you like him?"

I nod. "Yes."

"Okay, so then give this thing a shot."

Dr. Jeffers' comment from my session two days ago pops into my mind and I suck in a breath, peeking over my shoulder at the closed door as my heart races. Shit. Am I really going to do this?

"C'mon, Quinn. I have a good feeling about this guy."

Sighing, I meet her gaze and nod. "Okay. I'll agree to one date but that's it."

"Yes!" she squeals, jumping up and down excitedly. Shaking my head, I leave her to her victory party in the foyer as I step out onto the porch again. Lucas smiles as I meet his gaze.

"Okay," I say with a nod and his grin grows.

"Yeah?"

I nod again. "One date - that's all I'm agreeing to."

"That will do for now," he answers, pulling me into his arms and pressing his lips against my forehead. I say a little prayer to whoever is up there watching over me that he doesn't destroy me as I melt into him, already in way too deep.

A.M. Myers

It Ends Tonight

Chapter Seven
Quinn

Fuck.
Fuck.
Fuck.
What the hell am I doing?
I'm not ready for this.

"Alice!" I scream, blinking away tears as I flatten my shaking hands against the white lace of my dress. It is a little sexy, ending mid-thigh but with my cowboy boots, it doesn't look quite so risqué and I've spent the last hour and a half curling my hair and doing my makeup but I don't think I can do this. Alice runs into the room with Brooklyn on her hip.

"What's wrong?"

I turn to look at her and she sighs before closing the bedroom door and setting Brooklyn down on the floor.

"I have to call and cancel."

She shakes her head, a determined look on her face. "There's no way in hell I'm letting you do that. You can do this, Sis."

"I can't," I whisper, my hands shaking even harder. I don't know what the hell I was thinking when I agreed to this date last night but I can't actually go through with it. She plops down on the bed.

"Why not?"

I turn back to the mirror and inspect myself again. "I'm not ready."

"That's just fear, Quinn. It doesn't mean that you're not ready and if you cling to that excuse, you'll never find love. Next."

"It's not good for Brooklyn for me to be going out…"

"Yeah, I'm calling bullshit right now," she interrupts me, holding her hand up. "Brooklyn is a baby and will never remember this one date, if that's all it is but if it's more, I'm damn sure that having more people to love her will never be a bad thing. Next."

I suck in a breath. "He won't tell me anything about his past…"

"That's the point of the date, big sister. You guys go out and eat or see a movie and you get to know each other. Besides, I highly doubt you've spilled everything about yourself."

"I told him about Grams and Mom and Dad."

She scoffs. "That's the easy stuff and you know it."

"I am scared, Al."

Alice crosses her legs on the bed and nods like she knew that all along. I sigh and turn to face her again.

"What are you scared of, Quinn?"

"Showing him all the broken pieces," I answer, staring down at my hands.

"No, that's not it…"

Sucking in a breath, I meet her eyes and glare because damn her for being right all the time. "I'm scared that he won't accept all the broken pieces."

"Because?"

"Because I really like him - more than anyone else I've ever met."

Smiling, she points at me. "And there it is."

"You're annoying."

"But effective," she replies and I laugh despite the urge to stay mad at her. "Feeling better?"

I shrug. "I suppose."

"Seriously, Quinn. It's just one date. Go out and have fun with Lucas - who, by the way, I happen to think is someone special."

"You do?" I don't know why I need her validation but hearing her say that he seems different than any other guy I've brought home makes a difference to me. She nods.

"Definitely. The man sat in a hospital for hours just to make sure you were okay. I know you've been out of the dating game for a while but dudes like him don't come around all that often."

The doorbell rings, pulling both of our gazes toward the door and Alice hops off the bed before scooping Brooklyn up in her arms.

"I'll stall him for a few minutes. Take a breath, get yourself together, and then make a stunning entrance, 'kay?"

I laugh and nod. "Okay."

She kisses my cheek and ducks out of the room as I turn back to the mirror and suck in a breath.

It is just one date.

I repeat that mantra in my head a few times before touching up my makeup and running a hand gently through my hair to break up the curls. When I'm feeling steadier, I grab my bag and walk out of my bedroom. Lucas's voice drifts up from the foyer and I stop at the top of the stairs, listening to his conversation with Alice.

"You'd better treat my sister right," Alice warns and I smile, shaking my head. "She's been through a lot and she deserves the world."

"You have nothing to worry about," he assures her, his warm voice drifting up the stairs, sending goose bumps across my skin. Butterflies stir in my belly as I start down the stairs.

"You're damn right I don't," Alice adds. "I meant what I said about burying you in the yard."

He laughs. "Noted."

"Alice, stop threatening him," I say as I reach the bottom of the steps and they both turn to me. Alice grins as Lucas's gaze slowly drops down my body and back up again before we start moving toward each other, meeting in the middle of the foyer.

"These are for you." He holds out a bouquet of red roses and I take them, burying my nose in them as I hum in approval.

"Thank you," I reply, peeking up at him. "They're gorgeous."

"No, sweetheart. I'm pretty sure that's you."

Heat rises to my cheeks as our gazes connect and I suck in a breath as my heart gallops wildly in my chest. His lips part and my gaze drops to his mouth as his tongue darts out and runs along his bottom lip. Lord, I don't think anything has ever looked so obscene and so innocent at the same time. My legs feel like Jell-O and I fight the urge to lean into him as I remember how good it felt to have his arms around me yesterday.

"I'll just take these," Alice sings, snapping us both out of a daze as she plucks the flowers from my hand and winks at me. "You two have fun."

We watch her disappear into the kitchen with Brooklyn on her hip before Lucas turns back to me with a bemused smirk on his face.

"Uh... you ready to go?"

I nod. "Yeah. Where are we going?"

"That's a surprise."

I wrinkle my nose and glance down at my dress. "Well, am I dressed okay?"

"Babe, even if your outfit was wildly inappropriate for our date, I wouldn't tell you because I'm enjoying the view too damn much."

"Don't try and sweet talk me, Lucas," I tease, rolling my eyes as he laughs and pulls me into his arms.

"Would it be bad form to kiss you at the beginning of the date?" His nose brushes against mine, stealing the air from my lungs as I grip his arms and nod.

"Yes."

"What if I can't resist?" he asks, his minty breath hitting my face as my body floods with warmth and my heart hammers against my rib cage.

"Try harder. Besides, it will give you something to look forward to."

"Are y'all still here?" Alice yells and I jump back as Lucas shakes his head, holding his hand out to me.

"We were just on our way out." My nerves melt away as he laces our fingers together and I shoot a look over my shoulder at my annoying little sister. She grins back at me.

"Don't do anything I wouldn't do!"

Lucas laughs as we step out onto the porch. "Why do I get the feeling there isn't much she wouldn't do?"

"She's full of it since I practically had to force her out of the house on the Fourth."

"Ah, I see," he muses. "So she's just messing with

you?"

I shrug. "I think she was trying to make me think about something other than how nervous I am."

He stops next to his truck and pulls me into his arms again with a scowl. "I'm making you nervous?"

"Not you, really… It's just that… Well, do you remember when I told you I knew a thing or two about dark and complicated?"

He nods, his expression growing more concerned. "Yeah."

"The truth is it's been a really long time since I've done this and I'm a different person than I was then."

"I understand. But, for what it's worth, I like who you are now."

I drop my gaze to his chest as his arms tighten around me. "You didn't know me then."

"Doesn't matter. It's not like you can go back and if we're going to move forward, this is the girl I'd like to move forward with," he says, brushing his thumb over my cheek and I peek up at him as my heart melts.

"All right, then."

He grins. "Are you ready to go out on our date now?"

"Yes," I answer with a nod and he opens the passenger door for me before helping me climb up. I smile as he rounds the front of the truck and as he slips behind the wheel, I realize that my nerves are mostly gone. The excited butterflies remain but the outright panic that I was feeling before he showed up is gone. I don't know if it was Alice's distraction or just Lucas himself that makes my fears flee but I'm glad that I can just focus on having a good time with him tonight.

"Hey," he says, pulling my attention to him as we pull out onto the road and I glance over at him.

"Yeah?"

"There's something I need to ask you…" He leaves the statement hanging in the air and my belly does a little flip as I nod.

"Okay."

"When you said you hadn't done this in a really long time… how long are we talking?"

I suck in a breath. "Two years, give or take, since my last relationship."

"Did it end badly?"

"No," I answer, shaking my head. "The breakup was just the start of a lot of bad things in my life."

"Were y'all together for a long time?"

I glance across the truck and meet his gaze. "You really want to know?"

"Yeah."

"Danny and I were together for three years and we were engaged."

It's clear from the look on his face that I've stunned him so I wait, biting my lip while I give him a minute to process.

"Is he Brooklyn's dad?"

I shake my head, fighting back memories. "No."

He nods, staring out at the road again for a second and in the same way that thunder always follows lightning, I know what question is coming next.

"Is her dad in the picture?"

"Nope. Are we getting dinner first? I'm starving."

He stares at me for a second before, thankfully, ignoring my change of topic and nodding. "Dinner may be included in my plans for the evening."

"Well, that's cryptic," I mutter and he laughs, reaching across the cab to grab my hand.

"I'm sorry if I pushed too hard."

I shake my head, meeting his gaze. "I want to tell you all about myself but I just need to do it in my own time. There are things that I've never told anyone besides Alice and my therapist so opening up isn't always the easiest thing for me."

"So, what you're saying is that you need to take this slow?"

"Yes," I answer, relief washing through me as I nod. "I need to take this slow."

He nods. "Okay."

"That easy, huh?"

We pull into a parking lot and he parks the truck toward the back of the lot before turning to me. "Yeah, Quinn, that easy."

Before I can say anything else, he jumps out, rounds the back of the truck, and opens my door. He helps me down and as I turn around, I gasp at the Ferris wheel towering above us from the fairgrounds.

"You brought me to the fair?"

He nods, a shy smile replacing his usual cocky grin. "Yeah, I thought it seemed like fun but we can go somewhere else if you want."

"No, this is perfect. Actually, the first concert I ever went to was a Garth Brooks concert here with my dad."

"Yeah? How old were you?"

"Oh, gosh," I reply as we walk toward the front gate hand in hand. "Five, maybe. I haven't been back here since they died."

"How come?"

I shrug. "It was just sad for me. I don't think I even realized how much I missed it until I saw the Ferris wheel."

"We can go somewhere else…"

"No!" I exclaim, cutting him off. "I don't want to go. Besides, I think it's way past time for me to make new memories."

He grins, giving my hand a squeeze as we step up to the gate. "I like the sound of that."

"How many?" the attendant asks.

"Two," Lucas answers, sneaking glances back at me as he pulls his wallet out of his pocket. After he pays, he takes my hand again and leads me past the gate before throwing his arm over my shoulders.

"So, what first? Food or dancing?"

I sputter out a surprised laugh. "You dance?"

"You'll just have to wait and see," he teases with a wiggle of his eyebrows and I laugh again.

"Well, as tempting as that is, food first because my stomach is currently in the process of digesting itself."

"We can't have that," he says, nodding to the path in front of us. "Any preference?"

I stare up at the rows of different food trucks, my mind blank. "Uh...no?"

He laughs, pulling me closer and I relish in the feeling of being tucked into his side. "Okay, what did you always get when you used to come with your parents?"

"Corn dogs," I answer. "But I think I'm a little too old for that."

"Bullshit. Let's go find corn dogs."

I giggle as he pulls me along, intent on finding me my childhood favorite. We pass by so many trucks I lose count before he stops at a pizza truck.

"What can I get you guys?" the guy manning the truck asks.

"Yeah, can you tell me where I could find some corn dogs?"

He shoots us a glare. "Man, do you want pizza or not?"

"Lucas," I whisper, poking his side. "It's fine. We can just get pizza."

"Naw, we're good," he says, ignoring my comment and I roll my eyes as we set off again. We pass a few more trucks before I spot a kettle corn stand and let out a squeal before pulling Lucas to it.

"Hey, can I get two bags?" I ask when the woman at the register looks up at me. She smiles and turns to scoop two large bags of popcorn as I release Lucas's hand to dig in my wallet for money.

"I got it," he cuts in, laying some money on the counter and I turn to him with a scowl.

"I can pay for my own food."

Shaking his head, he pulls me into his arms as his gaze drops to my lips for a second before meeting my eyes. "Not when you're with me, you don't. Besides, I'd buy the whole damn stand just to hear that cute little squeal again."

"Shut up." I laugh, shoving him away as the lady behind the counter hands us the kettle corn. I flash her a smile. "Thank you."

"Have a nice day," she chirps.

"You, too," I call over my shoulder as we turn away and set off down the path again. We make it a few more stands down before my stomach growls loudly and I turn to Lucas. "I don't know that we're going to find corn dogs."

He scoffs. "It's like a fair staple so they've got to be around here somewhere."

"I appreciate the effort but I don't *need* corn dogs. We can just find something else. Look, there's a Mexican place."

"Who said anything about you?" he asks as he pulls me off to the side of the path by a little picnic area and wraps his arms around me. "*I* want corn dogs."

"Oh, well then, by all means, let's keep searching."

He glances down the path before turning back to me. "Why don't you sit down and eat some kettle corn and I'll hunt down our dinner?"

"Are you sure?"

"Yeah," he answers, leading me over to one of the tables and setting the bag of kettle corn in his hand down. "I'll be right back, okay?"

I nod. "Okay."

His fingers dive into my hair and he pulls me closer, pressing his lips against my forehead and I melt into him, my heart fluttering at the sweet gesture and when he pulls away, I have to fight the urge to yank him back to me.

"Sit," he orders, gesturing to the picnic table. "I'll be right back."

Nodding, I sit down and watch him as he strides away from me, unable to wipe the smile off my face. It's crazy to think about how much has changed in the last five days. Even thinking that stuns me. No matter how much I think about it, it doesn't feel like only five days. It feels like I've known Lucas for so much longer and if I try to imagine how I would feel if we get nothing more than tonight, there's an ache in my chest that I'm too scared to investigate. I think I knew, before I ever agreed to this date, that I would agree to a second and third and however many he asks me for… which is scary. I don't like letting him have that much power over my emotions but if there was any way to stop it, I would have done it by now. My fear was so potent earlier this evening that I was ready to sabotage everything.

My phone buzzes in my purse and I pull it out, laughing at the text from Alice.

Alice:
Are you two crazy kids hopelessly in love and married yet?

Me:
No, but I am having a good time.
Thanks for talking me down.

Sighing, I turn to look out across the fairgrounds. There's a pond next to the picnic area and a lift strung out in the air across it, carrying folks from one side of the park to the other and a memory of riding it with my parents hits me. They died when I was eight and Alice was Brooklyn's age so she doesn't have the same memories with them that I do but sometimes, I think that's easier. You can't miss what you never had, right?

My phone buzzes again.

Alice:
That's what I'm here for.
Have fun.

She sends a second text with a kissy face emoji and I smile as I tuck my phone back into my purse and stare out at the rides as the sun begins to sink below the horizon.

"Victory," Lucas calls and I turn to him, laughing as he holds up two containers full of mini corn dogs, fries, and a drink tray with two sodas. He sets one of the containers and a drink down in front of me before sitting across from me and I nod.

"I admire your dedication."

He winks. "Thank you."

"Your time is up, though."

"Oh, yeah? My time is up for what?"

I pop a fry into my mouth and study him as I chew. He arches a brow, fighting back a smile as he waits for my reply.

"We're officially out on our first date and usually, on dates, people get to know each other so it's time for you to spill."

He nods thoughtfully, leaning back as he takes a sip of soda. "You think, huh?"

"I do."

"And what if I disagree?"

Feeling playful, I dip a fry into my ketchup as I

133

mimic his nod. "That's your right but usually, girls decide if they're going to agree to a second date based on how well the first date goes and being so elusive is a big red flag."

"Elusive, huh?" he asks, looking out across the fairgrounds as emotion skates over his face.

"Just tell me one thing. Something real."

Our gazes meet over the table and the rest of the world melts away for a second. "One real thing... Okay. I've never felt more myself than when I'm with you."

"You mean that?" I ask and he nods, sincerity shining through his blue eyes.

"I do. Now, tell me one thing about you."

I roll my eyes to cover up my racing heart and rosy cheeks. "You already know things about me."

"I know but I want to know more."

I mull over his words as I bite a corn dog in half and chew. "Okay, when my parents were alive, we lived out in the country on this farm. I had a couple horses, two goats, and a pig."

"I can picture you out on a farm," he says with a smile. "Pigtails in your hair and little cowgirl boots on your feet."

"You're actually not far off."

"That's fucking adorable. Please tell me there are pictures."

Laughing, I nod. "There might be."

"I have to get my hands on those."

"Yeah, I don't think so," I tease. He throws a fry across the table and it smacks me in the face as he laughs. "Now you're definitely not getting to see them."

"What if I say I'm sorry?" he asks, doing his best to look cute and damn it, it's working.

"Are you sorry?"

A grin stretches across his face as he shakes his head. "No."

"I didn't think so."

"What was your pig's name?" he asks, reaching across the table and grabbing my hand. I fight back a smile as my heart flutters.

"Piglet... I was in a Winnie the Pooh phase."

He laughs, that deep warm laugh that I'm quickly falling in love with. "And the goats?"

"Timon and Pumbaa. Lion King phase."

"Let me guess, for the horses you went with a Beauty and the Beast theme."

I shake my head. "Nope, close though. Cinderella. Their names were Jaq and Gus Gus."

"And your parents never tried to get you to name them something else?" he asks, his blue eyes shining with humor.

"Oh, of course they did but I was a very determined child."

"Who could say no to you?"

I beam. "Exactly."

"You ready to go on some rides?" he asks, glancing

down at my almost empty container and I shake my head.

"Oh, no, mister. You teased me with dancing and now that I'm fed, I'm not missing that."

Chuckling, he releases my hand and starts collecting all our trash. "You're not going to let me forget that, huh?"

"Not a chance."

When he's finished gathering up our things, he drops the trash in a bin near the picnic table before reaching for my hand and leading me away from the food trucks, toward the sound of music. We round the corner and there is a little pavilion with a stage on one side and a dance floor on the other. On stage, a band plays older country songs and I pull Lucas to the dance floor where a few other couples are swaying back and forth. I gasp as Lucas spins me into his chest and places his hand on my hip as we start to dance along to the music.

"Hot damn, I guess you weren't lying."

Laughter bursts out of him and I can't help but smile. "You doubted me?"

"Yes. Yes, I did."

"I'm hurt," he whines, bringing our clasped hands to his chest and I shoot him a disbelieving look.

"You know I have to ask where you learned to dance, though."

His smile falls and our steps falter for just a second before he takes a deep breath and pulls me closer. Each time I bring up anything about his past, the tortured expression on his face kills me but I hope that I really am bringing him peace like he said I was.

"When I was a kid, I had pretty bad insomnia and Iris would stay up with me in the middle of the night to keep me company. We'd watch movies or play cards and she taught me how to dance."

"Who's Iris?"

"She was our guardian."

My nerves rear up as the next question pops into my mind but I press on. "What happened to your parents?"

"They... they died," he answers, looking away from me and my heart aches for him. I know his pain all too well and I know that nothing I could say right now would fix anything so I simply lean into him and offer him my silent support.

"What do you say we go on some rides?" I ask, peeking up at him and relief washes over his face as he nods.

"Let's do it."

The sky is lit up with oranges and pinks as he steps away from the ticket counter and I drag him over to the Ferris wheel to enjoy the sunset. In the car, he pulls me into his side and I cuddle closer, surprised by how much I'm enjoying the date.

"Hey, Quinn," he murmurs on our second trip around the wheel and I glance over at him. "I'm sorry that it's so hard for me to share my past with you but I want you to know that I'm trying."

I nod. "I do know that and if anyone understands, it's me."

"If we're taking things slow, does that mean I can't kiss you?"

I smile as we reach the top of the wheel. "No."

"I was really hoping you'd say that," he whispers as he leans in and cups my cheek. Our gazes meet in the space between us and he smiles before leaning in and claiming my lips in a soft kiss. I melt into him, sighing as a feeling that I can't quite explain rocks through me and when he pulls away, we're both quietly gasping for air.

"One date isn't going to be enough for me," he admits and I nod.

"I know."

It Ends Tonight

Chapter Eight
Lucas

Storm nudges me as we walk across the wet grass of the graveyard and I glance over at him, nodding in acknowledgement.

"Keep your eyes open today, yeah?"

"You think this bastard's gonna show up here?" I ask, glancing out at the crowd of people dressed in black gathering around the casket.

"Not ruling anything out at this point."

We move to the back of the crowd as I nod. "Yeah, you got it."

Ever since I ran into Rodriguez at the station, we've had people checking in on him everyday. The reports remain the same - he's grieving and determined to find whoever killed Laney and make them pay to the point that he's obsessed. We're all worried but putting myself in his shoes, I think he's handling it all pretty well or at least, as well as any of the rest of us would. I can't imagine how much Storm, Chance, or Kodiak would lose it if anything happened to the women they love.

My thoughts drift to Quinn and I fight back a smile that's not at all appropriate for this funeral. After riding the rides for over an hour last night, we walked over to the booths and I threw down over a hundred dollars to win a little teddy bear for Brooklyn but damn was it worth it to see the smile on Quinn's face when I handed it to her. I think I'd do just about anything for that smile. Fuck, this girl is doing me in. Not that I care. Being with her just feels right and after all the shit in my life, I'm not going to question it. Especially since I've never been able to hang onto anything good for very long.

The music dies down as the preacher steps forward and begins delivering the sermon but my focus is on the guests. I roam the crowd, looking for anything out of place but I don't see anything. Laney's parents are sitting by Rodriguez, sobbing over their daughter as Rodriguez struggles to keep it together. The club has formed somewhat of a barrier around the back to watch over everything and I glance over my shoulder to check behind me. A man that looks vaguely familiar is standing about seventy yards back and I scowl, trying to place him before turning to Storm.

"Five o'clock," I whisper to him but when we both turn to look back again, he's gone. Storm moves closer as he scans the crowd in front of us.

"Did you recognize him?"

I shake my head. "I'm not sure. Maybe, but I couldn't tell you where from. It would be incredibly stupid to show up here though if he was the guy."

"Yeah," he agrees. "Unless he couldn't enjoy his victory without seeing Diego's pain."

"This is so fucked up."

The club has been dealing with some heavy shit for the past six years but this feels different.

"I'll tell you one thing," Storm whispers as the pastor goes on about God always being with us and I roll my eyes. "I'm getting damn tired of going to funerals."

"I'm with you there." This is the second funeral in the last year and I'll be happy if we don't lose anyone else anytime soon. Dana was someone the club helped escape her abusive ex and her death hit us all hard. No matter how many we save, the ones we don't haunt us all.

"What did he look like?"

I shrug. "Like the most average white guy you've ever seen. Kinda tall, brown hair, slim."

"Perfect," he grumbles as his wife, Ali, walks up to him and grabs his hand, her pregnant belly poking out in front of her.

"Is everything okay?" she asks, glancing between the two of us.

"Yeah, kitten," he assures her. "Everything is fine."

Her gaze snaps to mine before drifting back to her husband. She flashes him a determined look and I lean back against the tree to watch the show, fighting back a smile.

"Logan James Chambers, don't you dare lie to me."

He growls and pulls her into his body. "We will discuss this later, woman."

Laney's parents stand with Rodriguez right on their heels as they approach the casket and each lay a single rose on top. Rodriguez lingers for a minute, his hand pressed against the closed lid of the casket and a single tear falls down his cheek. He quickly wipes it away and returns to his seat as the second row of chairs lays more roses on the top followed by the third and so on until there is a pile of flowers adorning her coffin.

The preacher finishes his sermon and steps back as two men in work uniforms step forward and start lowering the casket into the ground amid the sound of sniffles and tears. Kodiak and Moose make their way through the crowd and join our group.

"You guys see anything?" Kodiak asks.

"Maybe. He disappeared before I could get a good look, though."

He sighs and nods. "Shit."

"My thoughts exactly. Where's your lady?"

"She wanted to come but said she couldn't do another funeral." Kodiak met Tate six months ago when her mom passed away and I don't blame her for skipping this one.

I nod.

"Y'all headed back to the clubhouse for the wake?" Moose asks and I shake my head.

"I gotta go try and find my brother."

Kodiak sighs and I shake my head.

"Don't fucking start with me."

"You're killing yourself with this and he doesn't even care, Smith."

"I said "don't"," I grumble even though he's right. Clay doesn't care that his addiction is eating away at me just as much as it is him but what else can I do? Abandon him?

"Just give it a break. At least for today," he reasons and I shake my head.

"Can't. Tell Rodriguez I'm sorry I couldn't make it," I say as I back away from them. No one tries to stop me as I walk to my truck and once I'm inside, I lay my head against the headrest and take a deep breath.

My phone buzzes with a text and I dig it out of my pocket.

Quinn:
Thank you for last night.

I smile, my stress melting away for a second as I type out my reply.

Me:
Pretty sure that's my line.
When can I see you again?

Instead of waiting for her reply, I decide to get my search over with so I can hopefully stop by and see Quinn and Brooklyn tonight. On my list of to-dos, that is the only thing I really want to do.

I pull away from the cemetery as the rest of the guys climb on their bikes and I turn toward Clay's favorite place to get high, hoping I don't have to search too hard tonight. Kodiak's statement keeps repeating in my head and the more I think about it, the angrier I get. I know that he's absolutely right. Clay doesn't care about anything but the drugs. It is his sole focus and nothing else matters, not even me and each night I go out searching for him, I want to throw in the towel. Why am I killing myself when he doesn't give a shit? But I know if I gave up and he died from an overdose, I would never forgive myself. Sometimes, though, that just makes me hate him more.

Pulling into the parking lot of a dingy old bar on the outskirts of town, one of Clay's favorite hang-outs, I park my truck in the back of the lot and smash my fists against the steering wheel again and again until my hands drop weakly into my lap. As I look up at the door to the bar, I consider leaving and never looking back but something, maybe my guilt or the fear of being completely alone, keeps me moving forward. With a heavy sigh, I turn off the truck and climb out. There are a few people hanging out around the entrance but other than that, the lot is quiet. No one would come to a place like this unless they were looking for trouble. Which is exactly why Clay likes it.

As soon as I walk in, I want to turn right around and leave but I press on, working my way into the smoke-filled room as my eyes adjust to the dim lighting. A painfully thin woman glances up at me from behind the bar and I nod.

"Clay here?"

She points to the back room and I mutter a "thank you" as I pass her. As I step into the back room, I stop and take in the scene, my stomach turning at the bodies draped over every available surface - their eyes glassy and vacant.

Jesus Christ.

My gaze drifts to the corner of the room and I release a breath at the sight of Clay curled up in a chair. His hair is greasy and it looks like he hasn't eaten anything since he walked away from me four days ago. Sighing, I run my hand through my hair before making my way across the room and crouching down in front of him.

"Clay?" I whisper, shaking him a little and his head slowly turns to look at me but his eyes are empty. There's a pipe in his lap and I shake my head as I grab it and set it on the coffee table behind me as a deep, aching sadness takes hold of me. How did everything go so wrong? How did we end up here? Pushing down my pain, I put my hands around my brother and pull him out of the chair. I try to encourage him to support his own weight but it becomes clear fairly quickly that he can't and tears burn my eyes as I lift him into my arms and turn toward the door.

"Luke," he whispers, his eyes drifting closed and I jostle him to keep him conscious as I carry him back into the bar.

"Yeah, I'm here, bud. Stay with me."

He opens his eyes and licks his dry, cracked lips. "I'm sorry."

"Don't worry about it," I assure him and his eyes close again. It's dark when I step outside and once I get him to the truck, I buckle him into the passenger seat and press my fingers to his neck to check his pulse. I release a breath when the steady beat of his heart pounds against my fingers and I drop my head, a mix of relief and anger flooding my body. I've gotten so used to this, so accustomed that I'd forgotten how fucked up it was to spend my night hunting the city for my drugged out brother. It wasn't until I met Quinn that I was able to look at this all with new eyes and it makes me sick.

Glancing up again, I stare at his face as I try to decide where to take him tonight. Usually, we'd go back to the clubhouse but I don't want to interrupt the wake and I'm in no mood to be around a bunch of people right now.

That only leaves one option but it's one I've been avoiding. With a sigh, I push off the truck and slam the door before rounding the front and slipping behind the wheel. He doesn't even stir as I fire the truck up and pull out of the parking lot.

As I drive toward Iris's house, I try to think of what I'm going to say to her, how I'm going to explain all this but I know no matter what I say or how I say it, she's going to be disappointed in me and that kills me. I've failed at protecting my brother and I certainly don't need her to tell me that but I also know that I can't do this alone anymore.

Her house is dark as I pull into the driveway but as I turn the truck off, the front porch lights turn on and Iris steps out of the house, clutching her robe around her.

"Lucas? What are you doing here so late?" she asks, squinting into the darkness as her voice drifts in through the open window. I open the door and climb down.

"I need your help."

Her gaze darts to the passenger seat. I don't know how well she can see Clay through the windshield but after a moment, she nods and I walk around to the other door and yank it open. Clay opens his eyes for a second before they drift closed again and I lift him out of the truck.

"Oh my god," Iris breathes as I step around the front of the truck with Clay's body in my arms and she runs over to me, fear marring her pretty face. "What's wrong with him?"

"He's high," I answer, my voice lifeless as I continue walking to the front door and her soft gasp drives a stake through my heart. She's stunned but after a second, she catches up with me and holds the front door open for me as I carry Clay into the house.

"Take him to his old bedroom."

I nod and turn toward the hallway, leaving her in the dining room. Clay's room is just as he left it and I guess that makes sense since neither one of us technically moved out. I lay him in his bed and pull the covers over him before checking his pulse again. His heart is still beating steadily and I sigh as I step away from the bed and leave him to sleep.

Iris is in the kitchen, brewing tea when I find her and she casts a disapproving look over her shoulder when I walk in.

"I take it this is the thing you wanted to talk to me about?"

I nod. "Yeah."

"How long?" She pours tea into a mug for herself and holds up a second one to me. I nod again and she pours water in it before handing it to me.

"Six years."

"What the fuck, Lucas?"

I stare down at the mug in my hand. "I know, Iris. I just… I thought I could handle it myself. Make him stop and then, at some point, it just became my life."

"You should have known better. Addiction runs in your family, Lucas, and you're better than this."

"I just wanted to protect him. That's all I've ever wanted," I say, my voice cracking and she sighs, setting her cup down on the counter. Iris crosses the kitchen and pulls me into her arms.

"I know but this isn't the way to do it. He needs real help - more than either you or I can give him and you deserve a life that's made up of more than taking care of your baby brother."

Nodding, I pull away. "You're right."

"Listen, I have to go to work in the morning but I'll come home early and we can all sit down and have a talk, okay? We've got to convince him to get help because I never want to see him like this again."

"Me either," I agree.

"It's getting late so I need to try and get some sleep. Do you need anything before I crash?"

I shake my head. "No, Riz. I'm good."

She studies me for a minute before nodding and giving me another hug. Once she leaves the kitchen, I collapse into one of the dining chairs and set my cup of tea down on the table.

Fuck.

What a day.

My phone buzzes in my pocket and I pull it out, hoping it's a text from Quinn.

Quinn:
How fast can you get over here?

I decide to call her instead of texting her back.

"Hey," she answers and at the sound of her voice, a sense of calm washes over me and I sigh.

"You have no idea how good it is to talk to you."

"Yeah?" she asks. "Bad day?"

I nod. "The fucking worst."

"Tell me about it."

"It's just my brother," I answer like somehow she'll accept that answer and she sighs.

"Tell me about it, Lucas."

Before I know it, I'm spilling my guts and feeling better than I have since I dropped her off last night after our date but that's what she does for me. Something about her makes all the shit just melt away. She's the only thing that's keeping me going lately and I don't know what I'd do if I lost her.

*   *   *   *

"Sleeping beauty awake yet?" Iris asks, walking into the kitchen and I shake my head as I take a sip of coffee.

"Nope. Still out like a light."

She fills her travel mug with coffee before turning to me. "Have you checked on him?"

"Yeah, when I woke up."

"You look tired," she comments, sitting across from me at the table. "Did you sleep much last night?"

I shake my head. "No, I never do when I'm keeping an eye on him."

"Lucas," she whispers, picking at the corner of the table before her green eyes meet mine. "Was I too easy on you guys? I never wanted to drive you away but since you showed up last night, I can't help thinking that I should have been more strict with the two of you when you were growing up."

I reach across the table and grab her hand. "Don't ever fucking think you didn't do enough for us, Riz. We were homeless when you found us and I think we'd both probably be dead right now if it wasn't for you."

"But…"

"No," I snap, cutting her off as I shake my head. "Clay and I were dealt a bad hand before you came into our lives. You're the only reason we're both still breathing."

She nods, wiping away a tear and it shreds me. Iris may not be related to Clay or me biologically but she's the only mother we've known for the longest time and I hate seeing her blame herself for this.

"I love you boys, you know."

I nod. "I know and we love you, too."

"Okay," she breathes, releasing my hand and standing up before brushing her hands over her skirt. "I'd better get going to work. I'll try to come home after lunchtime and we'll all talk, okay?"

"Sounds good."

Turning away from me, she grabs her purse off the counter before holding her coffee cup up in the air. "Thanks for the coffee, by the way."

"You're welcome," I call as she walks into the living room. After she leaves, I relax back into my chair as open the paper, trying to do anything to distract myself from the impromptu intervention we're having today.

"Motherfucker!" Clay's voice bellows from down the hallway and I sigh as I set the paper down and wait for him to come into the kitchen. A few seconds later, he stomps in and slaps his hand against the wall. "You brought me to Iris's?!"

"What else should I have done when I found you unconscious in the back room of a bar?"

His eyes narrow. "Take me to the club, just like every other fucking time, asshole."

"That's never worked before so I thought I'd try something different. Besides, the clubhouse was being used for something else."

Sighing, he walks over to the coffee maker and pulls a mug out of the cabinet before slamming the door and I clench my teeth to avoid losing my shit over his hissy fit.

"I take it she left for work?" he asks after filling up his mug and I nod.

"Yeah, but she'll be back after lunch."

He shrugs. "Whatever. I won't be here."

"Actually, you fucking will."

"Actually," he sneers. "You don't get to fucking tell me what to do anymore."

Sucking in a breath, I mentally count to ten to get control of my anger before meeting his eyes. "Why are you doing this, Clay? We just want to help you."

"I don't want your goddamn help. Why don't you just go back to your new family and forget I ever existed?"

"What are you talking about?" I ask.

"The club. As soon as you left home, you went and made yourself a new family so why don't you just worry about them."

"Is that what all of this is about? You feel alone?"

He laughs but it's hollow. "Nothing in my life has anything to do with you."

"The guys would welcome you with open arms."

"No," he mutters. "They wouldn't."

I nod. "They would if you were clean and I'd love nothing more than to have my brother back."

I see the sharp retort right on the tip of his tongue but he pauses and I notice the longing in his eyes. It gives me a spark of hope.

"It's your choice, Clay. You can choose something

different. You can choose to have a family again and yeah, it's not conventional but who cares? The family we were dealt kind of sucked so let's make a new one."

He eyes me warily as he drinks his coffee and my heart pounds as I wait for his answer. Hope wells up inside me despite the fact that I know better.

"There's something I need to tell you," he finally says and I nod.

"Okay. What's up?"

He shifts back and forth on his feet, staring down at his coffee mug. "I drove up to the prison to see him."

"What?" I breathe, blinking at him in shock as a chunk of ice imbeds itself in my stomach. "Why would you do that?"

"I… I just needed to talk to him."

"And what could you possibly need to talk to him about?"

He clears his throat. "He wrote me a letter a couple weeks back. He says he's innocent."

"He's fucking lying!" I roar, slamming my fist on the table as I jerk to my feet. Clay jumps before his eyes narrow and he takes a step toward me.

"You don't fucking know that."

"Have you lost your goddamn mind? Have you done so many drugs that it's literally melted your brain cells? Of course, I fucking know that he's lying because I watched it happen. I saw everything with my own two eyes."

"So you say but I believe him."

I sink into my chair with a huff, shaking my head. "You've got to be kidding me? He's literally sitting in jail for what he did and you think he's innocent?"

"You don't have to believe me," he grits out, tossing his coffee mug into the sink where I hear it shatter. "But I'm going to find proof."

Before I can stop him, he runs out of the house and I bury my face in my hands, trying to wrap my mind around the last ten minutes but no matter how much I go over it, it still doesn't make sense. My muscles tense and my knee shakes as I keep repeating what Clay said, over and over again, until I feel like I'm losing my mind. Standing up, I grab a piece of paper off the counter and leave a note for Iris before I run out to my truck and fire it up.

There's only one person who has answers for me and it doesn't matter how much I don't want to ever speak to him again. For Clay, I will.

The hour long drive to the prison passes in a blur of memories and pain and as I pull into the lot, my stomach flips. I haven't set eyes on the man in years and I never thought I'd be here. My hands shake as I walk across the lot and step into the lobby, where I sign in. After an officer pats me down and I leave my cell phone and keys at the front desk, they lead me back to a room with plexiglass dividing it in half and phones in each cubby.

I take one of the chairs on the end and wipe my

sweaty palms on my jeans as I wait for the guards to bring him out. My heart races and memories start to overwhelm me. The door in the back of the room opens and he steps out, dressed in an orange jumpsuit and cuffs around his wrists and ankles. His gaze zeroes in on me and I feel like throwing up and running from the room but I stay seated, leveling him with a steely glare despite the chaos raging through my soul.

He sits across from me with a surprised expression and we both pick up the phones at the same time and press them to our ears.

"Lucas?" he asks, his voice just like I remember from all those years ago and I nod.

"Hi, Dad."

It Ends Tonight

Chapter Nine
Quinn

"Quinn, I have Nick, the lead singer from The Renegades, on line one again," Willa says, poking her head in my office and I sigh as I look up from the paperwork on my desk. This is the third time he's called today and each call starts out with a silly question about the event before he starts flirting with me and before I'm able to end the call, he asks me out.

"What does he want this time?"

She shakes her head. "I'm not sure."

"Just uh… just tell him I'm in a meeting and answer any question he has," I say with a tired sigh.

"You got it."

"Oh, and, Willa? Please remove him from our vendor list so we don't have this problem again."

She laughs. "It's already done. You're too nice,

Quinn."

"You might be right about that."

"Do you want me to go grab you some lunch?" she asks but before I can answer, the front door opens and she turns away from me. "Can I help you?"

"Yeah," a voice answers from the front office and I smile. "I'm looking for Quinn."

"Your name?"

"Lucas Smith."

Willa glances back at me and I try to hide the wide smile on my face as I nod but when she narrows her eyes, I know I failed. She studies me with a quirked brow for a second before she turns back to the front door.

"Go ahead."

As soon as Lucas walks into my office, my heart flutters in my chest and I drop my attempts to hide my grin as my gaze drops down his body and back up again. How the hell does the man make a t-shirt and jeans look better than anyone else?

"Hey, gorgeous."

I toss my pen down on the desk. "Hi. What are you doing here?"

"Should I be somewhere else?" he asks, a playful smile on his face and I shake my head.

"You know, now that you mention it, I think this is exactly where you should be."

"Good to know. Are you hungry? I was hoping I could take you out to lunch."

"I'm starving," I answer and he crosses the office until he's leaning over me as I sit in my chair.

"Can I steal you away for an hour?"

I purse my lips as I meet his eyes. "Only if you kiss me first."

"Well, I don't know, Miss Dawson… that's a difficult request."

"Difficult to kiss me?" I ask, arching a brow. "I'm offended."

He shakes his head and leans in until his lips gently brush against mine. "No, difficult to stop kissing you once I start."

I'm reminded of the other night when he dropped me off after our date and the ten minutes we spent making out on my front porch like a couple of teenagers before Alice interrupted us.

"Good answer."

His lips stretch into a smile against mine before he leans down and steals a kiss. My entire body relaxes at his touch like my soul is letting out the most content sigh and I reach up to grip his shirt, hoping to hold onto the feeling forever.

A throat clearing interrupts us and I jerk back. Lucas licks his lips and slowly turns to look at the doorway as I follow his gaze. Willa flashes me a knowing, indulgent smile and a quirked brow.

"I was just going to go grab lunch if you don't need anything else."

I shake my head. "No, I'm good."

"I bet you are," she mutters under her breath and I shoot her a look as she winks and leaves the room. Lucas laughs and his breath brushes against my ear.

"She's going to be impossible to rein in after she gets back."

"Regretting your decision to kiss me at work?"

I turn and meet his gaze, smiling softly. "Never."

"Good," he answers, standing up and holding his hand out to me. "Ready for lunch?"

I nod and grab my purse from under the desk before grabbing his hand. He pulls me out of my chair and wraps his arm around my waist before slipping his hand into the back pocket of my jeans.

"So, is there anything good around here?" he asks as we step outside and I nod as I lock the office door.

"Yeah, there's a deli on the next block over that has the best sandwiches," I say, pointing to the right before turning left. "Or, there's a burger place down there that I love."

He takes my hand and laces our fingers together. "What are you in the mood for?"

"Let's go to the deli."

He pulls me into his side as we turn for the deli. "So, how's your day?"

"Busy."

"But good?" he asks and I nod.

"Yeah. What about you? I haven't seen you in a

couple days."

He smiles and arches a brow. "Miss me?"

"Maybe. Is that crazy?" I know we haven't known each other that long but I really do love spending time with him and he's been too busy to stop by the last couple nights and texting only helps so much.

"If it is, then I'm right there with you. I wanted to come see you more than you know."

A blush creeps up my cheeks and I look down at the sidewalk to hide my smile. After all I've been through, it means so much to me that he isn't playing games with me. He's honest and upfront with how he's feeling and it's exactly what I need.

"What kept you away?"

He sighs. "Clay."

"How is he?"

"Last time I saw him, he was just fine but that was days ago."

"I'm so sorry, Lucas," I whisper as we stop in front of the deli. He pastes a smile on his face but I can see the stress wearing on him. As he opens the door, he brings our intertwined hands to his lips and kisses the back of mine.

"Don't worry about it, babe. It is what it is."

I nod. "Well, I'm here if you want to talk about it."

"I know. Now," he says as we step up to the front counter, "tell me what's good here."

"My favorite is the honey bear sandwich," I reply,

pointing to the menu board up on the wall. He nods as he reads the description with an adorable pucker to his lips.

"Sounds good."

A young woman stops in front of us with an expectant expression. "What can I get for you two?"

"I'll get the honey bear sandwich, a side of fries, and a water," I say before glancing back at Lucas, who nods.

"Same, please."

She rings it up and reads out the total. Lucas grabs his wallet out of his pocket and when I open my mouth to protest, he shoots me a look before handing over some cash. I stare at him for a second before pulling my wallet out of my purse and grabbing a ten-dollar bill. He glances back at me as I step up to the counter and slip the money in the tip jar. His jaw ticks as he watches me step back and then he smiles and shakes his head, pulling me into his arms as she hands him his change and receipt.

"Defiant, aren't you?"

I arch a brow. "Only if you are."

"Me? Defiant?"

"Well," I mutter, wrapping my arms around his waist. "Maybe defiant isn't the right word but you could let me pay for a meal every once in a while."

He shakes his head. "No, I couldn't. Iris would have my head... and my balls if I ever made a lady pay for her own food."

"I see... so you're going to pay for every woman's lunch?" I ask, gesturing to the line forming at the counter and he laughs.

"If I have to, to prove a point."

I flash him a skeptical look and he grins as he pulls some twenties out of his wallet and goes back up to the register where he whispers something to the cashier before handing her the money. The first woman in line watches him, wide-eyed, as he struts back over to me and I laugh.

"Feeling proud of yourself?"

He nods. "Yeah, I am."

"Smith," the cashier calls, holding up a bag with our food in it. He flashes me a wink before strolling back up to the counter to grab it. When he comes back, we head out to the patio and find an open table as he lays out our sandwiches, fries, and bottles of water.

"So," he says as we sit down across from each other. "I have a question for you."

"Shoot."

"Tomorrow night… I was hoping to take you and Brooklyn to dinner at Iris's house."

"Oh," I whisper, surprised by his question.

"If this is moving too fast for you, just say the word, Quinn, but I'd really like to introduce her to the two of you."

Our eyes meet across the table and the hopeful expression on his face pulls at my heart. Maybe it is moving too fast but I can't deny how I feel about him, even after such a short time, and I can tell that this is important to him. I nod.

"I'd really like that."

He flashes me a satisfied smile. "I'll let Iris know."

As I peel back the wrapper around my sandwich, I suck in a breath, suddenly feeling nervous about meeting Iris tomorrow night. It's clear from how Lucas speaks about her that she means a lot to him and I want to impress her.

"You okay?" he asks and I nod.

"Yeah, just a little nervous, I guess. I want her to like me."

He reaches across the table and grabs my hand. "Of course, she's going to like you. How could she not?"

"I... I just don't want her to think badly of me. I know how people see me - a single woman raising my child on my own."

"First off, Iris isn't like that and second, anyone who is doesn't deserve to know you. I may not know what happened with Brooklyn's father but I know you well enough to know that you wouldn't be raising her by yourself if you had any other choice."

"Thank you," I whisper as my heart pounds in my chest. I glance down at the table for a second as a blush creeps up my cheeks before meeting his eyes again. "Tell me about her."

"Iris?"

I nod and he laughs as he pulls his hand back and pops a French fry into his mouth. "Let's see... she's worked as a manager at this little grocery store as long as I've known her and she's super laid back, which is exactly what I needed as a kid. She likes to drink tea and watch movies - that's something we used to do together when I couldn't sleep…"

"I can't see you drinking tea," I interrupt and he laughs.

"To be honest, it wasn't for me so she'd make me hot cocoa and we'd watch her chick flicks."

I laugh, shaking my head. "I can't see that either."

"I know. No one can but I have a plethora of movie references up here," he says, tapping the side of his forehead.

"Plethora, huh? I'm impressed."

He nods with a wink as he grabs another French fry. "You should be."

"How did you meet Iris? Was she fostering other kids?"

"Uh," he mutters before clearing his throat. "No. Her house backs up to the woods and there's this old railway that used to run through there but they don't use it anymore. Clay and I found an old boxcar sitting on the abandoned track and we were living there when she found us."

"Oh my god, Lucas," I whisper, imagining my own baby out in the woods, living in a boxcar and tears sting my eyes. "I'm so sorry."

As he glances down at the table, he shakes his head.

"It's okay. I mean, it all worked out, right?"

"Still, no kid should have to go through something like that. How did you end up there?"

"I think that's enough sadness for one day, don't you?" he replies, lifting his head and the pain in his eyes breaks my heart. There's so much depth to this man as well as pain and tragedy that I haven't discovered yet and what I already know makes me want to pull him into my arms and fix it for him. "There's something that I wanted to ask you, though."

"What?"

"Your ex fiancé... what happened with him?"

I sigh and pick at my sandwich. "Nothing really, which I guess was the problem. I met Danny just before the start of my sophomore year of college and he was the kind of guy that everyone expected me to end up with. Like if you saw us, you would just assume we were together because we looked like we fit but in every other area of our relationship, it was just... boring, expected."

"So you ended it?"

I nod. "Yeah. I just wanted something... more. Besides, if I had to listen to one more golf story, I would have blown my brains out."

"No golf stories, got it," he murmurs with a grin and I laugh, playfully scowling at him.

"I'll believe the movie thing but there's no way you have golf stories."

"Okay, you've got me on that one. So, if you don't

want golf stories and the expected, what is it that you do want?"

"I want to be someone's whole world. I want to be loved so fiercely that it takes my breath away sometimes and I want to build a beautiful family on the basis of that love."

His brows shoot up. "Wow."

"Yeah," I answer with a smile as I drop my gaze for a second before peeking back up at him. "What about you? What do you want?"

"I want to get my brother clean."

I shake my head. "No, what do *you* want? When you reach the end of your life, what is going to be the thing that you look back on and say "I did good"?"

He opens his mouth to respond before snapping it shut again as a scowl takes over his features.

"What?" I ask and he shakes his head.

"Honestly, I don't know. My whole life for the last six years has been Clay and I think I've completely forgotten about me."

"You need to figure out what is going to make you happy."

He nods. "Yeah, I guess I do."

Watching him, my heart breaks. It's clear to me that Lucas has one of the biggest hearts I've ever encountered but he hides it behind jokes and charm while he silently suffers through so much pain that I'm not even sure how he's standing. In some ways, he and I are so alike and but it feels like he's given up hope at ever having a normal life, which is something I still desperately cling to.

"I hope this doesn't upset you but your brother is his own person and he's going to do whatever he wants to do. It's clear to me that you carry around an immense amount of pain from your past but you can't carry his, too. The reason he turns to drugs is because he doesn't know how else to deal with that pain in a healthy way but that's what he has to learn if he's ever going to get clean."

"Are you saying I shouldn't help him?" he asks, his jaw ticking and I shake my head as I reach across the table and grab his hand.

"No, not at all, but just like your brother uses drugs to bury his pain, you use him to avoid yours and you'll never be happy or free until you let him go enough to become your own person and have your own life."

He clears his throat and stands abruptly, knocking the chair back a little. It scrapes against the floor and I feel like every eye on the street turns to look at us. "I've... uh, I've got to go."

I watch him as he walks back into the deli and stomps out the front door without ever looking back at me. Once he's out of sight, I lean back in my chair and release a heavy breath. "Shit."

It Ends Tonight

*   *   *   *

"You got any plans tonight?" Alice asks as she plops down next to me on the couch. I glance down at the jeans and nice shirt I changed into after work on the off chance that Lucas shows up to take Brooklyn and me to dinner tonight.

"Not sure."

She arches a brow as her gaze dips to my outfit. "How are you not sure?"

"Well… Lucas invited Brooklyn and me over for dinner but then I'm pretty sure I put my foot in my mouth."

"Did you text him?"

I nod. "Yeah, and I tried calling him today."

"I'll get the wine," she replies, patting my leg as she jumps off the couch and I sigh. The doorbell rings before she makes it into the kitchen and she stops in the hallway before slowly turning to me.

"You want me to get that?"

I peek over the back of the couch to the front door. "Maybe just go see who it is first."

"Okay, 'cause that won't make you look like a crazy person. You know we don't have a peephole."

"I told you we should have bought that video doorbell thing," I grumble as I get off the couch and meet her in the hallway.

"You gonna go answer it?" she asks as the bell rings again.

"I don't know. What if he's just here to break up with me?"

She shakes her head, giving me a little shove toward the door. "Guys don't break up in person anymore. If that's what he was doing, he would have texted you or just ghosted you."

"Good to know."

He knocks on the door and I sigh before dragging myself across the foyer, my heart racing as I silently plead to the heavens to not let him dump me. I know we've only gone on one real date, but boy do I like him. As I wrap my hand around the doorknob, I suck in a breath and count to three before yanking it open. Lucas glances up at me and surprises me as he flashes me a smile that makes my knees a little weak.

"Hey, you ready?"

I narrow my eyes. "Uh, maybe?"

"Maybe?"

"Um," I mutter, glancing over my shoulder to where Alice is standing, listening to our every word. "Do you think we could talk outside?"

"Sure."

We step outside and I shut the door behind me as butterflies flap around in my belly.

"What's up?" he asks.

"I, uh… I just wanted to apologize for yesterday. I didn't mean to upset you…"

He presses his finger to my lips, silencing me as he takes a step forward, closing the space between us. "Please don't apologize for what you said. It was essentially what my brothers in the club have been saying to me for years but the way you said it, it stuck with me. I was up all night thinking about it and meeting you has made me realize that I do want a life. Not that I know what I want in that life yet but I do want it."

"So…" I say, studying him. "We're good?"

"Yeah, we're good," he answers with a nod and I release a breath. "Now, are you and Brooklyn ready to go?"

I glance down at my outfit as I nod absentmindedly. "Just give me like two minutes."

He nods and follows me as I turn back to the house and step inside. Alice is waiting right where I left her and she shoots me an "I told you so" look as she crosses her arms over her chest.

"Shut up," I whisper as I race past her into the living room where Brooklyn is quietly playing with blocks. "Hey, baby girl. You ready to go?"

She looks up before dropping her block on the floor and reaching for me. Before I can grab her, Lucas laughs at something Alice says and her head whips in the direction of the foyer. She's off like a bolt of lightning, quickly crawling out of the living room and into the foyer. A squeal greets me as Lucas laughs again and when I step into the hallway, my heart almost seizes at the sight of him holding her in his arms.

God, what is it about a sexy man holding a baby that sends ovaries into overdrive?

"Ready?" he asks and I nod, grabbing my purse off the table.

"Yeah, let's go."

"Y'all have fun now, ya hear?" Alice calls in a smug voice as we walk out of the house and I flip her off behind my back. Her laughter reaches me just before the door closes and I shake my head, fighting back a smile. I hate when Alice is right because that girl can gloat like no one else so I know I'll be hearing about this for the next month, at least.

"I feel like I need to clear something up," Lucas says as he climbs behind the wheel of my car after buckling Brooklyn into her car seat.

"What's that?"

"Earlier, when you thought I was here to break up with you… Well, I just can't see that happening anytime soon. Or maybe even ever if I'm being honest. We're taking this slow because that's what you need not because of the way I'm feeling about you."

I blink, surprised but not unhappy with his declaration. The fear that I expected isn't there either. "Oh."

"Shit. Now I scared you by saying that."

I shake my head and reach out to grab his hand. "You don't scare me, Lucas. And if we're being honest, I don't even know what I meant when I asked you to take this slow. It's just been so long since I've dated and I'm a different person now than I was then but I'm comfortable with the pace we're at now and in case you haven't noticed, I really, really like you."

"Yeah?" he asks with a shy smile that pulls at my heart strings. I nod.

"Yeah."

His smile grows as he reaches across the car and brushes my hair from my face. "What are the rules on kissing you?"

"Oh, the rule on kissing is simple."

"Is it?" he asks, arching a brow. "Why don't you enlighten me?"

"The rule is that you should kiss me as frequently and passionately as you want."

He nods slowly, like he's thinking over what I said before he meets my eyes again. The spark of playfulness in his gaze makes my heart skip a beat. "So, what you're really saying, is that I've been dropping the ball?"

"Yes... I think you have."

Warmth rushes through me and my body hums in anticipation as he leans in and just when his lips brush against mine, Brooklyn lets out a squeal from the back seat. Lucas drops his head and chuckles before turning to my daughter.

"No one forgot you were here, baby girl."

"Guess you'll have to save that kiss for later," I whisper, tracing my finger over his bottom lip after he glances back up at me. His blue eyes darken and the hunger in his gaze feels like a bolt of electricity running through my veins but he doesn't move. "Lucas?"

"We're going to be late for dinner," he growls before opening his door and climbing out of the car. I watch him, open-mouthed, as he rounds the front of the car and opens my door. Reaching into the car, he pulls me to my feet and closes the door before pressing my back to the car. There's a flash of fear that lances through me and he picks up on it immediately, brushing his fingers across my face. "Tell me what happened to you, baby."

"Now really isn't the time or place, Lucas," I whisper and he nods, studying me for a moment.

"Listen, I've worked with enough women who have been hurt by men to know that something bad happened to you and the last thing I would ever want to do is push you past your limits so I want you to always remember that, no matter what, you're the one in control here. Say you understand that."

I nod without even a moment's hesitation. "Yes."

"I'm gonna kiss you now," he replies, holding my face as he leans in and my eyes flutter closed as our lips connect. I sigh. His arms slip around my waist and he pulls me close. I trail my fingers across his chest, reveling in the feeling of his firm muscles and the low hum that vibrates in the back of his throat from my touch.

"Get a room!" a voice yells and we both jerk back. I glare up at the front porch where Alice flashes me a grin.

"Go away!" I yell back and she laughs as she turns away from us. We watch her disappear into the house before Lucas turns back to me and steals another quick kiss.

"Come on. Iris will have my ass if we're late."

I arch a brow as I fight back a smile. "You risked your ass just for a kiss?"

"Naw, Darlin'. Not just any kiss."

A wide smile stretches across my face and my cheeks heat as he opens my car door and after I slip inside, he closes it and rounds the front of the car again. Brooklyn squeals from the back seat as we pull out of the driveway and I laugh, turning my head to glance back at her.

"Why is it whenever you come around, I'm chopped liver to that girl?"

He laughs, peeking at her in the rearview mirror. "She's got good taste."

"So humble," I tease and he flashes me a grin before turning back to the road. Butterflies start to flap around in my belly and I press my hand against it as I suck in a breath. "I can't believe how nervous I am."

"Don't be nervous, sweetheart. Like I told you before, Iris is very chill."

I nod, reaching across the center console to hold his

hand. "But she's important to you, which means that I want to make a good first impression."

"Well, if it's any consolation, you made a fantastic first impression on me."

"Did I?" I laugh. "Tell me, was it the internal bleeding or panic attack that really won you over?"

"All of the above."

With a giggle, I shake my head. "I don't think those are going to work on Iris."

"That's true," he agrees with a nod. "But we've been hanging out for like two weeks now and I can confidently say that you are an easy person to love."

"Am I now?" I ask breathlessly. Does that mean that he…

"Definitely."

Turning to him, I study his face as he focuses on the road ahead of us, trying to discern what exactly he meant by that statement. Like he just said, we've only been hanging out for two weeks so surely he can't mean that he loves me. Right? Then again, I'm not all that sure how I feel about him. Saying I like him feels so inadequate for the thumping of my heart and the butterflies in my belly any time he comes around but do I love him? I don't know.

"We're here," he says and I turn as the cute little cottage comes into view.

"This is where you grew up?"

He nods as he pulls the car to a stop and puts it in

park. "Yep. You ready?"

"As I'll ever be," I answer with a nod and he shakes his head as he climbs out of the car. I suck in a breath before slipping out of the car and he's already at the back door, unbuckling Brooklyn. Once he has her out, he carries her over to me and grabs my hand. She lays her head down on his shoulder as she plops her thumb into her mouth and my heart aches at the sight of them. He's so damn good with her and she absolutely adores him - something that surprised me since she's usually so reserved around strangers but from the moment they met, she's been head over heels for the man.

"I don't think I've ever seen anything cuter," someone says and I turn toward the cottage, smiling at the dark haired woman in the doorway. Her gaze moves to me and she smiles. "You must be Quinn."

"I am. It's so nice to meet you," I tell her, holding my hand out but she bypasses it and wraps me up in a hug as the warm scent of apples and cinnamon surrounds me.

"Come on in," she urges as she pulls away and turns to Lucas. Brooklyn pops her head up, with her thumb still in her mouth, and stares at Iris, who smiles at her. "Hello, gorgeous girl."

Brooklyn smiles around her thumb and Iris lets out a chuckle before glancing back at Lucas.

"You look good with a baby on your hip, kid."

He peeks over at me with a grin. "You hear that, babe? I look good with a baby on my hip."

"She's not wrong," I answer, fighting back a smile. My stomach growls, drawing the attention of everyone on the porch and Iris backs up toward the door, ushering us to follow her.

"Come on, y'all. Pizza got here just before you did."

Lucas wraps his free arm around my waist as we step into the cottage. "Iris isn't much of a cook," he whispers and she turns to glare at him.

"I heard that."

"Tell me I'm wrong."

She sneers before turning back toward the kitchen and he laughs, pulling me into his side.

"Maybe if you're lucky, you'll even get to hear the Christmas ham story."

"Oh, Christ," she calls from the kitchen as a cupboard slams. "You're never going to let me live that down, are you?"

"Riz, we could have demoed a house with the thing after you got your hands on it." He laughs and she steps out of the kitchen with plates in her hands as she glares at him.

"So you say. Personally, I think it wasn't that bad."

"It broke a knife!" he exclaims, pulling me closer and I laugh as Iris rolls her eyes.

"You keep heckling me, boy, and I'm gonna kick you out on the front porch with no pizza."

He nods. "Okay, you win."

"Finally. Y'all sit down and I'll be right back with

the pizza. Quinn, I hope you like pepperoni."

"Sounds good," I tell her and she flashes me a smile before disappearing into the kitchen as Lucas and I sit down at the table. I turn to him and hold my hands out. "Here. You want me to take her?"

"Naw, baby. You relax; I've got her." He places her in his lap, facing the table and wraps his arm around her belly to keep her secure and my heart warms at how good he is with her. I reach into my bag and pull out the little container of fruit, crackers, and cheese I brought with me for Brooklyn's dinner and set it out in front of her. As soon as the food hits the table, she leans forward and snatches up a quartered grape before popping the piece into her mouth.

"Mmm," she hums and I smile as Lucas laughs.

"Is that good, pretty girl?" he asks her as she shoves another piece of grape into her mouth. I glance up and notice Iris watching us from the opening to the kitchen with a soft smile on her face and tears in her eyes. She dashes them away before motioning for me to be quiet as she steps into the room.

"Here we go," she calls and sets a box of pizza down in the middle of the table. I grab a slice of pizza and slip it onto a plate before setting it in front of Lucas.

He smiles and leans over to kiss my cheek. "Thanks, sweetheart."

"You're welcome." A blush creeps up my cheeks and when I glance across the table again, Iris is watching us with a wide smile on her face.

"You know, when Lucas told me he was bringing a girl home, I knew you must be special but seeing the two of you together is something else. You're so good for him," Iris says.

I peek over at Lucas as I fight back a smile. "You didn't like his other girlfriends?"

"Honey, he's never brought another girl home. You're the first and that alone earns you some major brownie points."

"Told you, Quinn," he whispers in my ear. "I'm all in."

I pull back enough for our eyes to meet as I try to discern what that means. Does he mean that he's all in for the long haul with not only me but my daughter, too? Or is he just trying to say that he's ready to kick things up a notch? Am I ready for that? He offers me a reassuring smile as my head swirls with questions.

"Mamamamama," Brooklyn babbles, drawing my attention down to her.

"How old is she?" Iris asks and I push back all my questions as I look up at her and smile.

"Thirteen months."

Iris smiles at Brooklyn, who watches her carefully. "She is just adorable and so sweet."

"Thank you."

"Excuse me if this is too bold, but I wanted to tell you how brave I think you are for raising her on your own. I know how hard it can be," she says, glancing over at Lucas with a fond smile. I nod, darker memories threatening to resurface.

"Thank you. She makes it all worth it."

She nods. "I hear you there. I never thought I'd end up with two young boys but I'd do it again in a heartbeat."

"All right, y'all. Enough mushy stuff. I'm starving," Lucas says, grabbing his slice of pizza and biting it in half as Iris laughs at him and grabs her own slice of pizza. The conversation flows easily as we eat and we sit around talking and laughing until Brooklyn falls asleep in Lucas's arms. As I watch her snoring on his broad chest, I know that he's stolen another little piece of my heart.

A.M. Myers

It Ends Tonight

Chapter Ten
Lucas

"Morning," Chance mumbles as I sink into the chair next to him with a steaming cup of coffee in my hand. I nod in agreement as I bring the mug to my lips and take a deep breath. Quinn, Brooklyn, and I stayed out at Iris's until almost midnight before I drove them back to their house and crashed at the clubhouse. Chance crosses his arms over his chest and sinks into his seat before letting his head fall back as his eyes close. He and Moose had an equally late night working a job and I'm surprised he's even awake at this hour.

"Got plans today?"

He shakes his head. "Nope, just couldn't sleep."

Before I can ask him why, the sound of yelling echoes down to the bar from upstairs and we both glance toward the stairs.

"Alison!" Storm roars, his voice booming through the clubhouse and anyone who is still sleeping upstairs won't be for long.

"Oh, hell," I mutter. Ever since Alison found out she was pregnant, Storm doesn't like to leave her alone so when we have work to do that goes into the night, he makes her sleep at the clubhouse, which means for the past few months, we've all had front row seats to their frequent fights. It would make all our lives so much easier if just one of them was a little less stubborn than the other but unfortunately, they are pretty evenly matched.

"Go fuck yourself, Logan," Ali calls as she waddles down the stairs, her belly hindering her tantrum. Storm is right behind her, his brows drawn together as he glares daggers into her back.

"Don't walk away from me, Kitten. This conversation isn't over."

Ali scoffs. "Yes, it is."

"Fucking hormones," Rooster, one of our new prospects, whispers under his breath from across the table and I glance at him with an incredulous look. If Alison heard his comment, she'd rip him a new one and that's tame compared to what Storm would do to him. Dude does not play when it comes to his lady. I kick his chair under the table and he jerks up before turning to me with wide eyes.

"Get up, prospect."

He stares at me for a second, like he might argue, before he scrambles up. As soon as his seat is free, Alison slips into it and I shake my head as he trudges over to one of the couches in the corner. Ali glares over her shoulder as Storm comes up behind her and crosses his arms.

"You wanna do this here then?"

She spins in her chair and crosses her arms over chest, matching him as she stares him down. "No. I've already told you my answer and that is the end of the discussion."

"Like hell it is, woman."

Ali arches a brow before turning to face me with a smile on her face. "Smith, you're coming to the baby shower, right?"

"Uh," I mutter, my gaze flicking to Storm as he continues looming over Ali's shoulder. He nods and I turn back to her. "Sure. When is it?"

"The twenty-ninth."

I nod and sip my coffee. What the hell do you even do at a baby shower? I bet Quinn would know…As soon as her face pops into my head, I'm fighting back a smile. I just saw her and Brooklyn last night but I already miss both of them. Maybe I should stop by her office later and take her to lunch…

"Holy shit," Ali gasps, drawing my attention back to her. At some point, Storm picked her up and claimed her seat before positioning her in his lap but I couldn't tell you when.

"What?"

A wide grin stretches across her face. "You met someone."

"Don't know what you're talking about," I answer and Chance laughs.

"The fuck you don't. I'd know that dumbass look anywhere."

"What's her name?" Ali asks, ignoring Chance's comment and I sigh as I glance across the table at her. She's not going to let this go.

"Quinn."

"And how did you meet her?" she asks, practically bouncing in Storm's lap. He casts an annoyed glance in her direction as he places a steadying hand on her belly that she ignores.

"Uh…Watched a truck run a red light and slam into her car."

She gasps. "Is she okay?"

"Yeah," I answer, nodding. "She had some internal bleeding and they kept her in the hospital overnight but she's good now."

"Oh my gosh, that's so scary. But leave it to one of y'all to woo a woman right after coming to her rescue."

We all chuckle as I shake my head.

"It didn't quite happen like that but you're not wrong."

"Well, you should bring her to the shower. I would

love to meet her."

Bringing the mug to my lips, I shrug. "I don't know. We're taking things slow."

"Yeah, right," she snorts. "When has that ever happened?"

"She needs to take things slow."

Understanding crosses her face but before she can say anything, the phone rings and we all turn to look at it. Chance looks over his shoulder at Rooster, who is passed out on the couch.

"Prospect!" he yells and Rooster jerks up, looking at us through heavy eyes. "Phone!"

Rooster gets up from the couch and grabs the phone off the bar before handing it to Chance with a scowl. Rooster, or Dalton as he was known before he came to us, has been prospecting for the club for the last five months or so and honestly, I'm not sure how well he's working out. Most of the time he's an all right guy but lately he's had an attitude anytime he has been asked to do anything but I suppose this is the reason for only taking him on as a prospect. All the brothers need to be sure that he's got their back one hundred percent before we patch him in.

Chance catches my gaze, the hard look on his face getting my attention before he turns to Storm and hangs up the phone. "We gotta go."

"What's going on?" Storm asks and he shakes his head.

"Not one hundred percent on the details but we need to go meet someone at a hotel on the edge of town."

"Who?"

He shakes his head. "A woman named Morgan and her two kids."

"And she didn't say what's going on?" I ask, adrenaline already pumping through my veins. I'd really like to know what we are walking in on, though.

"No, just that she needs our help."

I nod as I stand. "Just the three of us or should I go wake up Moose?"

"Just us. She didn't sound panicked on the phone so I think she's safe for the moment."

"Rooster," Storm barks as he stands and Rooster straightens as he meets Storm's gaze. I fight back a grin because at least someone can get Rooster to show some respect. "Keep an eye on my girl."

"I can take care of myself, Logan," Ali grumbles and he whips around to face her. She matches him, getting right in his face with an arched brow. He cups her face and pulls her close before whispering something to her and whatever he said, makes her melt. She nods and reaches up on her toes to kiss him before heading back up to their bedroom.

"Man, I thought for sure she was gonna rip your nuts off this time," I mutter as the three of us head out to the parking lot and he grins.

"That was just foreplay."

I groan and pick up my pace. "I really need to get my own place."

"You could probably borrow Kodiak's cabin since he's living with Tate now," Chance says before flashing a grin. "Then again, you might be moving in with your own girl soon."

Truthfully, I would love to spend more time with Quinn and Brooklyn but I know she still needs more time and I respect that even though it sucks.

"Naw, I don't think so. We're taking it slow, remember?"

He laughs. "Ali was right, brother. We don't do slow - especially when we find what we want. Shit, look at Storm now. That broody motherfucker was a brick wall before Ali walked into his life."

"I'm still a goddamn brick wall," Storm grumbles and Chance laughs.

"Sure you are, pussy."

I laugh as I nudge Chance. "Like you're any better these days. As far as I can tell, I'm the only one of the three of us that still has his balls."

"You sure about that?" Storm asks and Chance nods.

"Yeah, you looked like quite the smitten kitten back there."

I shove both of them as I reach my bike. "Shut the fuck up."

"Don't forget your helmet, Sweetie," Chance calls in a high-pitched voice as he swings his leg over his bike and fires it up. I flip him off as I start my bike.

"Assholes."

Despite my objections, I can't help but think that a world where Quinn and Brooklyn are my everything doesn't sound so bad. I mean, look at Storm, Chance, and Kodiak. I've never seen them happier or more at peace than when they met their ladies. And there's no doubt in my mind that Quinn does that for me. She's the only place of refuge in the raging storm that is my life. Shit... Now I just need to convince her of that.

As we pull out of the parking lot, my mind drifts to last night and the look in her eyes when I pushed her up against the car. It was only supposed to be a cute, somewhat sexy moment but the fear in her gaze was so real for a second and that was all it took to really drive home the fact that she's been through something terrible. I'm fucking dying to know what happened, who hurt her, and possibly fix it if I can - not that I have any idea how I would do that - but I want to. I want to give her the whole damn world and do anything it takes to keep her in mine.

We pull into the parking lot of the motel and park in front of room fifteen. I glance up just as someone peeks through the curtains in front of me. She locks eyes with me and the terrified look on her face reminds me why the club does what we do. What would happen to this woman if we weren't here to help her? How long could she hide out in this motel until whoever she's running from came looking for her? Where would she go?

"Come on," Chance says, climbing off his bike. "Let's go find out what we're dealing with."

Storm and I follow his lead and after climbing off our bikes, trail behind him as he approaches the door to room fifteen and knocks. Before he can even finish knocking, the door opens a crack, hindered by the chain as a woman peeks up at us.

"Morgan?" Chance asks and she nods.

"Chance?"

He nods and she closes the door in his face as the sound of the chain sliding pierces the door. When it opens again, she steps back to allow us into the room. Her gaze warily flicks to the parking lot until she closes the door behind us again and locks it.

"Have a seat," she murmurs, indicating to the two chairs positioned on either side of a round table on one side of the room. A little boy and a girl with dark hair are cuddled together in one bed and Storm and I sit on the edge of the other bed as Chance and Morgan sit in the chairs.

"Why don't you tell us what's going on?" Chance urges quietly, trying not to wake the kids. Morgan sucks in a breath and nods. When she glances down at her hands in her lap, I notice the bruise circling her entire wrist.

"Um… it's my husband. He's on these meds but he stopped taking them last week and then last night, he just

191

lost it…" Her voice breaks and images from my past come rushing back. Closing my eyes, I take a deep breath and force them back before opening my eyes again. Storm nudges me and flashes me a concerned look but I shake my head. The guys know all about my past but it's not something I like to talk about.

"Did he hurt you?" Chance asks and Morgan nods, holding her wrist out.

"Yes, but you have to understand that he never would have done this if he hadn't stop taking his meds."

Storm sighs. "And you have to understand how often we hear things like that. There's no excuse for him hurting you."

"I know that," she whispers, tears filling her eyes as she looks past us to where her kids are sleeping.

"Did he hurt the kids?" I ask and she shakes her head.

"No, thank God. They were sleeping through the whole thing."

Chance reaches across the table and gently grabs her hand. She jumps. "What is it that you want us to do?"

"I need to get him to the hospital so they can get him back on his meds."

Chance glances over at us. "Are you sure?"

"Yes."

Storm stands and pulls his phone out of his pocket. "Let me go make a phone call."

As he steps outside, Chance pulls one of our business cards out of his wallet and slides it across the table.

"We're gonna help you get him to the hospital but I want you to keep this. Just in case."

"Once he's back on his meds..."

"And I hope you're right," Chance interrupts her. "But in case you're not, take the card."

She scowls down at the card on the table. "He won't hurt me once he's back on his meds."

"Then it won't hurt to take the card and tuck it into your wallet for safe keeping."

"Fine," she mumbles with a sigh before scooping the card up. She may be fighting us but there's relief in her eyes from knowing she has a back-up plan. Storm walks back into the room and nods at Morgan.

"Police are on their way to your house to get your husband and take him to the hospital for a seventy-two hour hold. You need to meet them there to sign some paperwork but we can go with you if want us to."

She glances between the three of us before nodding. "Yeah, that'd be great, actually."

"Let's get you packed up, then."

The three of us get to work, helping her pack and loading her things into her car as she wakes the kids up and once they are loaded in the car, we follow behind her on our bikes to the hospital. She's shaking as she steps out of the car and her gaze follows a police cruiser that pulls to a stop in front of the hospital doors. Tears fill her eyes as the back door opens and the officer guides her husband out of the back seat. As soon as he sees her, his eyes widen before narrowing into a glare.

"You stupid slut!" he screams across the lot. "What did you do?"

"I'm so sorry," she answers, her voice breaking.

He starts to struggle against the handcuffs and the officer guiding him toward the doors. "Fuck you, bitch. You're not even close to sorry yet. I can't believe you'd do this to me. I thought you loved me. Fuck you…"

His voice trails off as they lead him into the hospital and Morgan gasps as tears start pouring down her face. My heart explodes with pain as I remember fights just like that from my own past and I glance over at Chance and Storm before motioning for them to stay with the kids. They nod and I approach Morgan.

"Come walk with me for a minute? There's something I'd like to tell you."

She studies me for a minute before nodding. As we walk away from the car, I suck in a breath and try to work myself up to telling this story. Around the side of the hospital is a little garden area and I lead her to a bench in the corner. When we sit down, she turns to me.

"What is it that you wanted to tell me? If you're thinking that you can talk me into leaving him, you won't."

I shake my head. "When I was ten years old, I… I watched my father kill my mother."

She gasps as memories flood my mind, bringing tears to my eyes.

"And the situation wasn't exactly the same because he had been using drugs for months but I need you to understand that all it takes is one time where things go too far and he's already voluntarily gone off his meds. I'm not here to tell you what to do and if you ever need our help, we're going to be here but I'd really prefer not to go to your funeral. And it would kill me to see those kids end up orphans just like I did."

"I'm so sorry that you went through that but it's not like that with us."

"Don't you think that every woman who's ever ended up in a bad spot has said that exact same thing? But like I said, I'm not telling you to do anything. Just think about it."

I stand and hold my hand out to her to lead her back to the car. For the time being, her mind is made up. I just hope that something I said sticks with her and she can make a change before it's too late.

A.M. Myers

It Ends Tonight

Chapter Eleven
Quinn

"Alice!" I call as I step into the foyer and set my purse down on the little bench by the door. The scent of something delicious greets me and I sniff the air.

"Hey, we're in here," Alice calls from the living room and I kick off my heels before following her voice. She smiles at me from the piano as Brooklyn plays on her mini keyboard, smashing the keys more than playing and I laugh.

"I see the lessons are going well."

Alice glances down at Brooklyn and nods. "I'm certain that she's a musical prodigy."

"Clearly." I laugh, my gaze falling to Brooklyn, who has the corner of the keyboard in her mouth. "What's that smell, by the way?"

"I've got Gram's rib recipe in the crockpot and

potatoes on the stove."

My stomach growls and I let out an appreciative moan. "Oh, lord, that sounds so good."

"Yeah, I woke up missing her this morning so I decided to do something in her memory."

I smile but before I can answer her, my phone starts ringing in my purse and I whisper a curse. "Hold on. I gotta get that."

Rushing back into the foyer, I grab my purse and dig my phone out of the side pocket, smiling when I glance down at the screen.

"Hey, you," I answer, butterflies in my belly just from seeing his name.

"Hey, baby," Lucas answers and his voice melts me on the spot. "What are y'all up to tonight?"

I spin and plop down on the bench next to the door before stretching my legs out in front of me. "Not much. Why?"

"Well, I have this problem…"

"Oh, yeah?" I ask. "What's that?"

"I am just missing you like crazy."

Giggling, I shake my head. "You're so damn cheesy."

"Should I stop?"

"No," I answer as a blush creeps up my cheeks. "But I do have to point out that you just saw us last night when you brought dinner over, remember?"

"Oh, I remember, but I kind of thought that I'd do it

again tonight."

Glancing through the hallway to the dining room, I imagine all of us seated around the table and I can't stop my smile. "Actually, how about I cook for you this time?"

"I think I could go for that. What time?"

"Mmm," I hum. "Give me like twenty minutes. Okay?"

"Sounds good, babe. I'll see you soon."

We hang up and I set my phone down on the bench next to me as my cheeks ache from my smile. It's been a few days since Lucas took Brooklyn and me over to Iris's house for dinner and it feels like our relationship has changed somehow. I feel more settled, more secure in us and my feelings for him, and I know it's time to tell him about my past. He needs to know the truth before we go any further but I have faith that I know him well enough to know that he'll take it well. At least, I hope so...

"Quinn and Lucas sittin' in a tree," Alice sings and I glance up as she leans against the archway into the living room.

"You, shush."

"Come on, Sis, admit it. You're totally falling in love with this guy."

I shake my head as I stand. "I just met him, Alice."

"You keep saying that like it means anything. Time has absolutely nothing to do with the smile on your face or the sparkle in your eyes since you met him."

"It's just… he doesn't know about my past yet… I was going to tell him tonight."

She nods in understanding as she pushes off the archway and walks over to me, wrapping me up in a hug. "I know you're scared but he's a good man, Quinn. That isn't going to phase him at all."

"I'm just nervous."

"Trust me, it will be okay," she assures me as she grabs her backpack off the hook on the wall. "But I've got to get going now. Save me some ribs."

After I promise to save her a plate, she leaves for class and I retreat into the kitchen to check on the food. I grab a fork and check to see how tender the potatoes are before slipping into the living room where Brooklyn is still playing with her keyboard. When she sees me, she starts crawling over to me and I smile.

"Hey, baby girl."

She stops at my feet and I pick her up before tickling her belly. She giggles and my heart aches with love.

"Did you have fun with Auntie Alice today?" I ask.

"Babababa," she babbles and I nod.

"Really?" I gasp as I turn back to the kitchen with her in my arms. "What else did you do today?"

I put her in her high chair, sprinkle some Cheerios on the tray, and work on finishing up dinner as she babbles on. When the potatoes are done, I drain the water and dump them into a bowl before adding a generous helping of butter and milk and mashing them. Once the potatoes are done, I throw a bag of vegetables into the microwave and turn to check the ribs. Before I can even take the lid off of the crockpot, the doorbell rings and Brooklyn's head whips in the direction of the foyer.

"Lalalala," she sings and I can't help but think she's trying to say Lucas.

"Who's here, pretty girl?" I ask as I wipe my hands on a towel and pass by her high chair.

"Lalalala."

I laugh and snag one of her Cheerios. "You think so?"

I step into the foyer and my heart starts to race as butterflies flap around in my belly. A smile stretches across my face as I grab the doorknob and it doesn't even matter that I haven't even seen him yet because just knowing that he's on the other side of that door is enough to reduce me to a grinning, bubbly mess. Sucking in a breath to calm the electricity zipping through my body, I open the door and my grin grows as he steps into the house and lifts me up into his arms despite my squeal.

"Lucas!" I gasp, slapping his shoulder and he laughs as he slides me down the front of his body, igniting every single nerve ending under my skin. My breath catches as our eyes meet and I can smell the spearmint gum in his mouth as he leans in. His arm slips around my waist and he pulls me so close that I'm not sure where I end and he begins but I can't bring myself to pull away - not when being in his arms feels like the only place I'm meant to be. Ever so slowly, he closes the distance between us and the moment his lips touch mine, I sigh because kissing him is like coming home.

"Mmm," he hums as he pulls back just enough to touch the tip of his nose to mine. "I can't decide if I want to keep kissing you or find out what the hell smells so damn good."

"You know, I think I would be offended if the best damn ribs you've ever had weren't waiting for us in the kitchen."

He pulls back and smiles as he laces our fingers together and shuts the front door. "Lead the way, then."

Brooklyn's eyes light up when we walk into the kitchen and she smiles, raising her arms above her head as Lucas chuckles.

"Hey, girlie. Did you miss me?"

"Dada," she babbles and I suck in a breath, unsure how he'll react but it doesn't seem to faze him at all as he unbuckles her from the high chair and scoops her up into his arms before raising her above his head. She squeals and kicks her legs as she giggles and any qualms I have about telling Lucas about my past vanish. Despite the fact that we've only known each other for a short time, the truth is that I do know him and I know he'll be just as amazing about everything I have to tell him today as he's been all this time that I've been asking him to take things slow.

"You want to move her chair up to the table?" I ask as I turn to grab a couple plates.

"Sure."

I start dishing food up onto plates and grabbing silverware when I feel his arms wrap around my waist. He pulls me into his body and presses his lips to my neck, sending a shiver down my spine.

"Anything you need help with?"

I hold up a plate. "You could help me carry plates over to the table."

"You got it, baby."

Between the two of us, we get the three plates, silverware, and glasses over to the table and as he gives Brooklyn a bite of mashed potatoes, I fill up her sippy cup with milk before joining them. I sigh as I sink into my chair.

"Long day?" he asks and I nod.

"I have a charity gala to put on in five days so every day is crazy this week."

He nods as he picks up his fork. "Sounds stressful. Anything I can do to help?"

"You mean besides showing up every night to hang out with Brooklyn and me?" I ask since he has been doing that most nights anyway. He nods.

"Well, yeah, since that's for me, not y'all."

I bark out a laugh. "That's not for us?"

"No," he answers, shaking his head with a grin. "It is an entirely selfish move."

"And here I thought you just liked me."

He shakes his head again and my heart stalls in my chest. "Naw, baby. The word 'like' implies some middle school shit that doesn't even come close to how I feel about you."

"Oh, I see," I whisper, a wide smile stretching across my face as my heart races in my chest. "Well, in that case, there is something you can do for me."

"What's that?"

"You can go rent a tux."

His brows furrow as he studies me. "A tux?"

"Yeah. So you can be my date for the gala."

"Done. Anything else?" he asks, his smile bright. I shake my head, surprised by how easily he agreed to be dragged along to my work function.

"Not at the moment."

Our eyes meet across the table and he winks. "Well, you just let me know if there's anything else."

"I'll be sure to do that," I answer, fighting back a grin. Brooklyn shrieks, pulling our attention to her as she slaps her hands down on her tray and reaches for the plate of mashed potatoes. Lucas laughs and grabs the spoon.

"I'm sorry, Darlin'. Did we forget about you for a minute?"

She squeals and opens her mouth as he holds the spoon in front of her. As he gives her the bite of potatoes, I sprinkle some green beans on her tray and she quickly scoops one up and bites it in half.

"So, how's your brother?" I ask and Lucas shakes his head.

"Honestly, I don't know. I've gone out to look for him a couple times and I've put the word out that I'm looking for him but what you said about figuring out what I wanted really resonated with me and I've been trying to do just that."

I smile as a feeling of pride wells up inside me. "Any progress?"

"Maybe," he teases, meeting my eyes but when he doesn't say anymore, I lose my nerve and decide not to push him. I'm in way too deep now and no matter how much I tell myself that I don't need him to decide that I'm something he wants in his life, I'm dying to hear those words. We fit so well together and he makes me happier than I can remember being in a long time so it's not hard to imagine a future for us. But what if he does all this soul searching I sent him on and realizes that he needs something else?

We finish our meal, making comfortable chitchat in between Lucas playing with Brooklyn and each time he turns to give her equal attention, my heart feels like it might explode from happiness. And the closer we get to the end of our meal, and the information I vowed to reveal to him tonight, the more nervous I get. Aside from Gram, Alice, and my therapist, I've never told anyone else this and just the thought of forcing the words out of my mouth makes my heart race and my mouth go dry.

"Damn, babe. You were right. These were the best damn ribs I've ever had," Lucas says as he finishes his meal and I smile.

"It was my grandma's recipe."

He nods thoughtfully before sitting forward. "I just figured out something that I want."

"Yeah? What is it?"

"I want family recipes. I want that history to pass down to my kids... which I guess means that I want kids, too."

I glance over at Brooklyn. "I think, based on how good you are with her, that it would be a damn shame if you didn't have kids. You're going to make an incredible dad."

"You really think so?" he asks and the vulnerability that I don't usually get to see from him makes my heart ache for a whole new reason. Most of the time, it's so easy to forget the crap that he carries around with him on a daily basis because he's spent his whole life learning how to act fine while he's slowly dying on the inside. It's a side of him that I'm certain most people don't get to see and the fact that he so willingly shows it to me means the world. I nod.

"I'm certain of it."

He reaches across the table with a shy smile on his face as he grabs my hand. "Thanks, gorgeous."

Brooklyn lets out a big yawn and we both turn to

look at her as Lucas chuckles.

"I think someone is tired."

I nod. "I think you're right."

As Lucas begins clearing plates from the table, I stand and unbuckle Brooklyn from her high chair but when I try to lift her into my arms, she starts fussing and reaching for Lucas.

"Looks like I'm chopped liver tonight," I tell him and he glances over his shoulder. Brooklyn strains as she reaches for him and he chuckles as he sets the plates down on the counter and walks over to us.

"Is that better?" he asks after he picks her up. She shoves her thumb into her mouth and lays her head down on his shoulder as she looks up at me, her eyelids growing heavy.

"She's going to pass out any second. Do you mind putting her to bed?" I would do it myself but I'm pretty sure that she'd just start fussing again. A part of me loves how much she likes Lucas but there's a tiny little part that's heartbroken she wants someone other than me. For thirteen months, it's just been the two of us and Alice and I wasn't prepared for this.

Lucas grabs my hand, pulling my gaze up to his. "Come on."

We walk up the stairs hand in hand as Brooklyn starts to drift off in Lucas's arms and I stand back by the door to Brooklyn's room as Lucas carries her over to her crib and lays her down in her bed.

"Blanket?" he whispers, turning back to look at me and I point to the dresser next to her crib. Grabbing the folded blanket off the top, he shakes it out and lays it gently over her before turning back to me and sneaking out of her room.

"Is she out already?"

He nods and my nerves kick in again as we walk back down the stairs. When we reach the bottom, I turn to him and suck in a breath.

"Do you want to go sit on the porch? There is something I want to talk to you about."

"Sure," he answers as his gaze flicks across my face, studying me. I'm sure I look just as nervous as I feel right now.

He takes my hand again and we walk out onto the front porch before sitting on the swing. I curl my legs underneath me as he pulls me close and we just swing in silence for a few seconds before he nudges me.

"What did you want to talk about?"

I draw in a ragged breath and wring my hands together. "Um... I just... uh..."

"Hey, it's okay," he urges, rubbing his hand along my arm and a sense of calm washes over me as I glance over at him.

"The truth is, Lucas, I think I'm falling for you and you need to know what you're getting into before that happens."

He nods, understanding crossing his face. "The

reason we're taking things slow?"

"Yes. See… the thing is… I…" My hands tremble as I suck in another breath and focus on the feeling of his hand skating over my skin. "I don't know who Brooklyn's dad is…"

I bite my lip as I peek over at him and his shocked look makes my belly flip. Finally, he nods.

"Uh, okay… that's not what I was expecting but I can't say that I was a saint before I met you."

Shit.

That's not what I meant.

I shake my head, trying desperately to clear my thoughts and explain the situation to Lucas clearly. "No, you don't understand. After I broke up with Danny, I was a little lost because all the plans I had for my life had just fallen down around me."

"Hey, you don't have to explain yourself to me, baby," he interrupts me and I grab his hand, giving it a squeeze.

"No, I really do. It's not what you think."

He nods for me to continue.

"One night, about three months after we had broken up, I was feeling really down so my girlfriends talked me into going out. They said there was this new bar they wanted to try and it was supposed to be amazing. Well, when we got there, it was anything but amazing. It was run down and kind of sketchy but they were intent on trying to cheer me up so we started drinking and I got wasted. I honestly don't remember a lot of the night but around one in the morning, I went outside to get some fresh air and that's where he found me."

"He who?" Lucas asks, his voice tight but I don't have the strength to answer his questions right now. I only want to have to tell this story once.

"I was leaning up against the wall of the bar, looking up at the sky when he pulled me into the side alley. Everything from there happened so fast. One minute I was standing there and the next he was on top of me..." My voice cracks as tears well up in my eyes. "And he had shoved my dress up and cut my panties off. He was probably only on top of me for two minutes or less but it felt like an eternity and when he was finished, he stood up and smiled down at me before just leaving me there."

"Quinn," he whispers, pulling me into his arms as his body shakes with rage. I can feel his anger vibrating through every cell of his body but I've never felt safer and the tears start to flow as memories from that night come rushing back.

"My friends found me not long after that and they rushed me to the emergency room where they did a rape kit and called the police. Five weeks later, I found out I was pregnant with that sweet perfect little girl upstairs but they never found who did it."

"I'm so sorry, baby," he says, his hand threading through the hair at the back of my head as he presses his lips to my forehead.

"That's why I needed to take things slow, Lucas. I've spent the last two years just trying to heal and focusing on Brooklyn because she was the best thing that ever happened to me even if her conception was the worst."

He pulls back to lock eyes with me and wipes away my tears with his thumbs. "You don't have to explain anything else to me, sweetheart. I understand completely and I feel like a giant ass for assuming that you slept with a lot of people."

"It's okay." I laugh, gripping his t-shirt and pulling him closer to me. "I wasn't explaining myself very well."

"Listen, I won't push you for anything, okay? You don't have to talk about it and if I've been too aggressive at all, just tell me and I'll back off. We'll take this as slow as you want and I'm not going anywhere."

"No, Lucas. The reason I told you everything is because I'm ready to move forward. I don't want that moment to define the rest of my life and meeting you has been the biggest blessing. I'm happy again and it's all because you came into my life so I'm ready to make this thing official if you are."

His smile is blinding and I can't help copying it. "Baby, I've been waiting weeks to hear you say that."

"Then kiss me."

"Yes, ma'am," he murmurs, pulling me to his lips and when he kisses me this time, there's no restraint. Knowing that he held back before out of respect for me and my needs makes giving him another piece of my heart the easiest decision I never had a choice in making.

Chapter Twelve
Lucas

"All right, you degenerates!" Blaze bellows as he walks into the room. "Sit down. Let's get started."

The noise dies down and we all settle into our usual seats as Blaze sits at the head of the table and bangs the gavel on the top.

"Where are we at with the Laney investigation?"

I shake my head. "Stalled out."

We spent the last couple weeks pouring over the case and we can't find anything more than what Rodriguez did. It's gotten to the point where I'm wondering if Owen wasn't really behind it despite the feeling in my gut that there's more going on.

"If there's evidence to find, we're not finding it," Storm adds, frustration splayed across his face.

"Keep digging," Blaze instructs. "We promised

Rodriguez some answers."

"Have we considered the possibility that the two things aren't related?" Moose asks and Blaze turns to him.

"Meaning?"

"Meaning that all the evidence points to this guy that Rodriguez locked up so are we sure that her death and her stalker are connected?"

I point at him from across the table. "It's too neat, though. There's no way that if this guy actually did it that he'd leave so many clues for us to find."

"Both are a possibility," Streak adds. "But if it's a set-up, it's one of the best damn ones I've ever seen."

"So what are you saying?"

He shakes his head, letting out a breath. "Nothing. Just that if someone did set him up and that's a big if, they'd have to have an intimate knowledge of not only Rodriguez but the way the police work. All the clues pointed to Owen - not in an obvious way but he wasn't exactly hiding his tracks either. It's just believable enough that most people wouldn't dig further."

"Someone needs to talk to Rodriguez. Ask him if he's had issues with anyone lately," Blaze instructs and Storm nods.

"I'll handle it."

"Good," he answers before turning to me. "What do we have going on with the P.I. business this week?"

I shake my head. "Oh, you know, just the usual."

"Cheating husband?" Chance asks, his lip curling in disgust. Chance has made it perfectly clear in the past how much he despises working on the P.I. side of things because it seems like all we do is break up marriages but he is not exactly all that skilled with a wrench either, which eliminates the possibility of him working at the shop. I nod my head.

"Yep. I have to meet up with Tate in a few minutes for one of our cases."

Blaze nods thoughtfully. "How's she working out?"

"Good," I answer as I glance over at Kodiak. Tate first came into all our lives a few months ago when Blaze ordered Kodiak to watch her and it didn't take long for things to get a little out of control. There's still a little tension between Tate and Blaze after everything that went down but I have faith that they'll both come around. This is a family, after all. Blaze nods again before grabbing the gavel and banging it on the table.

"That's all I've got for y'all today. Get out of here."

I check my phone, hoping for a text from Quinn, as I step out into the bar but there's nothing and I shake my head. There was no way I was leaving her after everything she told me last night but I spent the whole night staring up at the ceiling in her bedroom as she slept cuddled up against my side. For hours, I imagined finding the monster who thought he had a right to put his hands on her and making him wish that he'd never been born. Even now, I want to go out and hunt him down despite the fact that she seemed happier, lighter this morning.

"You ready to go?"

I glance up and Tate arches a brow in my direction as Kodiak pulls her into his arms.

"Uh, yeah…"

"Everything okay?" Kodiak asks, his back straightening as he studies me and I nod, shaking off my thoughts.

"Yeah, it's all good. Now, release your woman so we can get to work."

He growls and pulls her closer. "Hold your fucking horses. I haven't seen her all damn day."

"I'm just going to wait out in the truck then," I grumble and roll my eyes as they start kissing. They don't even acknowledge me so I duck outside and climb into the truck before dialing Quinn's number.

"Hey, handsome," she answers and I grin.

"Hey, baby. What are you up to?"

She sighs and the image of her perfect pouty lips flash through my mind as my cock stirs. Fuck, it's been so hard to hold back with her when all I want to do is bury myself inside her.

"Just working."

"Yeah? How's the gala coming?"

"Well, I think everything will be ready by Saturday as long as I don't forget to pick up my dress with everything else I've got going on."

"Dress, huh? I can't wait to see you in it."

Her husky laugh goes straight to my cock. "Why does that sound dirty when you say it?"

"Maybe because I was imagining taking the dress off you at the end of the night."

"Lucas," she gasps, her voice a husky whisper and I bite back a groan.

"Baby, you can't say my name like that."

She giggles and the sound fills me with pride. I love making her laugh. "Why not?"

"Because I promised to take things slow and I don't want to be an ass, especially after what you shared with me last night."

"Forget the rules and taking things slow, Lucas. I told you last night that I'm all in."

"Quinn Dawson," I drawl. "Are you asking me to go steady?"

She laughs and I can just imagine the way her eyes sparkle when she smiles. "Yeah, I guess I am. What do you say?"

"I suppose we could give it a shot."

"I'm overjoyed by your enthusiastic response," she answers and I laugh as Tate walks out of the clubhouse.

"Truthfully, Darlin', I knew you were different right from the moment you looked at me. I've just been waitin' on you."

"You really mean that, don't you?"

I nod as Tate opens the passenger door to the truck.

"Yeah, I do. Told ya, I don't say things I don't mean."

"One of these days, that might just sink in. You want to come over for dinner tonight?"

"Yeah, I can do that," I reply as I feel Tate's gaze burrowing into the side of my face. Her brow quirks in question when I glance in her direction but I ignore it and turn back to the steering wheel.

"Perfect. I get off at five and I can pick something up on my way home."

Something about the way she says home does something to me and I can't help but picture truly having a home with her and Brooklyn someday. Damn, that's a pretty picture even if it's only in my imagination.

"Don't worry about it, babe. I'll grab something before I come over. What are you in the mood for?"

Tate sighs from the other side of the cab and I shoot a glare in her direction. The woman has no patience whatsoever..

"Surprise me," Quinn answers and I nod.

"Okay. See you tonight."

We say good-bye and I hang up before tossing my phone in the cup holder and reversing out of the parking spot.

"Who was that?"

I glance over at Tate and shake my head. "None of your business."

"Oh, Lukie," she teases, grinning. "Have you forgotten that I could just make you tell me?"

"Do you remember the conversation we had about not causing bodily harm to the people you care about?" I say, narrowing my eyes at her and she laughs. I've never met anyone quite like Tate and she's quickly become one of my best friends, especially after Kodiak suggested that she try working for the P.I. side of the club. It's honestly been a perfect fit with her skill set but she's still a little too hot-headed to be out on her own. Tate has more of an act first, ask questions later attitude that can get her into trouble but that's the reason that Kodiak fell in love with her.

"Of course I do. Now, tell me who that was."

I sigh. "Quinn."

"Ohh, the girl from the car accident," she teases with a giggle. "Ali was telling me all about her. I take it from the part of the conversation I heard things are going well?"

"Yeah."

She leans across the cab, inspecting my face. "What's wrong? Is it not going well?"

"No, it's not that," I answer before sighing. "It's just that she told me something last night about her past... something traumatic, and it's just driving me crazy today. I want to fix it for her."

"Oh, for fuck's sake!" she exclaims, leaning back in her seat as she shakes her head. "Freaking men. You all want to fix everything but she didn't share that part of herself with you so you could fix it."

"I know…"

"No," she interrupts. "You don't know if it's still bugging you. When she told you whatever she told you, she was giving you a piece of herself, of her heart, and the only damn thing you need to do is protect and cherish it. Believe me, if she needs you to fix something, she'll let you know."

"How am I supposed to just listen to it, knowing that she's in so much pain and not do anything about it?"

She rolls her eyes. "Don't be dense, Luke. It's not a good look on you. By listening to her and holding her as she breaks down, you are fixing it. If she feels safe enough to open up to you, then you are fixing it every fucking day you're with her so all you gotta do is not fuck it up."

"Right," I say with a nod. "Don't fuck it up. Any other advice, nosey?"

We pull into Sunrise Diner where Tate used to work and where we're meeting our client, Kayla. Tate shakes her head. "Not right now but I'll let you know if I think of anything else."

"I'm sure you will."

She grabs the file of photos and receipts we're presenting to Kayla today and opens it, skimming through the shots I got last week.

"Shit," she hisses when she gets to a particularly lewd shot of Kayla's husband, Bobby, getting his dick sucked. "What an asshole."

It Ends Tonight

"You ready to do this?" I ask and she nods. I scan the parking lot as we climb out of the truck and spot Kayla's car on the far side of the lot. I never like these kinds of meetings but I get the feeling that Kayla's just looking for an excuse to leave her husband and that's exactly what I'm bringing her today. I'm not delivering terrible news or breaking someone's heart and it's a nice change of pace.

Tate nudges me as we walk into the diner, pointing to the back corner where Kayla is sitting, gazing out the window. She waves to a few of the employees as we make our way through the tables and Kayla looks up as we approach her table.

"Hi," she says, standing and shaking both of our hands.

"How are you doing, Darlin'?" I ask as we sit down and her lips part as she shrugs.

"Oh, you know... just going a little crazy. Did you guys find anything?"

I nod, sliding the folder across the table. "Yes, ma'am. We did."

She opens the folder, anger replacing her smile as she flicks through the photos. Finally, she slaps the folder closed and nods.

"Well, I suppose that's that, then."

"We're very sorry," Tate tells her. "We know no one likes to get this information."

Kayla shakes her head, seemingly shaking off her

anger at the same time. "Please don't apologize. This is what I hired you guys for." She reaches across the table and lays her hand on mine. "And I appreciate all your hard work."

"You're welcome," I answer, pulling my hand away.

"There's just the small matter of payment," Tate cuts in with a grin on her face.

Kayla nods. "Oh, yes, of course."

As she pulls out some cash and counts out enough bills for our fee, her gaze keeps drifting up to me and when she sees me looking at her, she smiles before tilting her head to the side slightly to expose her neck. I know exactly what she's doing but it's never going to fucking happen - not with a client and especially not with Quinn waiting at home for me.

*   *   *   *

"Lucas," she whispers as she opens the front door, a bright smile lighting up her gorgeous face and everything inside me urges me forward until I wrap my arms around her and pull her close.

"Hey, gorgeous. Miss me?"

She nods, pressing her hands flat against my chest as

she looks up at me. Fuck, the adoration in her ice blue eyes is a punch to the gut and I don't know how I will ever walk away from her. How the hell do I ever get anything done during the day when I know this is what is waiting for me?

"Terribly."

"Will you forgive me if I brought food?" I ask, holding up the dinner that I picked up on my way over here and she nods.

"I suppose I can let it slide this time."

I grin and dig my fingers into her side as she squeals. "How gracious of you."

"Lucas!" she screams, trying to wiggle out of my arms and I finally release her as a shriek comes from the living room.

"Brooklyn," I call out and laugh when another shriek echoes through the house.

"She's going to freak if you don't go in there to see her." Quinn laughs and I pull her tighter, molding her sexy body around mine as I lean down and claim her lips. She sighs and grips my t-shirt. When I pull away, her cheeks are pink and she is quietly gasping for air. All I can imagine as she licks her lips is finally getting her underneath me and I barely hold back a groan.

"Dada!" Brooklyn calls from the living room and Quinn shakes her head, reaching for the bag of food.

"Give me that and go see your girl."

Grinning, I hand her the bag of food and watch as she

walks into the kitchen, her hips swaying back and forth with each step.

"Dada!"

Brooklyn's shriek snaps me out of my daze and I can't help but smile as I walk into the living room and Brooklyn grins. I have no idea if her calling me "Dada" means anything or if she's just babbling but I can't lie - I love the way it sounds.

"Hey, baby girl," I say as I reach her playpen and she holds her hands up to me. I lift her into my arms and she immediately cuddles into my neck, shoving her tiny little thumb in her mouth. I rub her back as I carry her into the kitchen and Quinn's smile is soft when she turns and sees us.

"The two of you…" she mutters as she shakes her head. "Dinner's on the table."

I carry Brooklyn over to the table and buckle her into her high chair before sitting across from Quinn and pulling food out of the bag. Once everything is passed out, Quinn starts feeding Brooklyn her mashed potatoes and I study her, frowning at the dark circles under her eyes.

"Rough day?" I know she's been stressed with this gala coming up but I wish there was something I could do to help.

She nods. "Yeah. I didn't have very long to plan this thing so I'm being run a little ragged this week. I just need some sleep though."

"You sure?"

"Yes," she answers, offering me a reassuring smile. "I'm sure."

"Here, let me help with that," I say, taking the spoon from her hand and start feeding Brooklyn as Quinn digs into her food. She asks about my day as we eat and I tell her about Kayla's case, specifically leaving out the part where she hit on me and afterward when Tate told me I was already in deep and "totally screwed". Not like she's one to talk. She was all about avoiding relationships when she met Kodiak and that changed pretty quickly. Besides, I still don't know what is so bad about what they all have now.

I used to think that there wasn't room in my life for a relationship but meeting Quinn showed me differently and when she asked me about what I wanted in my life and I couldn't think of anything, I was floored. Somewhere along the way I had stopped being my own person and just became my brother's keeper - a title neither one of us wants me to have. Hell, I'm almost thirty and before she pushed me to search for answers, I had no idea what I wanted out of my life and no hope of ever discovering those answers.

"You want to watch a movie?" Quinn asks as we clean up dinner and I nod. I'll do just about anything to spend more time with her.

"Yeah, that sounds good. Should we put her down first?" I ask, motioning to a very sleepy Brooklyn and

Quinn shakes her head.

"Naw, let her cuddle up with us on the couch. Besides, she can pass out anywhere."

Once we get dinner cleaned up, I unbuckle Brooklyn from her high chair and join Quinn in the living room as she picks out a movie. The opening credits roll and Quinn cuddles into my side as Brooklyn lays her head down on my chest and plops her thumb into her mouth as I hold her steady with my free hand. Within minutes, she's snoring quietly on me and I nudge Quinn to show her. She doesn't answer and when I glance down and find her sleeping against my side, a feeling of contentment and peace washes over me. It's unlike anything I've ever felt before and I realize that this right here is exactly what I want out of my life. When I'm ninety years old on my death bed, if all I ever accomplished was loving these two with all my heart, I'll be able to smile and say I lived a damn good life.

It Ends Tonight

Chapter Thirteen
Quinn

"How are things looking, Ronald?" I ask as I step into the ballroom with a giant cup of coffee in my hand. People are working all around us and I survey what they've been able to get done since I left late last night.

"Good. I think we're about ready."

I scan the room again, nodding. "Looks really good. Thank you so much for all your hard work."

"No need to thank me, Quinn. Besides, I heard a little rumor that you were here until three in the morning working on all this."

I shrug as a traitorous yawn slips out of my mouth. "That's just part of the job. Now, what do we still have to do?"

"This way, please," he says, gesturing for me to follow him as he turns to one side of the room and points out some of the bigger decorations that are still in the final stages of being assembled before we turn toward the dining area.

"Chef Thomas has been hard at work all day and the waiters are getting the tables set up now."

I nod. "What about the art?"

"Once everything else is set up, we'll bring the auction pieces in and set them up along the outside of the room but we didn't want to risk bringing them in with some many people still working in here."

"Good. Have we heard anything from the band?"

"They should be here within the hour," he assures me and I nod, glancing around the room one more time.

"Okay, Ronald. I've got to go get ready but if there are any issues, I'm just upstairs in room two eighteen."

He nods. "We've got things under control down here."

"I'll be back before everything starts to check things over one last time. Thank you again for all your hard work."

"Of course, Quinn. It's been my pleasure to assist you."

I flash him a smile before turning toward the elevators as another yawn ambushes me. Once the elevator doors open and I step inside, I pull my phone out and send a text to Lucas.

Me:
The Plantation.
Room 208.
Meet me there in two hours.

Butterflies flap around in my belly after I press send
and I bite back a smile. After the most amazing week
with Lucas, I've decided that tonight is the night. I'm
finally going to sleep with him and while I'm nervous,
it's not as bad as I thought it would be. Maybe it's
because everything Lucas does makes me feel safe or
because he has systematically claimed pieces of my heart
since the moment we met. Whatever it is, I know this is
the right decision and I'm excited for this next step.

My phone buzzes as I unlock the door to my room
and the butterflies only get stronger so I take a deep
breath as I dump my bag on the bed and run my hand
over the plastic covering my dress before glancing down
at my phone.

Lucas:
Can't wait to see you, baby.

Last night was the first night in the past ten days that
Lucas didn't have dinner over at the house with Brooklyn
and me since I was busy setting up for the event and I'm
surprised how much I missed seeing him. I didn't expect
that. Then again, I also didn't expect to meet someone

and so quickly allow them to become an integral part of my day or so easily. Everything about this has been unexpected but kind of everything I needed, at the same time and now that I've decided to make things official with him, I can't help but imagine a future for us. I just hope he's feeling the same.

My phone buzzes again, pulling me out of my thoughts.

Holly:
Be there in twenty.

"Shit," I hiss, tossing my phone down on the bed. Holly is my hair stylist and I got so caught up thinking about Lucas that I forgot she was meeting me here to do my hair and makeup. Rushing into the bathroom, I quickly strip and turn on the shower before rushing through washing my hair and face. When I step out, I glance up at the clock and whisper another curse as I grab the silk robe off the hook in the bathroom and slip it on. My dress has a keyhole back so I'm not able to wear a bra but I slip a sexy pair of panties on underneath my robe just as someone knocks on the door. "Shit."

I check my reflection in the mirror, just to make sure I'm decent before running to the door and throwing it open. "Hey."

"Um… hi, crazy eyes." Holly laughs, arching a brow as she looks me over. "What the hell are you doing?

Running a marathon?"

I nod. "Feels like it. I lost track of time and had to rush to shower before you got here."

"Ah, the things we do for beauty," she muses as I stand back and hold the door open for her. As I close the door, she pulls the chair away from the desk in the corner of the room and gets her bags set up on the bed. "So, what are we thinking for your hair today?"

"I'm not sure. I was kind of thinking something half up but maybe you should look at my dress and tell me what you think."

She nods, pointing to the garment bag on the bed. "Let's see it."

Nodding, I cross the room and grab the hanger before hanging it on a hook by the closet and slowly pulling the plastic up to reveal the gorgeous midnight blue hand-beaded tulle trumpet gown I found in a little shop downtown. It feels very vintage with its illusion cap sleeves and neckline over a sweetheart bodice and the keyhole back. Holly gasps and I smile.

"Oh…my…god… that dress is stunning and I'm totally getting a vintage vibe from it. Like a nineteen twenties, Great Gatsby thing."

I nod. "That was exactly what I was thinking."

"Okay, so we'll do a low bun with curls and I've got the perfect band to put in your hair," she says, pulling out a headband with blue and white stones that complements the dress perfectly.

"That's gorgeous," I tell her and she nods as she gestures for me to sit in the chair before pulling a blow dryer and extension cord out of her bag.

"Come sit down and let me work my magic."

"Yes, ma'am," I answer, crossing the room and plopping down in the chair, eager to see how I look when she's finished with me.

"So," she says as she pulls my hair out of the towel and starts running a comb through it. "How's life?"

I can't hold back my smile as I stare at my reflection in the mirror. "Really good, actually."

"Well, look at you! You're glowing!"

"Am I?"

She slaps my shoulder playfully. "Yes, you are. What is putting this smile on your face?"

"Life is just good, you know."

My phone buzzes on the bed and I grab it, my heart skipping a beat at Lucas's name on the screen. I open the text and laugh.

Lucas:
Do I get a sneak peek of the dress?

Me:
Nope. You're just going to have to wait.

"Lucas, huh?" Holly asks and when I meet her gaze in the mirror, she wiggles her eyebrows. "Does he have anything to do with why your life is so good lately?"

A blush creeps up my cheeks. "Maybe."

"Well, in that case, let's make sure you knock him off his feet tonight," she answers with a determined look in her eyes and butterflies dance around in my belly as I think about seeing Lucas tonight and my plans for after the gala. The nerves are still there but so is this deep, steadfast feeling that tonight is going to be nothing short of perfection.

*   *   *   *

"Wow," I whisper, inspecting myself in the mirror as Holly stands back with a proud smirk on her face.

"You look incredible. I'm going to be pissed if your man is able to form words after seeing you."

I laugh as I gently run my hands over the beadwork on the front of the dress. "You know, I think I will be, too."

"When is he supposed to be here?" She fusses with my hair, making sure each piece is perfectly in place as I turn to look at the clock.

"Uh, five minutes."

"Shit," she whispers. "Well, let me get packed up and

I'll get out of here."

I turn away from the mirror as she starts throwing blow dryers, flat irons, bobby pins, hairspray, and combs back into her bag and when she's finished, she scans the room one last time.

"Okay, I think that's everything."

I nod. "Thank you so much for this. I feel like a movie star."

"Girl, you look like one. Text me tomorrow and let me know how long it takes the mister to pick his jaw up off of the floor," she teases as we move toward the door and I laugh.

"Oh, I definitely will."

She opens the door and turns back to me. "I would give you a hug but I don't want to smudge my masterpiece so we're just going to pretend."

We both go in for an air hug before giggling as we pull away and she shakes her head and steps out into the hallway.

"Have fun tonight!"

"You have anything planned for the evening?"

She nods, backing down the hallway slowly. "Yeah, big date tonight. Netflix and Chill with Jordy, my cat."

"Ooh, girl!"

"I know," she calls as she stops by the elevator and takes a bow. "Be jealous."

The elevator door opens and I wave as she steps inside. "Bye."

Once she's out of sight, I step back into my room and close my door behind me. The butterflies start up again as I check my watch and realize that Lucas will be here any second. Sucking in a breath, I walk over to the mirror and take one last look at the makeup Holly did for me. She kept it classic with thick liner and red lips and that combined with my side swept hair and the gorgeous dress I'm wearing, I look like I would seamlessly blend at a roaring twenties party.

Someone knocks on the door and my head whips toward it as I press a hand to my belly and fight back a smile.

"Here we go," I whisper before turning toward the door and walking confidently across the room. Lucas is just about to knock again when I open the door and as soon as he sees me, his jaw goes slack and he presses his hand to his chest.

"Holy fuck," he mutters, his blue gaze slowly sinking down my body and following every curve on the way back up. "Jesus Christ."

"Can you say anything else?" I ask, biting back a giggle and he shakes his head, still unable to meet my gaze.

"Uh... no, I don't think I can."

I plant my hands on my hips and slowly turn in front of him, savoring the whispered curses when he sees the back of my dress. "You like?"

"Baby..." he utters, taking a step toward me as I face

him again. "I fucking love. You look…"

"Good?" I ask and he shakes his head as he grabs my waist and pulls me into his body.

"No, better than that."

"Beautiful?"

"Always but that's not the word I was looking for."

I nod, laying my arms on his shoulders. "Well, maybe you could just show me."

"Fantastic idea," he murmurs, leaning in and sealing his lips over mine in a kiss that's far more aggressive than he's ever been before. I come alive in his hands and arch into his body, every cell pumping through my bloodstream screaming for me.

"Fuck, I want this dress off you," he growls and thrusts his hips forward, his erection digging into my hip. I gasp, clinging to the lapels of his tux and he pulls back as he shakes his head.

"Shit. I'm sorry, baby."

I shake my head and pull him closer. "No, please don't stop."

"Darlin'," he rasps, flashing me a grin as he swipes his thumb below my bottom lip. "You're running this show and now you've got to fix your makeup."

"Oh, shit." I glance at the clock behind me and I sigh as I slip out of his arms. "We're picking this up later."

He holds his hands up in surrender as he steps into the room and the door closes behind him. "You won't hear any complaints from me."

I finish fixing my makeup, aware of his intense stare the entire time and when I turn to face him again, I smile. His brow arches as I slowly walk toward him, putting a little extra swing in my hips and hoping I look as sexy as I feel. When I reach him, he pulls me into his arms again and molds my body to his.

"I have a surprise for you after the gala," I tease and he grins.

"Yeah? What is it?"

Shaking my head, I push away from him. "You're just going to have to wait and see."

"Oh, you're mean."

"Trust me, it'll be worth it," I call over my shoulder as I stop at the door and hold out my hand. "Now, are you coming?"

"Absolutely. I'm not letting you out of my sight tonight."

I laugh as we step out into the hallway and I tuck the hotel key into my clutch. "Why not?"

"Because this place is going to be crawling with men and you are a goddamn goddess. All these bastards need to know that you're mine."

"I like the sound of that," I whisper. It's the first time he's ever laid down a claim like that and I love the way it feels knowing that I belong to him. And there's not a single part of it that's demeaning or rude. I belong to him in the way he feels like home and the way he makes me feel like the only girl in the entire world.

We step into the elevator and he stands next to me, wrapping his arm around my waist and pulling me close until I can feel his warmth seeping into me.

"You know what I like?" he asks and I glance back at him.

"No. What?"

As the elevator doors close, he turns me to face him and slowly backs me up until my back presses against the wall of the car. His hand cups my face and he leans in, hovering his lips over mine and stealing the air from my lungs as our eyes meet.

"I love that you're all in now."

I smile. "I love that you made me feel safe enough to take that chance with you."

"Do you remember what I told you the night we went over to Iris's for dinner?" he asks and I think back to that night.

"That I'm in control?"

He nods. "That's right, baby. I'm not holding back anymore but I want you to always remember that, okay? You're the boss and if you're uncomfortable with anything, you just say the word and it stops."

"I trust you, Lucas," I whisper, gripping his wrist as he brushes his thumb over my face. He smiles.

"You have no idea how much I love hearing that."

Before I can say anything else, my phone buzzes and I scrunch up my nose. "Hold on one second."

"Time to work, huh?" he asks with a laugh as he

pulls away and positions me back at his side. I nod, digging my phone out of my bag.

"I guess so."

Willa:
T-Minus thirty minutes, boss lady.
Where are you?

"Everything okay?" Lucas asks, peeking over my shoulder as I read Willa's text and I nod.

"Yeah. My assistant is down there now getting things set up and I need to look things over one last time before guests start showing up."

He grabs my hand and laces his fingers with mine as the elevator doors slide open. "You just do what you need to do, babe, and I'll follow along."

"Are you sure you don't want to sit and get a drink?" I ask as we approach the ballroom. "I think the bar is probably already open."

"Nope. Told you, I'm not letting any of these fuckers near you."

"Lucas," I whisper with a laugh. "No one is going to be looking at me."

His brow arches and he pulls me closer. "Are you kidding me? It's a shame I didn't bring my gun."

"What?"

"Shit," he hisses with a wince. "Yeah, we'll talk about that later, okay?"

I open my mouth to protest as I spot Ronald and Willa crossing the ballroom to talk to me and I sigh.

"Yeah, we will talk about it later."

"Miss Dawson, you look stunning," Ronald says as he reaches us and I swear I hear Lucas growl behind me and I barely resist the urge to glare at him.

"Thank you, Ronald. How are things going down here?"

He nods and I glance over at Willa as she smirks at me and winks.

"Very well. We have just one little problem…"

"What?"

Willa steps forward and places her hand on my arm. "The band isn't here yet but I've called them and they promised me that they'll be here in ten minutes."

"Ten minutes?" I hiss. "We're going to have guests showing up in fifteen."

"It's not ideal," she answers, speaking in a calm tone that I think is supposed to tame my nerves but it doesn't work. This gala is one of the biggest events I've ever thrown and I still managed to pull it together with a shortened time table and after getting into a car accident so if the band tanks this thing, I'm going to ruin them.

"Get one or two of our regular bands on the phone and see if anyone's available as a back-up," I instruct Willa and she nods before running off to make phone calls. I turn back to Ronald and suck in a breath.

"Please tell me there are no more problems."

He shakes his head. "No, ma'am. Everything else has been running smoothly."

"Thank you, Ronald." Turning back to Lucas, I sigh and he pulls me into his arms.

"Anything I can do to help?"

I shake my head. "No."

"Quinn!" someone yells and I glance over toward the stage where Willa is pointing to the band as they unload their equipment.

"Thank fuck," I whisper before squaring my shoulders and marching across the room as I drag Lucas along with me.

"Shit," he mutters but I ignore him as I stop in front of the stage. Nick, the lead singer, turns to me and his eyes follow a leisurely path down my body that makes me feel all kinds of icky before he grins at me.

"Hey, gorgeous."

Lucas steps up next to me. "Fucking watch it."

"Let me ask you boys something… you are aware that you signed a contract, yes?"

"Yeah, and?" Nick asks, arching a defiant brow and I wish I could put him on my banned list a second time.

"And in that contract, it stated that you were to be here an hour early and yet here you are, setting up fifteen minutes before guests are set to arrive."

"Then why the fuck are you standing here, bugging us?"

My jaw tightens and I swear I can feel my eye

twitching. "Oh, I'll be out of your way in a second. I just thought I should let y'all know why you'll only be getting half your fee tonight."

"What?" Nick bellows, jumping down off the stage and Lucas is in front of me in an instant, putting himself between Nick and me as he charges toward me. "You can't do that, you little slut."

Lucas shoves him back and he stumbles before righting himself.

"Actually, I can. It was in the contract you signed and your conduct is completely unprofessional."

"Jackson. Rhett," the drummer says, stepping forward and the other two guys set their instruments down. "Get Nick out of here for a second."

They lead Nick out of the ballroom as the drummer approaches me. "Hello. I'm Dorian and I just want to apologize for Nick. I would say that he's not normally like this but I would be lying."

"Well, thank you for that, at least, and I hope you don't mind me saying that I think you guys are very talented but your lead singer is holding you back."

He nods, glancing over his shoulder. "I have to agree with you."

"Can you get set up in five minutes?" I ask, glancing at the time on my phone and he sighs.

"We'll give it our best shot."

I point to the door that the other two members dragged Nick through. "One more outburst like that and

I'll have you all removed. I already have back-up entertainment in place in case this doesn't go well."

"I understand, Miss Dawson."

He turns and walks out the same door the other three disappeared into and Lucas turns to me, rubbing his hands up and down my arms.

"You okay?"

I scoff. "Why don't you ask me again at the end of this night?"

A.M. Myers

It Ends Tonight

Chapter Fourteen
Quinn

Lucas pulls me into his arms and begins to sway back and forth as the band plays an instrumental version of *Perfect* by Ed Sheeran and I melt into him, relieved that this night is almost over. The band thankfully got their shit together just before the guests arrived and we managed to raise a ton of money for the children's hospital without any more drama. And, as an added bonus, I had several people come up to me tonight and ask for business cards because they were so impressed with my work.

"You ready to call it a night?" Lucas asks as he holds my hand to his chest and I shake my head.

"Not quite yet. Dance with me a little while longer."

He smiles. "I think I can do that. By the way, you

killed it tonight, babe. I'm so fucking proud of you."

"Thank you," I whisper, a blush creeping up my cheeks and a deep sense of satisfaction settling into my chest knowing that he's impressed with all my hard work. Who would have thought, three weeks ago, that his opinion would mean more to me than anything else. "And thanks for getting all dressed up and accompanying me."

"And miss seeing you in this dress? Not a chance in hell."

I lean back and our eyes meet. "You trying to butter me up, Smith?"

"Why?" He laughs. "Is it working?"

"A lady never tells."

"Quinn," Willa calls as she approaches us and I turn to her with a smile.

"Hey, girl. What ever happened to your date?"

She shakes her head with a sigh. "He bailed on me ten minutes before the event started."

"What a tool," Lucas tells her and I nod in agreement.

"Oh, don't you worry about it. You, sir, have renewed my faith in the opposite sex."

Lucas laughs, pulling me closer and I can't help but smile. "Well, glad I could help."

"And you," she says, pointing to me. "We have lots to talk about on Monday."

"I'm really looking forward to that," I quip, my tone

dry and she laughs. No doubt she'll spend the rest of the weekend thinking of questions to grill me with.

"Me, too. I'm going to take off and I'll be back in the morning to get all this broken down."

I nod and step out of Lucas's arms to give her a hug. "Thank you. Text me when you get home so I know you made it safe and I'll be around tomorrow if you run into any problems."

"Don't worry about it. I can handle it," she says before flashing me a grin. "So you two have a fun weekend."

"Subtle," I murmur and she laughs.

"That word is not in my vocabulary." She pulls away and takes a step back, waving as Lucas pulls me back into his body. "Bye, y'all."

When she's gone, I turn back to Lucas and yawn as I lay my head on his shoulder. We sway back and forth to *A Thousand Years* by Christina Perri. There are a few couples out on the dance floor and a few groups of people still milling around but the party is definitely winding down and although I'm exhausted, I'm incredibly proud of myself for throwing this together.

"Let's get you upstairs, gorgeous," Lucas whispers in my ear and I nod as I yawn again.

"Okay."

He grabs my hand and laces our fingers as we start slowly wandering out of the ballroom. "Is it time for my surprise now?"

"You're like a kid on Christmas," I tease with a laugh.

"Come on, baby. Just tell me what it is. I've been thinking about it all night."

I grab his arm and cuddle into his side as we stop in front of the elevator. "I think you can wait a few more minutes."

"Fine," he grumbles, looking more like a little boy than the man I've gotten to know over the past month and I giggle as the elevator doors open.

"So impatient."

We step into the elevator and as soon as the doors slide closed, he pushes my back up against the wall and runs his nose down the length of mine. "You know what else I've been waiting all night for?"

"What?"

He leans in and gently presses his lips to mine, letting them linger just long enough to make me want more before he pulls away. "That."

"Do it again."

"Look at you," he muses, leaning one hand against the wall by my head as he traces over my bottom lip with his finger. "Getting all demanding and shit."

"Kiss me, Lucas."

He shakes his head and drops his hand from my face. "I don't know, Darlin'. I kind of like hearing you beg like this."

"Don't press your luck," I murmur, arching my back

and pressing my hips into his. He sucks in a breath and a satisfied smile stretches across my face.

"What if I do?"

"Then I'll be sleeping alone tonight."

The door slides open and I arch a brow as I shove him off me and leave him standing in the elevator with a shocked look on his face. I peek over my shoulder as I dig the key out of my clutch and he follows after me, his gaze locked on my ass, and I turn back to the door with a grin on my face.

"The back of this fucking dress," he growls, stepping up behind me and gripping the fabric at the waist. "Is killing me."

"I would say I'm sorry…"

He shakes his head and presses his lips to my neck. "No, don't. I love it."

"Well," I muse as I slip the key into the lock and twist it. The door opens and I step inside before reaching out and pulling him along with me. As soon as the door closes, I feel bolder than I have all night and I press him up against the wall. "I think it's time for your surprise."

His eyes light up. "Yeah? What is it?"

Leaning in, I lay my hand flat against his chest and kiss his neck, lingering for a second before moving on to the next spot. A groan rumbles in his chest and his grip on my hips tightens.

"Darlin'," he rasps, his voice full of gravel. It sends shivers down my spine and my belly flips as moisture pools between my thighs. "If you keep kissing me like that…"

"Shut up, Lucas. No more warnings. No more holding back. No more rules. In the past month, you've proven to me countless times that you are the kind of man that I can trust with not only my body but my heart. My feelings for you are wild and overwhelming sometimes, given that we've only known each other for a short time but I told you I was ready for more and that's your surprise tonight."

His brows furrow. "What do you mean?"

"I guess I'll have to show you," I whisper, reaching under my arm and unhooking the top of the dress as our eyes lock. My heart thunders in my chest as I slowly lower the zipper and when I reach the bottom, I slip the dress off my shoulders. Lucas's gaze falls to my chest and he swallows hard as I let go of the dress and it glides down my body before pooling in a puddle at my feet.

"Fuck," he groans as his eyes slowly trail back up my body and I resist the urge to cover my bare breasts. It's been a long time since I've been willingly naked in front of a man but I meant everything I said. I trust him with everything - my heart, my body, my fears, my past. I've given it all to him.

He pushes himself off the wall as one arm wraps around my waist and pulls me into his body. We back up until my shoulders hit the opposite wall and he cups my face, brushing his thumb back and forth across my cheek.

"Do you remember what I told you?"

I shake my head. "No one needs to be in charge here, Lucas. I told you that I trust you and I meant it. If I'm uncomfortable with something, I'll let you know. Until then, stop holding back with me. I'm not going to break."

His eyes linger on mine for a second before he leans in and slams his lips to mine. I whimper and my knees tremble as I grip his arm and pull him closer, my lips parting. He nips at my bottom lip and my core clenches as a wave of need crashes over me. There is something deep down in my soul screaming for more from him, like it will never be enough. I'll never get him close enough. He'll never kiss me hard enough or long enough to satisfy this ache in my chest for him.

"Lucas," I whisper as he drags his lips across my skin and he groans, his hand gripping the back of my neck. We stumble away from the wall, our lips finding their way back to each other as I start frantically pulling at his tux, desperate to feel all of him against me. His jacket hits the floor quickly followed by his shirt as he kicks off his shoes. I hum as my fingers trail down his stomach and the tight muscles of his abs.

"Quinn," he breathes, his head dropping back. I continue down his body and unbutton his pants before shoving them down his legs. As he steps out of them, he wraps his arm around me and lifts me into the air before carrying me over to the bed. He lays me on my back and leans over me as he runs a hand down my chest. My nipple pebbles under his touch and he groans again.

"Tell me something," he says and I release a breath.

"You want to have a conversation right now?"

He nods. "Are you wet?"

A moan slips past my lips before I can respond and my cheeks heat. No one has ever talked to me like that before but it certainly works for me. Or maybe that's just Lucas.

"Was that a yes, gorgeous?"

"Yes," I breathe with a nod. He grins as his hand slowly crawls up the inside of my thigh.

"Are you going to tell me what you want?"

I meet his gaze. "You know what I want."

"Yeah," he muses with a glint in his eyes, totally in his element. It's a side to him that I've never seen and if I wasn't already addicted to him, I would be now. There's something about that little hint of danger in a man I know I can trust that thrills the part of me that still craves a rush. "I do."

He moves my panties to the side and strokes his thumb over my slit as my eyes roll back in my head and I moan.

"Do that again, baby," he whispers, repeating the move and I comply, moaning his name as a little voice in my head screams for more.

"Take them off." I hook my thumbs in the waistband of the lacy white panties I picked out for tonight and shove them down my hips as far as I can before Lucas takes over and tosses them across the room. He stands and removes his boxer briefs before crawling back over me and a moment of panic lances through me before I can stop it.

"Whoa, what was that?"

I shake my head and squeeze my eyes closed. "Nothing. Don't worry about it."

"Fuck that. Talk to me, baby," he says, grabbing my hand and pulling me up into a sitting position. I wrap my arms around my knees and suck in a breath.

"It's just… I haven't…"

"Since that night?" he finishes for me and I nod. "Do you want to stop?"

"No! I want to do this and I'm not even scared anymore. It was just like a second where I freaked out a little bit."

He studies me for a moment before nodding and I watch him as he props a couple pillows up against the headboard and leans back against them before holding his hand out to me. "Come here."

I crawl across the bed and allow him to pull me into his lap. His cock nudges against my core and I suck in a breath as he groans. Hooking his hand around the back of my neck, he pulls me forward until our lips connect and I sigh, any and all fear melting away in an instant.

"Better?" he whispers into my kiss and I nod. "You want more?"

"God, yes."

As he nips at my bottom lip, his thumb finds my clit and he circles it slowly as I grip his shoulders and fall apart in his lap, arching my back as I close my eyes and rock my hips against his hand.

"You good?"

I nod. "Yes."

"Ready for more?"

"Absolutely."

He releases my neck to stroke my cheek and I open my eyes, meeting his gaze. "Wrap your hand around my cock, sweetheart."

My heart hammers against my rib cage as I reach down and do as he instructs, grabbing his length before slowly pumping it up and down.

"Jesus Christ," he hisses, his eyes closing as his head falls back against the headboard. "Just like that, Quinn."

Leaning in, I kiss his neck as I continue working him up and down and he groans, his hands grabbing my hips and pulling me closer. Feeling a little bolder, I run my tongue up the column of his neck and he groans louder, his grip tightening.

"Shit, you're killin' me here."

I smile against his skin. "Oh? I'm so sorry."

"No, you're fucking not. I can feel you grinning."

Pulling back, I meet his eyes with the same smile on my face as I move up on my knees and press the tip of his cock against my entrance. He growls as his gaze drops to his lap. Holding him in place, I rub myself back and forth across the head a couple times. His eyes roll back in his head and I feel a little victorious as I slowly sink down on top of him.

"Wait! Shit. I need a condom."

I shake my head. "I'm on birth control and I don't want anything between us."

His gaze flicks to my face and he nods, giving me the go ahead as I take him inside me and release a low moan.

"Holy shit, you feel amazing," he groans, his fingers kneading my hips as he struggles to maintain control. "You good?"

"Yes, I'm good." Planting my hands on his shoulders, I start rocking my hips. "What did I say earlier? No holding back, no rules. Just let go."

He groans, his fingers gripping me harder as he grits his teeth. "I don't want to scare you."

"You don't scare me," I snap, grabbing his face and holding his gaze on me as I continue to bounce on his cock. "Take control."

Time seems to stand still as our eyes lock and I see the switch flip in him. With a growl, he wraps his arm around my waist and flips me to my back on the bed before pulling out of me and slamming back in.

"Is this what you want?" he snarls, weeks of pent up desire and frustration pouring out of him and I nod.

"Yes."

"Fuck," he groans, one hand gripping my hip and holding it down on the bed as he finds a punishing rhythm that leaves me gasping for air beneath him. It's steady and unrelenting and everything I need from him in this moment. I claw at his back as my hips try to buck off the bed, meeting him thrust for thrust, but his firm grip keeps me pinned to the mattress.

"Lucas," I moan and his answering groan sends a shiver through me.

"Christ, I love hearing you moan my name. I'm not going to last this time."

I shake my head. "Me either."

He releases my hip to lean down and kiss me as he drives into me faster and harder. My body tightens until I'm sure that I'm going to break. Just before I do, my release explodes through me and I gasp as I cling to him. He rips his lips from mine and thrusts a few more times before stilling and releasing a deep groan.

"Baby," he breathes, collapsing on top of me and I wrap my arms around him as a giggle slips past my lips. He growls and playfully nips at my neck. "Something funny?"

"No, not funny."

He pulls back and meets my gaze. "Why are you laughing then?"

"Because you make me really fucking happy."

A smile stretches across his face and his gaze heats as he glances down at my tits. "You give me five minutes and I'll make you really happy a second time."

I giggle again, nodding. "Deal."

It Ends Tonight

*   *   *   *

"Lucas," I whisper playfully as I walk my fingers up his bare chest and he grumbles something in his sleep before rolling away from me. Smiling, I cuddle in behind him and press my lips to his neck.

"Woman," he groans. "I don't even have to open my eyes to know that it's too fucking early to be awake. What the hell are you doing to me?"

"I want you," I whine. He sighs and rolls to his back before cracking one eye open and squinting up at me. In the past week or so, it's become very apparent that Lucas is not a morning person but he just looks so damn cute when he's sleepy that I can't stop myself from waking him up.

"I never thought I would complain about my girlfriend wanting too much sex."

I fight back a smile as I lean in and kiss him. "Say that again."

"What? That you want too much sex?" he asks and I giggle, shaking my head.

"No, the other part."

His large arms wrap around me and he pulls me

closer, opening both eyes as he flashes me a teasing smile. "The girlfriend part?"

"Yeah," I breathe with a nod, my heart on the verge of bursting as the word settles inside me.

"It feels kind of lame, doesn't it?"

"What does?"

He brushes my hair out of my face. "The word girlfriend, like we're a couple of teenagers."

"What would you call me then?"

"Hmm," he hums, studying me. "I don't know. Since I haven't asked you to marry me yet, I can't call you my fiancée…"

"Y…Yet?" I stutter, looking down at him with wide eyes and he nods.

"No more holding back, right?"

I nod.

"Then you've got to know I'm completely and totally in love with you, Quinn Dawson, and someday, I'm going to make you my wife."

I shake my head as my mouth drops open. "I don't… How can you…"

"A while back you asked me what I wanted out of my life and then the other night Brooklyn fell asleep on my chest and you were passed out next to me and looking down at the two of you, I realized that I already had everything. Nothing else matters as long as I get to spend my life with you."

Tears well up in my eyes as I stare at him, my heart

racing. "You mean that?"

"Baby, you know I don't…"

"Say things you don't mean," I finish for him as a tear rolls down my cheek. He brushes it away as his brows furrow.

"Why are you crying?"

"Because I'm the luckiest girl in the whole damn world. And because I never dreamed I would find this, find you, and now that I have, I feel like my heart just can't hold this much happiness. I love you, too."

He grins and pulls me into a tornado of a kiss that only reaffirms everything we just said to each other and when he finally pulls back, we're both gasping for air.

"Come take a shower with me," he commands and I nod, the thought of watching water slide down his muscular body almost driving me out of my mind with need.

"I hope you're gearing up for another round."

He shakes his head. "Jesus, woman. You really are insatiable and I'm going to need nourishment if you expect me to go again after the five times we did it last night."

"You know," I call, watching him as he flings the covers off his naked body and climbs out of bed. "Some men only get sex on their birthdays."

When he reaches back for me, I grab his hand and let him pull me to my knees before he drags me over to the edge of the bed and wraps his arms around my waist.

"How unfortunate for them. Thank God, I've got a girlfriend who's an undercover freak."

I scrunch up my nose. "You're right. I don't like that word. We should come up with something else."

"Okay," he muses, nodding his head. "What about mine?"

"Mine… I could get with that."

He nods and lifts me into the air and before I can ask him what he's doing, he throws me over his shoulder, slaps my ass, and carries me into the bathroom. I watch as he turns the water on and when it's warm, he steps inside with me still in his arms. Only when the glass shower door is closed does he slide me down the front of his body.

"Did I tell you how fucking gorgeous you are in the mornings?"

I shake my head. "No, I don't think you have."

"What an oversight because you're better than any sunrise I've ever been forced to endure."

I tsk and turn away from him to let the water run down the front of my body. "You're such a sweet talker."

"No, I'm serious," he rasps, stepping up behind me and wrapping his arms around my waist. "You make getting up early worth it."

"Aw," I tease, pressing my hand to my chest. "Now, that's love."

"You know what," he growls, spinning me back around to face him and lifting me in the air. He pins me against the shower wall and rubs his hardening cock against my pussy. "You're being awfully sassy this morning."

"Maybe it's because you haven't given me this," I whisper, rocking my hips against his as much as I can and he groans. With one arm securely wrapped around my hips, he thrusts his hand into my hair and pulls me down to his lips, searing his name into my very soul with his kiss. I gasp and his tongue teases mine for a second before he nips at my bottom lip.

"This what you want?" he asks, his voice full of fire. The sound settles right between my thighs and I moan as I imagine him sinking into my core just like he did all night long. I've never had sex like this and he may be right that I'm a little addicted to it but I don't care. He makes me feel things that I can't find words to explain and I don't want to stop.

"More."

He growls and drops me to my feet before spinning me to face the wall. "Plant your hands, baby."

"Why?"

His teeth nip at my earlobe and I gasp, goose bumps racing across my skin as he drags his lips down my neck and plants a kiss on my shoulder. "Just do what you're told, Quinn. You trust me, right?"

"Yes," I breathe, nodding and he grabs my hands before planting them above my head against the tile.

"Now, be a good girl and don't move."

I moan, closing my eyes as his hands slowly start traveling over my curves, his touch light enough to drive me out of my mind. Stepping up behind me, he presses his cock against my ass and his hands move to my belly, dropping lower and lower until he brushes his fingers over my clit.

"Lucas," I whisper and he nips at my ear again.

"You like that, Darlin'?"

I nod before dropping my head back on his shoulder. "You know I do."

Chuckling, he circles the sensitive little bundle of nerves with one hand as the other drags back up my body and squeezes my tit.

"You going to come for me?"

"Yes," I whisper, thrusting my hips back against him and he groans, his breath fanning out across my neck.

"Thought I told you not to move?"

I shrug, shaking my ass back and forth across his cock. "I'm not a good listener."

"Yeah, I've gathered that," he quips, the pressure on my clit increasing as he rubs faster and I gasp, my knuckles going white as I try to keep my grip on the wall. "We're going to have to fix that."

"Or…" I whisper, trying to organize my thought as my release builds deep in my belly. "You could just get used to it. Us Dawson women are very strong willed."

"I don't know about that," he growls, kissing my neck before his teeth sink into my skin and I gasp again.

My nipples pebble almost to the point of pain and I rock my hips against his hand, chasing an orgasm that's just out of reach.

"More, babe. Please," I beg and he groans as he releases my tit and grabs my chin, forcing my face to his before stealing a kiss. Just as I'm about to fall into the abyss of my release, his hand falls away from my core and I cry out.

"Shh, I've got you," he whispers, spinning me around and lifting me into his arms again. His cock presses against my entrance and he plunges forward as he pins my shoulders to the wall.

"Lucas!" I scream, gripping the back of his neck as he finds a steady rhythm that resurrects my abandoned orgasm in an instant. Pulling us away from the wall, he moves his hands to my ass and manipulates me up and down on his cock as he steps toward the water, grunting each time he sinks back into me.

"Oh my god," I moan, my muscles aching from holding on to him.

"Fuck," he groans. "Is that what you wanted? You needed this cock?"

I nod through my near constant moans. "Yes."

"Greedy girl," he growls, slamming me down harder and a rainbow of colors explodes through my vision as a release seizes my body. He roars, stumbling over to the wall and pinning me against the tile as he presses his forehead against my chest and continues driving into me.

263

"Goddamn it, baby."

I grip his hair and give it a little tug, forcing him to look up at me. His brows furrow in question but I ignore it as I lean down and kiss him hard. His grip on my hips tightens and he pulls away from me as a loud groan spills out of his mouth.

"Fuck!" he yells, thrusting into me one last time before he stills and groans my name, his voice echoing off the walls of the shower. After a second, he glances up at me and I can't help but smile.

"I love you," I whisper, reveling in the feeling of being able to say that to him and his answering smile that damn near blinds me.

"Darlin', I fucking love you more."

Wrapping my arms around his neck, I pull him close and press a quick kiss against his lips before going in for another.

"What do you say we finish showering and then go see our girl?"

He nods, leaning in for another kiss. "I can't think of anything better."

Chapter Fifteen
Lucas

"Oh, she's gonna do it," I say, sitting up a little straighter as Brooklyn stands and looks down at her feet. Quinn laughs from my arms and shakes her head.

"She's just teasing you, babe. She's probably going to start walking when no one is around to watch her."

I scoff and glance down at her. "No way. My girl is about to be a walking machine."

Instead of arguing with me, she just shakes her head again and cuddles into my side as we watch Brooklyn on the other side of the living room. If you had told me even a few months ago that this would be my life, I would have laughed. In fact, I think I did laugh when Ali insinuated that I would be next but meeting these two changed everything. There is peace in my soul where there once was chaos and my guilt has been replaced with love for the woman of my dreams and her perfect daughter.

My mind drifts back to yesterday. After we finished showering at the hotel, we came home but I wasn't ready to leave them so Quinn suggested we take Brooklyn to the zoo. We spent the whole day walking around, showing Brooklyn the animals and stuffing our faces with vendor food. I can't remember the last time I had so much fun and when Quinn took Brooklyn into the bathroom, a little old woman told me I had a beautiful family. Like a little bitch, I almost cried right in front of that stranger because it's been nineteen years since I felt like I had a family but as soon as she said it, it felt so right that I couldn't brush it off. Quinn and Brooklyn have become my family just like the guys in the club did when they took me in all those years back.

Quinn gasps and points across the room as Brooklyn lifts her little foot up, trying to take a step, but before she can set it down, she plops down to her butt and I sigh.

"I told you she was teasing."

I dig my fingers into her ribs and she squeals. "Yeah? What was all that gasping for, then?"

"Okay, so maybe she got me that time, too."

"That's what I thought," I murmur as I wrap my arms around her and kiss her forehead. Brooklyn stands again and claps her hands as she looks up at us.

"Oh, no, baby girl. I'm on to your games."

She laughs, flashing us a toothy grin and we both

chuckle as she glances down at her feet and takes a step forward. Quinn gasps, leaning forward and I'm right there with her, watching intently as Brooklyn takes another tentative step.

"Oh my god," she breathes, dropping down to her knees and holding out her hands. "Come on, sweet girl. You can do it."

Brooklyn glances over at me and I smile as she takes another step. I nudge Quinn and she flicks her gaze over her shoulder as I grin.

"What did I tell you? Walking machine."

Rolling her eyes, she turns away from me. "Smug bastard."

"Brooklyn," I call, laughing as I get down on my knees next to Quinn. "You got this, Princess."

Brooklyn takes a few more steps, surprised and delighted with herself each time her foot does what she wants it to do. She claps as she gets closer to us and I peek over to Quinn. There are tears shining in her eyes but she's wearing the biggest smile I've ever seen as she watches her daughter take her first steps.

God, I fucking love her.

I would move heaven and earth for either one of them. Reaching down, I feel the outline of the ring I've been carrying around in my pocket all day long and smile. I don't know how I'm going to do it yet or when but soon, I'll get down on one knee and ask her to spend the rest of her life with me.

"Oh my god," Quinn gushes. "Just one more step, baby."

Brooklyn squeals and looks over at me before taking the final step into her mama's arms and Quinn squeezes her to her chest as she praises her.

"You did it, baby girl. You're getting so big."

Brooklyn reaches for me and Quinn sighs as she rolls her eyes.

"Oh, of course. You just want Lucas."

"You can't blame her, Darlin'," I tell her, grinning as I pull the baby into my arms. "She's got damn good tastes."

I stand and sit down on the couch with Brooklyn in my arms and Quinn cuddles in next to me again as Brooke lays her head on my chest.

"I suppose that's true," she says, brushing her fingers across Brooklyn's chubby little cheek. "You are an excellent pillow."

I laugh and wrap my arm around her. "Oh, is that why the two of you are keeping me around?"

"Among other things."

"Like what?" I ask and she grins before dropping her gaze to my cock. Arching a brow, I pull her closer until my lips brush against her ear so the baby won't hear. "You dirty fucking girl."

She pulls back with a grin on her face and winks as she plays with the neckline on my t-shirt. "Put her to bed and I'll show you just how much."

"Sold," I call out, pressing a quick kiss to her lips before standing up. She follows behind me as we walk up the stairs to Brooklyn's room and I watch as Quinn changes her into her pajamas. Her eyes are droopy when we lay her down in her crib and cover her with her blanket but she's not asleep yet.

"Now, where were we?" Quinn asks, pulling me into her body in the hallway outside the nursery and I shake my head.

"Not yet, gorgeous. She's still awake."

She laughs. "Lucas, she'll be out in minutes."

"Nope, not risking it. Let's go watch TV or something for a little while."

Her eyes light up and she nods. "All right. I've got Pretty Woman downstairs and I've been waiting to test your movie knowledge."

"Big mistake," I say, imitating Julia Roberts' voice from the movie. "Huge."

"I'm willing to admit when I'm wrong," she answers with a giggle. "But it's going to take more than one line from the movie to convince me."

"Lead the way then, gorgeous."

We walk back downstairs and sit down on the couch. I pull her into my arms as she searches for the movie and starts playing it. As the opening credits roll, she grabs the blanket off the back of the couch and covers us with it as I reach over her head and hit the light switch.

When I start singing along to *The King of Wishful*

Thinking by Go West, she laughs and peeks up at me. "Still not totally convinced, sir."

"Just wait."

Cuddling together on the couch, we watch the movie and by the time Julia Roberts is singing in the bathtub, Quinn admits defeat.

"All right, so you've seen the movie a time or two."

I shake my head. "Try ten or twenty, at least. Insomnia, remember?"

"What kept you up when you were a kid?" she asks, her voice soft as she plays with the hair at the base of my neck and I suck in a breath, fighting back painful memories. Before I can answer her, my phone rings and she pauses the movie to allow me to answer it.

"Hello?"

"Luke?" Clay's disoriented voice answers and I sit up, offering Quinn an apologetic look for jostling her.

"Clay? What's going on?"

There's music thumping in the background and he moves somewhere a little quieter. "You're wrong."

"I'm wrong about what?"

"Dad is innocent. I know he is."

I drop my face in my hand and release a breath. "Clay, no, he's not."

"No! You don't know what you're talking about."

"How the fuck do I not know what I'm talking about?" I snap before remembering that Quinn is still behind me but when I glance back at her, the only expression on her face is a supportive one.

"You were just a kid and you have no idea what was really going on. I've been searching for evidence and I'm going to find it. I'm going to get Dad out of jail."

"Clay," I whisper, tears springing to my eyes as I think about our mother. "Don't you think if there actually was evidence to find, someone would have found it by now?"

"They set him up, Luke! The police and the judges and the lawyers, they all set him up."

"Why would they do that? Think about what you're saying, Clay. It doesn't make any sense."

He scoffs. "Then how do you explain it all?"

"Look, can we meet and talk about this? I'm worried about you."

"No. I'm not meeting you until I have the proof I need."

"Clay," I snap but the dial tone greets me. I grip the phone in my hand as I grit my teeth and let out a roar of frustration.

"Lucas," Quinn whispers and I glance back at her, expecting to see fear and feeling like shit for not being able to control my temper, just like my father, but instead, she scoots closer with furrowed brows and lays her hand on my back. "What's going on?"

"Shit," I hiss, turning back to look at her and this time I'm not even trying to hide the riot of emotions controlling my body right now. "There are things I haven't told you, Quinn."

She nods, vulnerability flicking through her eyes for a second and I hate to see it. "Okay. Tell me now."

"I don't…"

"No, Lucas. I can tell by your side of the conversation that this is serious and you're going to tell me what's going on."

I sigh. "Babe, I lied to you."

"About?" she asks with an edge to her voice that I've never heard before and my stomach rolls. Fuck, what if she doesn't want to be with me after I tell her everything? My past is dark and I couldn't blame her for not wanting this crazy in her life or her daughter's.

"About my past, my parents."

"They're not dead?"

I shake my head. "My mom is dead… and my dad is serving life in prison for murdering her."

"Oh, God," she gasps and when I look back at her again, there are tears in her eyes. I scoot back to her side and kiss her softly. When I pull back, she yanks me back to her and presses her forehead to mine and my fear subsides. "Will you tell me what happened?"

"Only if I can do it while holding you," I answer and she nods before climbing onto my lap and straddling my hips. I suck in a breath as I wonder where to start this story but before I can, she lays her hand flat against my chest, right over my racing heart and the same peace that I've felt since the moment I looked into her eyes settles inside me.

"You okay?" She grabs my other hand and holds it tight. I nod.

"Yeah, I'm good now."

She waits patiently for me to begin my story and when I'm finally ready, I take a deep breath and look up at her.

"I was ten years old when it happened and Clay was five. Dad had lost his job a few months before that and he and Mom had been fighting a lot. I used to lay in bed at night and listen to them scream at each other until the sun started coming up."

"Is that when the insomnia started?"

I shrug. "I always blamed it on the night she died but I guess it makes sense that it started even before that. Listening to the way they would go at it terrified me but I knew it scared Clay even more so I had to be the big brother. It was my job to protect him and tell him everything was going to be okay."

She nods and for the first time in my life, I don't question if she really understands because she's always understood Clay and my relationship more than anyone else.

"On this one stormy night, I remember that I just couldn't shake this feeling that something was really wrong and when Mom and Dad started fighting that night, something in me was telling me to run but I didn't listen to it. The screaming got louder and it woke Clay up. He laid in bed and cried and I tried so hard to keep him quiet because I didn't want Dad coming after us. And then there was this deafening bang and the whole house went silent, too silent, you know?"

A steady stream of tears pour down her face and I reach up, wiping them away before pulling her down for another kiss, this one a little salty.

"What happened after that?"

My hands shake as the memories flood my mind and she moves in closer, offering me her silent comfort. "Clay was damn near hysterical but I got him to cry into a pillow so Dad wouldn't hear him as I crept to the door and peeked down the hallway."

My voice breaks and a tear slips down my cheek as I stare down at our entwined hands.

"Mom was laying at the other end with a pool of blood around her head and Dad was kneeling next to her, staring at the gun in his hand like he had no idea how it got there."

"What did you do?" she whispers, cupping my cheek and wiping away tears as I work up the strength to continue my story.

"I knew we didn't have much time and I didn't know what he'd do to us once he snapped out of his daze so I snuck back into my room and just started throwing as much of our shit as I could into backpacks. Once they were stuffed full, we jumped out of the window and ran for it."

She leans down and presses her lips to mine. "I'm so glad you made it out safely. I don't know what I would do if I didn't have you."

"Seems you were doing just fine before I came along," I answer, slipping my hand into her hair and she shakes her head.

"I was surviving… barely. You saved me, Lucas."

"No more than you saved me, babe. Being around you gives me a feeling of peace I don't know if I've ever felt."

"I love you," she whispers, leaning in for another kiss and as her lips meet mine, I want to beat my chest and scream from the rooftops because she makes me feel like a goddamn king. Like I could rule the whole damn world.

"I love you more, gorgeous," I say when she pulls away and she smiles as she lays her head on my shoulder.

"How did you end up with Iris?"

"Clay and I ran all night long because I was convinced that if social services got ahold of us, I'd never see my brother again. Around dawn, we found this old boxcar along the unused portion of a track in the woods and I always liked to read The Boxcar Children to Clay so he begged me to stay there. I was exhausted at that point so I agreed and we stayed there for two weeks before Iris found us. The boxcar was on her property line and she heard Clay crying in the middle of the night. The next day she came searching for us and at first, I didn't trust her but slowly, she won us both over and became our official guardian."

"I knew I liked her."

I smile. "She really liked you, too. I've already gotten three phone calls about when I'm going to bring you and Brooklyn by next."

"What does all this have to do with Clay's phone call?" she asks and I run my free hand through my hair.

"Our dad sent him a letter a little while back, claiming he was innocent and because I never let Clay see our mother dead at the end of the hallway, he believes him. Said he's going to find evidence to prove our father's innocence."

I can feel her scowl against my neck.

"Why would he do that?"

"Clay?"

She shakes her head. "No, your father. What's the point of putting your brother through all that pain?"

"Believe me, baby, I've been asking myself that question every damn day. He used to be a drug addict like Clay is now but I think there's something else wrong with him. I think he likes watching our pain."

She pulls back to look me in the eye. "I'm so sorry."

"You, Darlin', have absolutely nothing to apologize for. My life is so much better, so much richer since the day you crashed in front of me and I know that no matter what happens with my brother or my dad, I'll be okay as long as I've got you."

"You've got me, Lucas. Always."

*   *   *   *

Pulling into the last space in the parking lot, I turn off my bike and stare up at the clubhouse as my knee bounces and my mind drifts to my conversation with Clay last night. Quinn and I stayed up late into the night talking about what I could do to help my brother and the one thing that stuck out was the fact that I can't do this alone. I have tried that route for years now and it's only made things worse so it's time to let go of some of this pain and guilt and ask my club, my family, for help. My stomach rolls as I climb off my bike and walk toward the door but I know this is the right decision. Clay is going to hate me for it but with any luck, he'll be clean and I can worry about our relationship after that.

"Well, well, well," someone calls as I step into the clubhouse and I glance in the corner where Ali, Storm, Chance, Carly, Kodiak, Tate, and Fuzz are hanging out on the couches. "Look who it is."

"Hey. What are y'all doing?"

"The better question," Tate says, studying me with

narrowed eyes. "Is where the hell have you been?"

I shrug. "Busy."

"Yeah?" Ali asks, grinning. "With a certain woman you met recently?"

"Maybe. What's with the third degree?"

"Are you guys still taking it slow?" she asks, completely ignoring my question and I roll my eyes.

"Not exactly."

"Ha!" Chance yells. "Pay up, suckers."

Storm, Kodiak and Fuzz all pass money over to Chance and I shake my head. "Are y'all seriously betting on my love life?"

Ali nods. "Yes, and I had faith that you wouldn't push that poor girl."

"Hold up, I didn't push her. She decided that she was ready for more."

Storm snaps at Chance. "Give me my money back."

"Hell, no," Chance snaps, stuffing the wad of cash in his pocket. "The bet was that they weren't taking things slow anymore."

"No," Kodiak growls. "The bet was that he would be just as pushy as you bastards and convince her to move faster."

"Don't sit here and act like you're not exactly the same way, Lincoln," Tate scoffs and he grins down at her.

"We're not talking about me right now."

"Maybe you should just give me the money and no

one wins," I suggest and they all laugh as Chance stands up and starts handing everyone their cash back.

"So," Ali prompts. "If you're not taking things slow, does that mean you'll bring her to the shower?"

"I don't know. I'll ask her but she might not be able to find a sitter."

Ali's eyes go wide and I can practically see the maternal instincts pouring out of her. "Aw, she has a kid?"

"Yeah, a little girl."

She presses her hand to her heart. "How old is she?"

"Like thirteen months, I think," I answer, shrugging my shoulder. I'm pretty sure that's how old Quinn said Brooklyn is.

"Fuck, dude. You're in so deep if you know how old her baby is in months." Chance laughs and Ali shoots him a look before sighing.

"Oh my gosh, that's so cute. She'll be able to play with Magnolia."

"Absolutely fucking not," Storm growls, shaking his head. "Fucking veto."

"What?" Ali asks, rubbing her belly. "It's a beautiful name."

"We are not naming our daughter Magnolia."

She crosses her arms over her chest and glares back at Storm, who shakes his head.

"No way in hell, Kitten. Think of another name."

"You look different," Tate adds, standing up from the

couch and standing in front of me. I shake my head.

"No, I don't."

"Yeah, you do actually," Carly says.

"He looks less sad," Ali adds and I sigh as I step away from the couches.

"Y'all need to get control of your women," I call as I turn toward Blaze's office and the girls all laugh.

"Listen, brother. The sooner you realize that's never going to happen, the easier your life will be."

I stop and turn to face them. "Yeah? Well, then… Storm, I can't wait to meet Magnolia."

"Absolutely fucking not!" he yells and I grin as I turn around and walk to Blaze's office, knocking on the door.

"Yeah," he calls and I open the door.

"You got a minute?"

He glances up from the paperwork in his hand and nods before pointing to the chair across from him. "Have a seat."

The yelling from the bar area is loud even after I close the door and he scowls. "What the hell is going on out there?"

"Storm and Ali," I mutter and he sighs.

"You know, that girl is family now but I'll be glad when she's not staying here."

I laugh. "Don't let Storm hear you say that."

"Boy, I wasn't born yesterday," he mutters before grinning. "Now, what can I help you with?"

Sighing, I run my hand through my hair and prop my

elbows on my knees. "Um, it's my brother… I need to find a rehab for him and I need help getting him there."

"Wow," Blaze whispers, his eyes wide. For years, I've refused the help of the club as I tried to fix things all on my own but I know now that I can't do this by myself. "This is huge. Does it have anything to do with the girl Ali says you met?"

"Quinn?… Yeah. She's opened my eyes in a lot of ways."

He nods. "Sounds serious."

I pull the two carat cushion cut diamond ring that I've been carrying around for the last two days out of my pocket and lay it on the table. Blaze's eyes widen and he lets out a whistle.

"Damn, kid. You dropped some serious coin for that ring."

I nod. "She's worth it."

"I don't doubt that she is. Does she know everything about you, your past, and what's going on with your brother?"

"Yeah," I answer with a nod. "I told her everything last night and she lost both of her parents when she and her sister were little so she understands me in ways that y'all never could… no offense."

He holds his hands up. "None taken, but you know we just wanted to help."

"I do know that and now I'm asking for it."

He turns to the filing cabinet and digs around for a

second before pulling out a folder. As soon as he opens it, I recognize the rehab facility on top. When the club decided to go legit all those years ago, Blaze's actions weighed heavy on him and there was a time when we helped the people that we had once sold drugs to as some sort of penance. Blaze slaps his hand down on the folder and stands.

"Leave it to me and I'll find the best place I can for your brother, okay?"

I grab the ring off the table and slip it back into my pocket before shaking his hand. "Thanks, Prez."

"Your family is our family, Smith. Always has been, always will be."

It Ends Tonight

Chapter Sixteen
Quinn

"Are you nervous?" Lucas asks, reaching for my hand as we approach the clubhouse and I peek over at him, shaking my head.

"No. Should I be?"

He makes a face and holds his hand out in the air, pulling a giggle out of me.

"You're supposed to make me feel better, not scare me."

"Well, truthfully," he says, adjusting Brooklyn in his arms as he stops and pulls me into his body. "Everyone is going to love you but… Ali has been dying to meet you for weeks now and she's not someone who doesn't get her way."

I nod, casting a faux nervous glance toward the door. "So, what you're saying is I'm about to be swarmed?"

"A little bit, yeah."

Sucking in a breath, I turn back to the door and square my shoulders. "I think I'm ready."

"You're so fucking cute," he teases, releasing my hand to wrap his arm around my shoulders before pulling me into his body. "And have I mentioned that this little skirt you're wearing makes me want to bend you over a table?"

My cheeks heat. "You know, I don't think you have."

"Oh, well it does." He nips at my ear and I suck in a breath as goose bumps race across my flesh and my nipples pebble.

"Good to know."

"One more thing…" he murmurs and I turn my head to meet his gaze. Our noses touch and he flashes me the kind of smile that can make me melt in an instant. "I love you."

"I love you, too."

Right on cue, Brooklyn squeals from Lucas's arms and he laughs as he pulls his arm off my shoulders to tickle her belly.

"You just can't stand when someone else is the center of attention, can you, Princess?"

She pats his face with her little hands and blows a raspberry. Both of us laugh and he blows one back at her, which sends her into a fit of giggles.

"Oh, Lord, she's really hammin' it up today," I say and Lucas reaches for my hand again as we step toward the door.

"Gee, wonder where she gets that from…"

I gasp. "Are you saying I'm a ham? I'm offended, sir."

The door to the clubhouse opens and a large man with dark hair and gray piercing eyes steps outside. He looks relieved when he spots us and Lucas laughs.

"She driving you crazy already, man?"

He shakes his head. "I don't know who that woman is in there but it's not my wife. I'll be glad when this pregnancy is over."

"True, but then you'll have two of them in your house."

His eyes widen. "Shit. Why didn't I think of that until now?"

"No clue," Lucas answers, laughing. "This is Quinn, by the way. Quinn, this is Storm."

I smile. "Hi, it's nice to meet you."

"You, too, Darlin'. Y'all better get in there. Ali is excited to meet you."

"What are you gonna do? Stay out here?" Lucas asks, quirking a brow and Storm blows out a breath.

"I'm seriously considering taking up smoking."

Lucas laughs as we turn back toward the door. "I'm gonna tell Ali that."

"Don't you fucking dare."

He walks out to the parking lot as we reach the door and I suck in a breath, my belly doing a little flip, as

Lucas opens the door and ushers me inside. The room is fairly open with a bar on one side and pool tables and couches on the other side with a few tables scattered throughout the space in between. One table near the entrance is piled high with gifts and I set ours down on top, thankful that I don't knock the rest over in the process.

"Is this a big party?" I ask, eyeing the stack of presents and Lucas chuckles as he shakes his head.

"No, but it's the first baby in the club in a long time and the guys went a little crazy."

I bury my head in his shoulder to hide my smile. "That's fucking adorable."

"Just don't tell anyone I told you," he whispers and I peek up at him as I nod.

"Your secret is safe with me."

"Lucas," someone yells and a little redhead bounces over to us with another large man following behind her. "And you must be Quinn. We've heard a lot about you."

"Oh?" I ask. "All good things I hope."

She grins and I peek over at Lucas as he rolls his eyes.

"Quinn, this is Tate and Kodiak."

"And who is this little cutie?" Tate asks, stepping forward and tickling Brooklyn's belly. Brooklyn giggles but it's a little reserved.

"This is Brooklyn," Lucas answers and she lays her head down on his shoulder, plopping her thumb in her mouth.

"Oh my god," Tate gushes. "If that's not the cutest goddamn thing I've ever seen…"

"Quinn!" another voice yells above the noise of the crowd and I scan the room with wide eyes. A bubbly blonde with a giant belly wiggles through the crowd. "You are Quinn, right?"

I laugh and nod. "I am."

"Oh, thank god. I'm Ali, it's so nice to meet you." She pulls me in for a hug and I glance back at Lucas, who grins.

"It's nice to meet you, too."

She releases me and turns to Lucas. Brooklyn peeks up at her and she smiles. "Hello, cutie. What's your name?"

"This is Brooklyn," Lucas answers and Ali makes a face at her and just like that, Brooklyn's shyness disappears as she copies the look. Everyone laughs and Ali taps her nose.

"Oh, I think you're going to fit in around here just fine, little girl." Ali turns to me again before looking around the room and frowning. "Hey, any of you seen my husband?"

"We passed him outside," Lucas answers and her scowl deepens.

"Well, what the hell was he doing out there?"

Lucas and I share a glance. "Uh, he was just getting a little air."

"Oh." She looks upset for a second before a smile slowly stretches across her face like every cartoon villain revealing their master plan that I've ever seen. "You want to know a secret?"

"Absolutely."

She giggles, shaking her head. "I've been doing everything I can to drive that man insane so he'll finally let me stay home when he's working late."

"Oh, what the fuck?" Lucas whispers before laughing.

"Fucking diabolical," Tate mutters with a grin on her face and Kodiak shakes his head.

My gaze bounces between all three of them before I turn back to Ali. "Wait, why won't he let you go home?"

"Ever since I got pregnant, he doesn't like me to be home alone so when he's working late with the club, he makes me sleep here and as you are well aware, pregnancy makes you very uncomfortable and the double bed he's got up in his room doesn't help anything. Not to mention that it's hard to get any work done with all these guys hanging around all the time."

"I'm gonna tell him," Lucas cuts in with a grin and she narrows her eyes into a glare as she points her finger at him.

"No, you're fucking not. I just want my bed, Smith. My big, comfy, king-size bed. Is that really too much to ask for?"

"Babe," I murmur, nudging him. "The correct answer

here is no. Just for future reference."

"I don't know. He's just trying to keep her safe," Kodiak adds. Tate peeks over her shoulder with a look that could kill.

"She is literally growing a person," she objects and I nod.

"And in… wait, how far are along are you?"

"Thirty-three weeks."

I nod. "Right. And in six-ish weeks, she's going to rip her body apart to give birth to that little person so if she wants her bed, she gets her bed."

"Here, here," Tate calls and Ali raises one in the air as the other cradles her belly.

"Preach, sisters."

Kodiak shares a look with Lucas. "We're getting outnumbered here, brother."

The three girls laugh as Storm walks back into the clubhouse. He scans the room and as soon as he spots his wife, he makes a beeline for her.

"Where you been, babe?" Ali asks as he pulls her into his side and he shakes his head.

"Just outside for a minute."

"Mm-hmm," she hums, meeting my gaze as I try to bite back my smile.

"Kitten…" Storm growls and she laughs, holding her hands up in the air.

"What? I didn't say anything."

"Ali, do you want to get the food started?" someone

asks, approaching the group and Ali nods.

"Yeah, we can do that. Oh, by the way, Carly, this is Quinn. Quinn, this is my best friend, Carly."

I hold my hand up and wave. "Hi."

"Hey," she answers, smiling at me before she turns to look at Lucas. "Wow, Smith. The dad thing works for you."

He glances down at Brooklyn with the sweetest smile on his face. "Thanks."

"I'm gonna go throw stuff on the grill. You need to sit down," Storm grumbles and Ali rolls her eyes.

"Yes, boss man. Right away, boss man."

"Kitten, I will spank your ass if you don't listen and rest your feet."

"I'm heading out, too," Kodiak says, kissing Tate on the head before he heads out with Storm. Lucas passes Brooklyn to me and presses a quick kiss against my lips as the rest of the guys file outside to cook.

"Would you look at them?" Ali grumbles. "Bunch of cavemen."

"He is right, though. You should sit down," Carly tells her and she nods.

"God, I know. My feet are fucking killing me."

Carly laughs and grabs her hand to guide her over to the couches and Tate and I follow behind them. Brooklyn starts to fuss as soon as I sit down and I pull the baggie of cereal out of my purse before handing it to her.

"Okay," Ali breathes after she gets settled and her

feet propped up. "Give it to me straight. How bad is labor?"

I laugh. "Um, bad... but the thing is, you forget how bad it was as soon as it's over and you're holding your baby in your arms. And when she takes her first step or says her first word, you'll be desperate to have another one."

"Well, that's comforting, I guess."

"Look at it this way... I would rather have another baby than get hit by a truck again."

She laughs. "I suppose that makes sense."

"That's how you met Smith, right?" Carly asks and I nod.

"Yeah, I had just gotten off work and I was driving home when this truck came out of nowhere. And then Lucas was there, keeping me calm until the ambulance arrived."

"That's Smith, for ya," Tate says and the other girls nod.

"So, you can totally tell me it's none of my business if you want but is her dad in the picture?" Ali asks, pointing to Brooklyn and I shake my head.

"No, he's not."

"That must be so hard for you. I know as much shit as I give him, I'd be lost in the pregnancy without Logan."

I shrug, smiling as I think about Grams. "I wasn't all by myself. My Grams was a huge support for me until she died and I've got my little sister Alice."

"It takes a village," Ali muses before flashing me a smile. "And now you've got all of us. It's easy to see that Lucas is head over heels for you, which means that you've just been added to this crazy family and we'd all do anything for each other."

"That's going to take some getting used to."

Carly lets out a laugh as she nods. "Yes, it will but one day, you'll look up and realize that it's the biggest blessing."

"That's true," Tate adds. "No family is perfect but what Blaze and the guys have built here comes pretty damn close."

"I kind of got that feeling from Lucas."

As soon as the words leave my mouth, Lucas strolls back into the room with Storm. Storm flashes a victorious grin at Ali when he finds her sitting down with her feet propped up and she rolls her eyes.

"God, he's going to be impossible now."

"Hey, Darlin'," Lucas says, sinking into the seat next to me and I smile at him.

"Hey."

Tate rolls her eyes and flashes Lucas a disgusted look. "God, the two of you are sickeningly cute."

"You're just jealous that you got stuck with that asshole outside," Lucas teases her and she flips him off.

"Don't think that just because it's a baby shower, I didn't bring my taser."

I peek over at Lucas with wide eyes and he shakes his head.

"Behave. We have company."

She rolls her eyes again before standing up and heading outside. The guys slowly start filtering in and out as they cook the food but Lucas stays by my side, talking to me and playing with Brooklyn.

"So, I have a question," I prompt and he nods.

"Shoot."

"The names - Kodiak, Storm, Moose... that's not their real names, correct?"

He laughs and nods. "Right. Those are road names."

"And why don't you have a road name?"

"Uh," he murmurs. "Smith is my road name, babe. My real last name is Julette but when I joined the club, I wanted to be anonymous, you know? I didn't want my father's sins following me around so Blaze called me Smith. But if anyone else asks, they think Smith is my real last name."

"Why not tell them?"

He shrugs. "Because I guess in a way, I've become Smith. That's the man I want to be and I've even looked into changing my name legally a few times."

"But you haven't?"

"I didn't want Clay to feel like I was abandoning him."

I offer him a soft smile as I cup his face in my hand. "Don't ever think that you're anything other than a damn

293

good man, Lucas Smith."

He leans in and presses his lips to mine as he runs his fingers through my hair. When he pulls away, he licks his lips and hums.

"I kinda wish we were at home right now."

I nod, leaning in. "Me, too."

Our lips meet again and he groans quietly as he grips the back of my neck.

"Smith!" someone yells and he jerks away from me, glancing over his shoulder as Kodiak waves him over. He sighs and kisses my forehead.

"Give me a second."

I nod. "Sure."

I watch him as he walks across the room and talks to Kodiak. Tate sinks into the seat across from me and I smile at her before turning back to look at him. A young man with dirty blond hair steps out of the back hallway and my stomach rolls as my entire body begins to shake. He glances in our direction and everything in me is screaming to run.

"Wh-Who is Lucas talking to?" I whisper, barely able to force the words out. Tate glances over at them before turning back to me with a scowl.

"His brother Clay. Why?"

My heart hammers relentlessly in my ears and I struggle to breathe as my mind goes blank.

No.

No.

No.

This can't be happening.

"Hey, are you okay?" Tate asks, reaching out and touching my arm. I jump and tears well up in my eyes as I look at her.

"I need you to get me out of here," I rasp and her scowl deepens.

"What's go…"

I shake my head. "No questions, please. I just need you to get me out of here without Lucas seeing me."

We both glance back to the hallway and both Lucas and his brother are gone and the air feels a little less heavy as I turn back to her. She studies my face for a moment before nodding.

"Okay, but I'll have to tell him that I took you home after I get back."

I nod. "That's okay."

When she agrees, I gather up my things and Brooklyn before following her outside. After I buckle Brooklyn into her car seat, she climbs behind the wheel of my car and I promise her that Alice will give her a ride back after giving her directions to my house.

"You have to tell me what's going on here, Quinn," she urges and I shake my head.

"I can't. Not yet." Hell, I can't even process it myself yet so there's no way I could coherently explain it to her. She sighs and nods, glancing over at me periodically as we drive to my house. I'm counting down the seconds until we get there as my insides feel like they're exploding.

Just one more mile, I tell myself, barely holding the tears at bay.

Just one more block.

Just one more street.

Just one more house.

By the time we pull into my driveway, my hands are shaking and my jaw aches from clenching my teeth to keep the scream at bay.

"I'll go get my sister," I whisper to Tate before jumping out of the car and running up the front steps as my stomach rolls. Alice pokes her head out of the kitchen as I burst in the door.

"What are you doing back so soon?"

I meet her gaze as the tears start to fall. "Alice…"

"Oh my god, Quinn," she gasps, dropping her plate on the island and rushing over to me. "What the hell happened?"

"Brooklyn is in the car and I need you to give Tate a ride back to the clubhouse."

She scowls. "Who the hell is Tate?"

I point over my shoulder and she peeks through the window.

"Please, Alice. I'll explain everything when you get back but I need you and Brooklyn to not be here right now and Tate needs a ride back to the clubhouse."

She studies me for a second before grabbing her

purse. Before she walks out the door, she lays her hand on my arm. "Are you okay?"

"No. Please go."

She nods, her gaze lingering for a second before she steps outside and I watch her get in the car. As soon as they drive away, a deep aching sob tears through me and I sink to my knees, gasping for air. Tears pour down my face and my hands shake as I press them against my racing heart and pain overwhelms me. It feels like a thousand dark hands, reaching up from the depths of hell. They grip my clothes, my arms, my legs, fighting desperately to drag me back into darkness and finish me off.

And this time, I might just let them.

A.M. Myers

It Ends Tonight

Chapter Seventeen
Lucas

Sighing, I glance over at the bed in my room at the clubhouse and sigh as Clay rolls away from me, snoring loudly. When he showed up here last night during the baby shower, looking for money, I wanted to get him out of here as soon as possible but it became clear, pretty quickly, that he was in no state to go anywhere. Kodiak and I hauled him up to my room and got him into bed. I was so fucking preoccupied that I didn't even notice Quinn was gone until Tate came upstairs to tell me that she hadn't been feeling well so she took her home. I glance at my watch and sigh again. It's only eight in the morning so I doubt he'll be awake anytime soon and I need to try and call Quinn. Tate said she wasn't feeling well at the party but I get the feeling that she might be mad at me for ditching her to take care of my brother.

Time to do damage control.

I leave Clay in my room and step into the hallway before dialing her number. As it rings, I lean my shoulder against the wall and tuck my hand into the pocket of my jeans. Truthfully, she has a right to be a little mad. Clay showed up and it's like I forgot all about her until Tate reminded me. He became my sole focus and it pisses me off that I let him.

"Hi, Lucas," she answers but her voice sounds different.

"Hey, darlin'. You okay?"

There's a pause and then she whispers, "Yeah, I'm fine."

"I'm sorry that I disappeared yesterday. My brother showed up at the clubhouse and I was taking care of him."

"It's okay," she answers but something is still off. She's normally so warm and affectionate but there's none of that coming through this time.

"You sure you're okay? You sound off."

She coughs. "Yeah, I'm just really sick."

"Shit, I'm sorry, babe. Let me deal with my brother and then I'll come over and bring you some soup."

"No."

I scowl. "You want something else? I could grab some ice cream or medicine or whatever you want."

"No, I don't want anything."

Worry eats away at me as I push off the wall and

walk down the hallway. "Maybe you should go see the doc, Quinn. You really don't sound good."

"I'll be okay. I just need sleep."

"Okay," I say, running my hand through my hair. "Well, give me like an hour or two and then I'll come hang out with Brooklyn so you can get some sleep."

"No. I don't want you to catch it."

"Babe, I don't give a shit about me," I tell her. "I'm worried about you."

She sighs. "I'll be fine, Lucas. Just worry about your brother."

"I'll deal with him and then I'm coming over."

"No!" she practically shouts and I pause, my eyes widening. "I really just don't want to get you sick, okay? Promise me you won't stop by the house?"

I stare at the wall for a second before sighing. "Okay, but you gotta text me and let me know how you're doing or I will come over there."

"Okay, I will."

"I'm serious, Quinn. I want hourly updates and if you need anything, you better call me. It doesn't matter what else I'm doing, you come first."

"I love you," she whispers and I swear I hear her voice crack just a little, but before I can say anything else, she hangs up on me and I pull the phone away from my ear, gaping. I don't care how many times she tells me she's fine. There is definitely something wrong.

I stare at my phone for a minute before dialing Tate's

number.

"Hey, what's up?"

"How was Quinn when you took her home last night?"

She sucks in a breath. "I mean, she was acting like she didn't feel very well."

"Tate, come on. I have this feeling that something is going on but no one is talking about it."

"Look, I'm sorry but I really don't know anything. She said she wasn't feeling well and asked me to take her home. You had disappeared so I agreed."

I still can't shake the feeling that she's not telling me everything but I have no proof so I sigh and try to forget it.

"Yeah, okay."

"Sorry I couldn't be more help."

I shake my head. "Naw, it's okay. I'll talk to you later, okay?"

"Sounds good."

We hang up and I shove my phone in my pocket before stopping in front of my door and leaning back against the wall across from it and before my thoughts can even fall down the rabbit hole of why my woman is ignoring me, something crashes inside my room. Sucking in a breath, I push off the wall.

"Here we go," I whisper to myself before stepping forward and opening the door. Clay is in the corner of the room, looking through the books on my bookshelf and his head snaps up as I walk in the room.

"Looking for my cash?"

He tosses the book in his hand down on the floor and glares at me. "Come on, big bro. I just need a little bit."

"No, you don't," I answer, grabbing his shirt off the chair and tossing it at him. "Get dressed."

"Why?"

"There is somewhere I want to take you."

He takes a step back and shakes his head. "I'm not going to rehab."

"Believe me, Clay, I'd love nothing more than to drag your ass to rehab but that's not where we're going today. Now, get dressed."

"Aren't you going to give me a little privacy?"

"Why?" I growl. "So you can sneak out of the clubhouse and go get high again. I don't fucking think so."

"Motherfucker," he mutters, shoving his arms in the sleeves of his t-shirt before grabbing his jeans and pulling them on. When he has his tennis shoes on, he stands and flashes me an expectant look. "Willing to tell me where we're going now?"

I shake my head. "Nope. Let's go."

I have to push him out of the room and continually nudge him down the stairs and outside to my truck. Once he's in the passenger seat, I sigh and round the hood before jumping in and firing it up.

"Are we going to see Dad?" he asks as I pull out of

the parking lot and I barely avoid glaring in his direction.

"No."

We're silent for the rest of the trip and when I pull up to the cemetery, I feel his shocked gaze whip to my face.

"What the fuck are we doing here?"

I put the truck in park and turn it off. "We're here to see Mom."

"I don't want to do that," he whispers, shaking his head. The fear in his eyes is exactly the same as all those years ago as I packed up our things and pushed him out of our bedroom window. Maybe this is exactly what he needs or maybe this will send him off the deep end but I know that it's time for me to do something other than what I've been doing for the past six years.

"Tough shit. Get out of the truck."

He seems smaller as he gets out and meets me on the other side, like all this time he's still been the five-year-old little boy who went on the run after his father killed his mother.

"Why are we here, Luke?"

I sigh and we start walking along one of the paths. "I've never told you what happened that night."

"And you're going to tell me now?" he scoffs and I nod, glancing over at him.

"Yeah, I am."

We stop in front of our mother's grave and I suck in a breath as I read her name on the tombstone:

It Ends Tonight

Amanda Julette
Devoted Wife and Mother

"What do you remember from the night she died?"

He shakes his head. "Just yelling and being scared but my earliest clear memory is running through the forest with you and finding the boxcar."

"The night she died, it had been raining all day and around dinner time, these thunderstorms rolled in. The thunder was so loud that it shook the walls in our bedroom and I laid there for hours, unable to fall asleep so I heard them as soon as they started fighting. It had been happening a lot before that and I found out later that Dad had been using drugs."

"No," Clay snaps, backing away from me as he shakes his head. "Dad isn't an addict."

I nod. "Yeah, he is. That's why he lost his job a few months before Mom died and why they were fighting so much."

"I don't believe you."

"I know you don't," I whisper, turning back to her grave. "We'd been in bed for a few hours when the fighting got louder, scarier than anything else I could remember and it got so bad that it woke you up, too."

"What else?" he asks, his voice rough and my hands shake as I suck in a breath.

"You were laying in bed, crying, and I was trying so hard to get you to be quiet because I knew if Dad heard you, he'd come after us and I couldn't let that happen. As I was trying to calm you down, there was this bang, so fucking loud that my ears were ringing, and then it was silent. That silence, I've never heard anything more terrifying in my life."

Clay steps forward and lays his hand on Mom's grave. "I don't remember her."

"She was like sunshine - always cheerful even when everything was going wrong. She'd find a way to make us laugh and make it all seem okay and she was so warm. All you had to do was be near her to feel her love because it just radiated off her."

"I've spent my whole life jealous of you for being able to remember her."

I wipe away a tear. "I'm sorry, Clay, but I was a kid, too, and I couldn't stop what happened anymore than you could have."

"What happened next?"

"The bang just made you scream louder and I made you shove your face in a pillow 'cause I didn't know what was happening yet and I crept toward the door. When I opened our bedroom door, I saw her. Mom was laying at the other end of the hall with a hole in her head and a puddle of blood all around her body. Dad was next to her, holding the gun in his hand and covered in her blood. It was everywhere, Clay. All over the walls, the floor, all I could see was red."

"But you didn't see him pull the trigger," Clay

breathes like I've just unveiled some forgotten clue and I grit my teeth.

"It doesn't matter! He killed her."

He shakes his head, backing away from me. "You don't know that for sure. Unless you watched him pull the trigger, you don't know."

"You've got to stop this, Clay. This isn't healthy for either one of us."

He takes another step back. "I'm going to find the truth, Luke. It's like one of those movies Iris likes to watch. No one believes me but I'm going to prove you all wrong and get our dad out of jail."

"Just stop!" I roar, balling my fists at my sides. "This isn't a goddamn movie and you can't prove him innocent because he's guilty, Clay. What you need to focus on is getting clean. Blaze is looking for a good rehab facility for you and we're going to get you better."

"No," he snaps, taking a few more steps back. "I'm not going and you can't make me."

"Actually, I can and this is what is best for you."

Without another word, he turns and takes off running.

"Fuck," I growl, chasing after him but he's faster than me and it's not long before I lose him in the maze of graves. I skid to a stop and squeeze my eyes shut before spinning around and slamming my fist into the tree on the side of the path. "Fuck!"

As I catch my breath, I walk back to Mom's grave and drop to my knees in front of it.

"Hey, Mom," I whisper, tears welling up in my eyes again. I remember all the times Clay and I would fight when we were kids and Mom would pull us apart, telling us that we had to look after each other, not fight. I lay my hand flat against the stone and sigh. "I'm trying, Mom. I'm trying so hard."

I sit in front of her grave and tell her all about Quinn and Brooklyn before promising to keep trying to help Clay and as I'm leaving, I spot a cardinal in a tree on the edge of the cemetery. It looks right at me before flying off and I watch it until it disappears.

When I get in the truck, I pull out my phone and send a text to Quinn.

Me:
Hey, babe.
How are you feeling?

Quinn:
Fine.

I read her message and throw the phone across the cab of my truck before leaning my head back against the headrest and closing my eyes.

"Fine, my ass," I whisper, determined to figure out what the hell is going on.

Chapter Eighteen
Lucas

My eyes burn as I lean back in my chair and lift my coffee mug to my lips. I'm on my fourth damn cup of this stuff but it's still not helping. Of course, it would be best if I had gotten any sleep last night but between trying to check on Quinn and looking for my brother, that didn't happen. I glance down at my phone on the table, irritated that she still hasn't answered my last text. When I wasn't driving around this whole damn city looking for Clay, who's honestly probably so high he can't see straight, I was texting her and her answers were always vague one or two word responses that tell me something is seriously wrong.

"You okay, bud?" Chance asks, sitting down across from me and I shake my head.

"Nope. Been a pretty shit night, actually."

He nods. "Your brother?"

"And my woman."

"What the hell is going on with Quinn?" he asks as he leans back in his chair and crosses his arms over his chest. I sigh.

"No fucking clue. She disappeared from the baby shower and now she's saying that she's sick and doesn't want me to come around."

"Maybe she's just sick…"

I shake my head. "No. She's not acting anything like herself, barely talking to me and when she does, it's all vague and noncommittal."

"Ah," he whispers with a nod. "You remember when I first met Carly?"

"Barely."

"Well, she was… difficult to say the least - constantly pushing me away and running from what she was feeling."

I shake my head as I glance down at my phone again. "I don't think that's what Quinn is doing."

"Maybe not but the point is, if you want a long term with her, you may have to chase her a little."

I scoff. "I already have chased her. We were together and then this happens."

"So, what? You're going to give up? The good ones are never easy, dude. Trust me."

He stands as I sigh as he walks away, my gaze falling to my phone again before I scoop it up and dial her number. Irritation eats away at me as it rings and when her voice mail picks up, I let out a growl.

Time to make a move.

If she's truly sick, I should be there with her despite all her objections and if she's not, I'm going to get some fucking answers as to why she's avoiding me. It just doesn't make any sense. We were having such a good time at the baby shower and then, just like that, she's gone and I can't get her to pick up the damn phone.

"Hey, you headed somewhere?" Blaze asks as I stand up and set my coffee cup on the bar. I nod and slip my phone into my pocket.

"Yeah, I was just leaving. Why?"

He looks down at the folder in his hand. "Just need someone to run down this lead on Laney."

"Chance is upstairs, not doing anything," I tell him, nodding to the stairs and he nods.

"I'll put him on it. How's your brother?"

I sigh. "Missing again. I brought up rehab and he flipped out."

"Shit."

"Yeah." I nod. "I got other things to worry about right now, though."

His eyebrows shoot up. "When has anything ever been more important than your brother?"

"Since someone made me realize there has to be more to my life than being his keeper."

"Sounds like a smart woman," he says with a smile

and I nod.

"Yes, she is."

He nods and turns toward the hallway to go find Chance. "Good luck."

"Who says I need luck?"

"That determined look on your face says it all," he answers with a laugh. "Stubborn ass women will do that to you every time."

I shake my head as he disappears into the hallway and I turn toward the door, ready to bulldoze my way into her house if I have to. On my way out to the truck, I dial her number again one last time and her voice mail picks up almost immediately. I pull the phone away from my ear and hang up.

"Are you fucking kidding me?" I whisper, staring down at the screen. "You're screening my calls now, gorgeous?"

I climb in the truck and as she fires to life, *Die a Happy Man* by Thomas Rhett starts playing over the radio.

Shit.

She's taken over my life in every single way and I have no clue what I'll do if I lose her, which is the thought that's been plaguing me since the baby shower. Maybe she got a taste of my world and decided that it wasn't for her. I shake my head before backing out of the spot and driving out of the parking lot.

I know the club isn't a traditional version of family

but they'll be there through thick and thin, they'll always have my back, and they'll welcome Quinn and Brooklyn in without hesitation. If that's what is going on, if she's having doubts about the club, I just have to make her see how great it could be to have people to call on for anything.

As I pull up in front of her house, I let out a breath and put the truck in park before climbing out. I don't even make it to the first step before Alice steps out of the house and crosses her arms over her chest.

"What are you doing here, Lucas?"

"I'm here to see Quinn."

She shakes her head. "She's still sick."

"Okay, well, let me in to see her. I've been worried."

"She doesn't want you to come in," she answers. A look of sympathy flashes across her face before she steps forward, further blocking my way.

"Alice, what the fuck is going on? I don't believe that she's sick."

Alice shrugs. "Well, she is and she wants to be left alone."

"Quinn!" I yell, stepping back to look up at the windows on the top floor. I swear the curtains move just a fraction of an inch in her bedroom. "Quinn!"

"Stop, Lucas," Alice hisses. "I'm sorry but you need to leave."

I shake my head as I meet her gaze. "I just want to talk to her."

"She'll talk to you when she's ready."

Fuck.

I knew there was more going on here.

"Will you please tell me what the fuck is going on?"

She shakes her head. "I can't. She'll contact you when she's ready to talk."

"What the hell do you mean…"

Alice marches down the step and gives me a little shove, pushing me away from the house. "You need to go, Lucas. Before I call the cops."

"Call the cops. I don't give a shit. Let me talk to her."

"Fine." She pulls her phone out of her pocket and begins dialing. I whisper a curse and back away from her, my gaze flicking to Quinn's empty bedroom window again.

"Fuck! Hang up the phone. I'm leaving," I snap, rounding the hood of the truck. She flashes me a sympathetic look as she shoves the phone back in her pocket.

"I'm sorry, Lucas. She just needs time."

"Time for what?" I ask, my voice desperate as panic rips through me. My heart belongs to that woman upstairs and if she's done with me, I'll be fucking ruined.

"I'm sorry," Alice answers again, turning back to the house and I glance up at the windows one last time, stalling when I meet a set of ice blue eyes that own me completely. Her eyes are red and tears steadily drip down her cheeks as she turns away from me. When the curtain falls back into place, my stomach rolls and I climb in my truck, vowing to be back tomorrow.

And the next day.

And the next

And the next.

Every day until she finally agrees to talk to me because there is no vision of my future that doesn't have her in it.

*   *   *   *

A car horn blares behind me and I jump, turning away from the EQA Events sign to glance over my shoulder as I blow out a breath. My eyes burn from another night of barely any sleep since I've spent the last twelve hours camped out here, waiting for a glimpse of her. I'm fucking frustrated, on edge, and more than ready to get some goddamn answers from the woman I love with everything I've got. Quinn's assistant, Willa, arrived ten minutes ago and now I'm just waiting to see her. I've spent the last two days wondering why she won't talk to me and if she's even half as miserable as I am. I finally understand what Storm, Chance, and Kodiak went through with their own women now that the current pain in my ass and love of my goddamn life is avoiding me like the plague. This is probably some karmic retribution for giving them so much shit at the time.

A flash of blonde hair catches my attention and I watch as she climb out of her new car and rounds the hood. She's just as gorgeous as always but the dark circles under her eyes give her away and as much as I hate to see her in pain, it makes me feel a little bit better that this isn't easy for her. She glances out at the street and I duck down in my truck, whispering a curse, but she doesn't see me or if she does, she doesn't acknowledge my presence. Sadness is etched into every curve of her stunning face and my stomach rolls.

What the fuck happened to put that look in her eyes?

I watch her until she disappears into the office and run my hand through my hair as I suck in a breath. I'll give her a few minutes and then, it's showtime. I'm not leaving without some damn answers and if I have to beg her for another chance or forgiveness, I'll do it. Not that I have any clue what I might be apologizing for. Pulling the engagement ring out of my pocket, I stare at it and wonder if I'm ever going to be able to slip it on her finger. When I saw it in the store, I knew it was fucking perfect for her and I imagined a whole life for us - all three of us since Brooklyn has stolen my heart just as much as her mama has. The thought of spending my life without the two of them...

No.

Fuck that mess.

I've never been more sure of anything in my life and if I'm going down, I'll go down fighting.

Blowing out a breath, I turn off the car I borrowed from Blaze and open the door before stepping outside and squaring my shoulders. As I cross the street, all the questions that have been running through my head since I left her house yesterday return and I ball my fists at my sides. There is no scenario where I don't get the answers I need today. It's not an option. And then once I know what we're dealing with, I can start to fix it.

The bell on the door jingles as I pull it open and step inside. Willa continues staring at something on her desk as she smiles.

"Hi. What can I help you with?" She glances up and her eyes widen. "What are you doing here, Lucas?"

"I need to see her," I answer. She shakes her head.

"I can't let you do that."

I take a step forward and she stands. "I need to see her, Willa."

She shakes her head again, her gaze hardening. "And I said no. You need to leave."

"That's not going to happen."

"Lucas, don't make me call security. She'll talk to you when she's ready." She reaches for the phone and the last of my patience slips away. I don't give a damn who she calls and I'm not leaving this damn building until I see Quinn. She grabs the receiver and I let out a grunt of frustration as I march toward Quinn's office door. She steps in front of me.

"Lucas!" she yells as I dodge her and approach Quinn's office door. "I'm calling security."

I turn and shoot a glare over my shoulder. "So call them."

"Willa," Quinn's voice crackles through the phone's speaker. "Let him in."

Fucking finally.

I open the door to the office and step inside before stopping dead in my tracks. Quinn is seated behind the desk and just like yesterday, she's crying. It fucking rips through me like claws and I can't fight the pulling sensation deep down in my gut, telling me to go to her and wrap my arms around her. Crossing the room in three quick strides, I stop next to her chair and do just that.

"God, I missed you, baby," I whisper into her hair and a sob bubbles out of her but I ignore it. Whatever is going on is serious and I need just a few more seconds to hold her before I find out what it is.

"Lucas," she gasps, clinging to my shirt so I hold her tighter, hoping to take just a little bit of her pain away as worry eats away at me. Pulling back, I meet her eyes and try to force a smile to my face.

"You wanna tell me what's going on here, baby? Why I had to hunt you down at work just to get you to talk to me?"

Another sob spills out of her mouth and she nods as she presses the back of her fingers to her lips. "You should sit."

"Think I'll stand," I growl. Her eyes beg me for compliance and I pull her back to me, pressing my lips against her forehead before releasing her and rounding the desk. We both sink into our chairs and she sucks in a breath.

"I don't know where to start."

I nod, running the tip of my finger along my bottom lip as I study her. "Why don't you start with what happened at the baby shower?"

"We…uh, we have to start before that."

"Meaning?" I ask, arching a brow.

"Do you remember when I told you about Brooklyn's father?"

My stomach turns as I remember the night she told me about her past and I nod. "Yeah, I remember, babe."

"The man who raped me… he was never found and I've never seen him again…" She sucks in a breath as more tears fall down her cheeks. "Until we were at the baby shower."

I blink and stare at her, my mind stalling on her words. "Are you saying one of the guys raped you? Quinn, they would fucking never…"

"No, Lucas," she whispers, her tears falling faster. "It wasn't one of the guys."

"There was no one else…"

My sluggish thoughts screech to a halt and I stare at her for a second, searching for any kind of clue that she's not implying what I think she's implying.

"No," I whisper and she nods, staring down at her shaking hands as she presses them to the table and another sob rips through her.

"I'm so sorry, Lucas."

I jerk out of my seat, knocking it backward as I stumble away from her. "No." She meets my eyes and I can see the certainty in her gaze. I run my hand through my hair as I pace back and forth across her office. "No. It's not possible."

"You have no idea," she says as she stands, "how much I wish it weren't true but as soon as I saw him, I knew. Your brother is the man who raped me."

"No!" I scream, shaking my head. My thoughts are heavy as I try to piece it all together, make it all make sense because she has to be mistaken. There is no way that Clay is her rapist. "You're wrong. You didn't get a good look at him."

"Lucas," she says, her tone grave. "For those two minutes, I stared your brother in the face as he violated me and I will never forget him. Not even when I'm old and gray. I know this is hard for you but don't ever insinuate that I don't know who the monster who raped me is."

I take another step back and shake my head. "He's not a monster. He's my brother."

"To you, he isn't but to me…"

"No. He had to have been high at the time. He probably didn't even know…"

"And that makes it any better?" she asks, interrupting me and I shake my head.

I don't know what to do.

I don't know what to think.

Blowing out a breath, I continue my pacing and pull at my hair, wishing there was someone I could punch nearby just to do something with the thunderstorm of emotions rocking through me.

"No," I breathe, shaking my head. "Of course, it doesn't make it better but…"

She steps forward and holds her hand up. "Please just stop. Nothing you could say is going to fix what he did."

"Baby…" I whisper, meeting her gaze and it hits me as her pain rips through me again just like before. My baby brother raped her. All this time I've been killing myself to save him, to find him some piece of redemption but maybe he was too far gone all along. Staring at my girl, I imagine her that night, shoved into an alley while he had his way with her and tears burn my eyes as I shake my head. "I'm so sorry."

She releases a stuttered breath as fresh tears drip down her face. "You have nothing to apologize for."

"Are you going to go to the police?"

"That's what I've been trying to figure out for the last three days. If he was anyone else, I would have already reported him but he's not. He's your brother and I don't know how to do anything that wouldn't hurt you."

I open my mouth to answer her before realizing that I don't know what to say. I'm being torn in half by my love for her and my love for my brother and she's right. If he was anyone else, I would be right there beside her, turning him into the police. Taking a step toward the door, I grab the handle and shake my head. "I… I have to go."

She meets my eyes, sobbing again as she nods and I turn toward the door as my stomach twists into knots. I hesitate only for a second before yanking it open and practically running out of the office and to my truck. I can't deal with this now. I need time to think and sort this all out because either way, I fucking lose.

I mean, what the hell am I supposed to do?

Do I betray the woman I love or the only blood I have left?

*   *   *   *

A clap of thunder rattles the walls as lightning streaks across the sky and a whimper greets me in the darkness from the other side of the room. Clay has always been scared of storms but I can't be sure that's the reason he's uneasy tonight. I clutch my blanket tighter and stare up at the green glow in the dark stars Mom helped me put on the ceiling last Christmas, praying for daylight. Something about the darkness always makes the fighting seem worse.

"Luke?" Clay whispers, his voice wavering with unshed tears. I force down the fear creeping up the back of my spine and turn my head to look at him.

"It's just thunder, Clay. Go back to sleep."

His little lip wobbles as he meets my gaze. "Why are they fighting this time?"

The sound of breaking glass pierces the silence and echoes down the hallway, punctuating his question and I shake my head.

"I don't know."

Staring at the door, I strain my ears, trying to hear anything from the front of the house but it's quiet. Too quiet. It's almost as if the crickets and frogs that usually chirp outside our bedroom window can sense the approaching storm. Or maybe they can sense the same thing that's been making my tummy feel funny all night long.

"Goddamn it, Amanda!" Dad's voice booms, full of anger, and I shrink into myself, my heart pounding as I grip the blanket tighter. I wish I could say this was new but Mom and Dad have been fighting a lot lately and it scares me but I have to be tough for Clay. Dad wasn't always like this – so grumpy and short-tempered – but when he lost his job a year ago, everything started to change. I think Mom hoped that when he found work

again, things would get better but they've only gotten worse. He's unpredictable and when he loses his temper, I'm terrified of him.

"Ray, please don't do this!" Mom's wail reverberates through the house and Clay lets out another whimper. With my heart pounding in my ears, I turn to him and bring my finger to my lips. He nods, tears welling up in his eyes. As scary as this is for me, I know it's got to be worse for him. He's only five and he looks at me as his protector so that's what I have to be.

"No!"

A loud bang rips through the house, making me jump out of my skin as Clay cries out. Without thinking, I throw the covers off of me and race to his bedside before placing my hand over his mouth. He stares up at me, his eyes full of terror, and I press my finger to my lips, desperate to shut him up before Dad hears. My heart hammers in my chest and tears well up in my eyes but I hand him a pillow to cry into before stepping away from his bed and moving toward the door, careful to avoid the floorboards that creak. I creep over to the door, careful not to make any noise as I crouch down behind it and pry it open before peeking down the hallway.

Mom is laying in a heap at the other end of the hallway and Dad is on his knees next to her, covered in blood, and holding a gun in his hand. Dark red blood pools under her and pain rips through my chest.

No.

No.

No.

Mom!

It Ends Tonight

"Fuck," Dad chokes out, his voice like nothing I've ever heard before and he grabs the gun again, staring down at it as his finger wraps around the trigger. I have no idea what he's going to do next but I know Clay and I can't be around to find out. When I try to move, my gaze drops back down to Mom and tears slip down my cheeks.

Mom...

A scream echoes through my head as more tears fall and I mash my lips together. Every part of my body wants to run to her, shake her, force her to wake up but the gun in Dad's hand keeps me rooted to this spot. Taking a step back, I carefully shut the door and turn to Clay as silent tears fall down my face.

"Get dressed now and be quiet."

He shakes his head. "What's going on, Luke? Where's Mom? I want Mom."

I choke back a sob and shake my head, crossing the room to his bed. I grab his arms and hold them firmly. "This is important, Clay. You have to be quiet and we have to go, now. Get dressed."

"What about Mom?" he asks again and I shake my head.

"We'll come back for Mom tomorrow but for now, she's safe." I hate lying to him but I have to get him out of here. When he nods, I release him and go to the closet, grabbing my backpack before I start shoving clothes in it. When it's full and I'm dressed, I zip it up and turn back to Clay as I throw it on my back.

He shifts on his feet, looking between me and the door and I shake my head, pointing to the window.

"This way."

He glances at the door. "Are you sure, Luke?"

"Hey, I'm your big brother. Would I ever lie to you?"

He shakes his head. "No. Never."

"Smith?" someone asks, jerking me awake, and I blink into the harsh overhead lights of the clubhouse as I open my eyes. Blaze arches a brow and glances down at the half empty bottle of whiskey on the table in front of me and I sigh as I lean forward, grab it, and raise the bottle to my lips. "What's going on, brother?"

I shake my head, tears welling up in my eyes as I remember leaving Quinn in her office hours ago. "I...Fuck. It's all fucked, Blaze."

"What's going on, Smith?" he asks, his voice taking on a serious tone as he sits down next to me and I take another swig of liquor.

"My brother...." It's all I can choke out without a deluge of unbearable emotions drowning me.

"Did something happen? Is he okay?"

I shake my head. "Quinn was raped a couple years ago. That's how she got pregnant with Brooklyn."

"Okay..."

"They never caught her rapist."

His brows furrow as he studies me. "Where the hell is this going, Luke?"

"Clay is the man who raped her. She saw him at the baby shower and recognized him instantly."

"Oh, fuck," he whispers, running a hand through his hair. "Jesus Christ."

I nod, taking another swig of whiskey. This damn

thing was full when I started drinking but it's still not enough to dull the pain.

"What are you going to do?"

I let out a humorless laugh before pouring more alcohol down my throat. "I'll let you know when I figure it out."

A.M. Myers

It Ends Tonight

Chapter Nineteen
Quinn

I stumble out of the bar and press my hand along the rough brick of the building as I stop and lean against it, sucking in a breath before I drop my head back and stare up at the few stars that I can see through the city lights. Music pumps from the bar as the door opens again and I fight back a smile. Despite my reluctance to come out tonight and the rough start to our evening, I'm glad my girls talked me into going out with them. It's exactly what I needed after moping over my breakup with Danny for the past couple months - not that I regret it. Ending things was the right choice but I had our future mapped out in my mind and losing that has left me feeling a little lost. Tonight feels like the start of something really good though and for the first time in a while, I'm excited for what's to come. Grams signed EQA Events over to me last week and officially retired. I'm scared to take the business she built from the ground up into my hands but I also haven't felt this alive in a long time - before things ended with Danny - and it tells me I'm finally on the right track. Hell, I would even be open to dating again if the opportunity presented itself so I think that means I'm doing all right.

A scraping sound draws my attention back to the door. There's a man by the door but he's completely oblivious to me, staring at the sidewalk and smoking a cigarette so I turn back to the sky as a warm breeze brushes over my skin. I should get back inside before the girls come out looking for me. My head is still spinning though and I think I'm about ready to call it a night. I push off the wall and turn toward the door but before I can take a step, two large arms wrap around me and I scream.

"Shut up," his voice hisses in my ear as a hand clamps down on my mouth and he starts pulling me away from the door. I search for the man that was smoking a cigarette, hoping he can help me, but the sidewalk is empty. I scream against the hand on my lips and kick my legs, trying desperately to escape. He's too strong. My heart thunders against my rip cage as he pulls me into the alley on the side of the bar and tears sting my eyes.

"No!" I scream as soon as he uncovers my mouth. He lets out a grunt as I continue jerking against his hold. Pain explodes in my chest and my vision blurs as we fall

*to the ground. He pins me to the concrete with one hand
around each of my wrists and my chest feels tight.*
"Help!"

*"Shh," he whispers, leaning down over me and
taking a deep breath. "Mm, you smell so good."*

I buck my hips, trying to throw him off me. "Help!"

*He shoves my dress up to my belly and a sob tears
through me as I thrash and kick, my stomach rolling. No,
this can't be happening to me right now. As I stare up
into his dull blue eyes, and the vacant expression on his
face, a wave of icy coldness hits me right in my chest.*

*"Please don't do this," I beg, tears flowing freely
down my cheeks. He smiles.*

"Don't worry. I'll make it good for you."

*He moves my hands together and uses one hand to
press them back against the concrete as he reaches
behind him and pulls out a pocket knife. My stomach
drops and my chest feels heavy as my pleas turns to sobs
and I jerk against his hold. His gaze falls to my panties
and the cold feeling that started in my chest is seeping
into the rest of my body. I shake my head back and forth,
silently begging for help. When he slices through one
side of my panties with the knife, I sob again and my
body stills as he slices the other side. He meets my eyes
and smiles as he pulls the panties away from my body.
His hand starts creeping down my stomach and I gag.*

"No!" I scream, jerking forward in bed. Gasping for
air, I grip the blanket as tears pour down my cheeks and

images from that night continue playing in my mind.

"Breathe, Quinn. Just breathe," I whisper to myself, focusing on each breath I draw into my lungs as my heart rate slowly returns to normal. Once my breathing returns to normal, I fall back to the pillow and release a breath, tears welling up in my eyes. It's been three days since I told Lucas the truth and I haven't heard from him once since. Not that I can blame him. I knew as soon as I found out who Clay was that we were in trouble but I guess I stupidly hoped that maybe he would choose me. God, how selfish is that though? Lucas and his brother have been all each other had for so long and then I just wanted him to choose me? I never stood a chance.

Brooklyn lets out a cry from her room and I sigh as I turn to the baby monitor and watch her stand up, bracing her hands on the edge of the crib. Sighing, I fling the covers off my legs and glance out of the window as I stand. Sunlight streaks across the floor and I wipe away my tears, shoving my emotions into a box so I can be bright and cheery for my little girl. Fake it 'til you make it and all that. Brooklyn yells from her room and I grab my silk robe off the end of the bed and pull it on as I leave my bedroom and walk down the hallway to Brooklyn's room.

"Good morning, gorgeous girl," I sing as I step into her room, trying desperately to hang on to my smile for Brooklyn. She lets out another yell when she sees me and rattles the side of her crib. "Well, you're feisty this morning, aren't you?"

She pushes her bottom lip out in a pout and rubs at her eyes with a closed fist as big, crocodile tears well up in her eyes. They slide slowly down her chubby little cheeks and my heart breaks. Picking her up out of her crib, I cuddle her in my arms as I turn toward the rocking chair in the corner of the room. As I rock her back and forth, I hum a song and she lays her head on my shoulder, letting out a heavy, tearful sigh. I rub my hand across her back.

"What's wrong, sweet baby?"

"Dada," she mumbles before shoving her thumb in her mouth and I suck in a breath, tears stinging my eyes. Lord, how did we end up here? Only last week, I was blissfully in love and planning such a grand future for Brooklyn, Lucas, and me. Now, I don't even know if we're together, let alone if we have a future. I mean, how the hell could we?

"I know, sweetie," I whisper, pressing my lips to her soft blonde hair. "What do you say we change your diaper and go find Auntie Alice for breakfast, huh?"

She lets out another sigh and I fight back tears as I stand and carry her over to her changing table. The cute little dress I laid out for her last night is laying on top of her dresser and I grab it before peeling her out of her pajamas and changing her diaper.

"Dada," she says again, reaching toward the door and I spin around, my heart jumping into my throat only to fall when I see the empty doorway. Sucking in a breath as I turn back to Brooklyn, I shake my head and wipe a tear from her cheek.

"You got my hopes up, little girl."

She reaches toward the door again. "Dada."

"I miss him, too, Brookie."

"Seems he's missing you, too, if the truck parked across the street everyday for the last few days is any indication," Alice says, stepping into the room and leaning against the doorframe. "You've seen it, right?"

I glance over at her and nod. "I've seen it."

For the past few days, I've noticed Lucas's truck periodically parked outside the house but he hasn't gotten out and I haven't worked up the nerve to go talk to him.

"Have you tried to talk to him?"

"No," I scoff, my lip wobbling as I look away from her. "Too afraid that I'll go out there and he'll tell me that we're done."

"I don't think he'll do that, Quinn," she whispers and I shake my head as I meet her eyes.

"You didn't see his face, Al. I don't know how we get past this."

She nods. "Time will tell. Are you ready to go to the police?"

"I don't know," I mutter. Ever since seeing Clay's face in the clubhouse, I've been trying to force myself to go down to the police station and pass the information along to a detective but I can't seem to do it even though I know it has to be done. If it were any other man, he'd already be behind bars but it's not any other man and it kills me to think about Lucas's heartbreak over this whole thing.

"You need to do it. Just get it over with."

I shake my head with a sigh. "You don't understand."

"I understand perfectly but your love for Lucas doesn't change the fact that his brother attacked you!"

"It changes everything, Alice."

She sighs, shaking her head in disgust. "So, what? You're just going to let him get away with what he did because you fell in love with his brother? I was here with you the whole time, Quinn, and I know how much this stuff still affects you. Don't think I didn't hear you yelling in your sleep just twenty minutes ago."

"Just give me a little more time."

"And what if he's out there hurting some other poor girl?" she asks and I turn to glare at her.

"Don't you think I've already thought of that? I know what's at stake here, Alice, but it's not as easy as you're making it out to be."

She throws her hands up with a sigh. "But it is, Quinn. And I'm almost certain that with a little time, Lucas will understand why you had to do it."

Brooklyn lets out a cry and I sigh as I finish buttoning her dress and pull her into my arms. Maybe she's right. Maybe he would understand but if he doesn't, if I lose him in this process, then turning my rapist over to the cops doesn't feel like the victory that it should.

"I can't talk about this any more right now."

"Okay," Alice sighs, holding her hands out for Brooklyn. "Pass her to me and I'll get her some breakfast while you get ready for work but just know, that this conversation is not over."

"I expected nothing less."

She takes Brooklyn downstairs. I sigh as I go back to my room and rush through my morning routine all while trying to keep my mind off of Lucas and his brother. It's not an easy task but I manage to shower and do my hair and makeup without tears welling up in my eyes. By the time I get dressed and walk downstairs, Brooklyn is playing in the living room with Alice watching over her.

"I'm sorry," she says as I step into the room and I nod.

"I know."

She wraps her arms around herself. "I just want justice for you, Sis. What happened to you… it can't go unpunished."

"I know that, too. None of this is as simple as it should be."

"Yeah, I get that," she sighs. "I left some eggs and hash browns on a plate for you in the kitchen if you're hungry."

I shake my head, grabbing my bag. "No. I'll just grab something on my way."

"You don't have to leave so early on my account. I'll shut up about this for now."

Sighing, I glance toward the front door. "I just need some fresh air to clear my head."

"Are you okay? I mean, obviously, this whole situation is fucked up on every level but are you really okay?"

"I don't know how to answer that question, Alice. I was so happy, you know. So damn happy and I thought I had found the one person I could spend the rest of my life with and then we went to that baby shower. Now, I haven't heard from him in days and I have to go down to the police station and send his brother to jail." I let out a breath and brace my hands on the back of a chair as tears well up in my eyes. "This was supposed to be easy. I find the man who raped me and I go to the police so this all could finally be over. I just never expected the end of one nightmare to be the beginning of another."

A tear slips down her cheek. She stands and wipes it away as she crosses the room and wraps her arms around me. A sob racks my body and I cling to her as the tears fall from both of our eyes.

"Have I told you lately how proud I am to be your sister?" she whispers. I shake my head.

"N-No, I don't think you have."

She pulls back and meets my eyes. "You've handled everything that's been thrown at you with grace and so much strength. If it had been me, I think I would have just fallen apart but not you. You persevered when you had every reason to not to and I know you can do this, too, even though it feels impossible right now."

"I don't want to lose him," I tell her, more tears falling as pain radiates from my chest and she nods.

"I know."

My phone buzzes in my purse and I pull away from her as I suck in a breath and wipe the tears from my cheeks, clenching my teeth in an attempt to stop new ones from falling. "Ugh, God, I don't have time for this right now. I have to get going."

"Maybe you should take the day off. I'm sure Willa can handle everything for one day."

"No," I answer, shaking my head. "I can't just sit here moping all day. I need a distraction. I'll be home before you have to leave for class, though."

She nods and I peek down at Brooklyn, who's staring up at me with concerned eyes and I suck in a breath, forcing a smile to my face.

"Have a good day with Auntie Alice, baby." I blow her a kiss but the scowl doesn't leave her face as she watches me. My smart girl knows something serious is going on. Even at only fourteen months old, we can't slip anything past her.

"I'll put Beauty and the Beast on to try and cheer her up a little," Alice assures me and I nod, hoping that her favorite movie will be able to distract her from the fact that Lucas is this giant gaping hole in our lives right now.

"Okay, I'm leaving, then." I turn toward the door and pull my phone out of my purse. There's a text from Willa and I read it as I open the door and step outside.

Willa:
Coming into work today, boss lady?

Me:
On my way now.

I sigh as I put my phone back in my purse and instead of walking down the steps to my car, I turn toward the swing on the far end of the porch. As I sink into the seat and sway back and forth, a few tears slip down my cheeks. Alice is right - I need to go to the police and finally put an end to this two year long nightmare. I'm just terrified that it's going to cost me everything that I've been building for my life.

My mind drifts to the morning after being raped. Grams was by my side through the night as they administered the rape kit and she held me as I cried. I can still hear her telling me that I was too strong to let this beat me. As I suck in a breath, I feel a little bit of that strength returning and I know it's time to handle this. Despite what happens between Lucas and me, I do deserve justice.

I pull my phone out of my purse and hesitate for a second before dialing Lucas's number. His voice mail picks up and I close my eyes, summoning the courage I need to leave this message. When the beep sounds, I take a deep breath and open my eyes.

"Hi. It's me. I just… I wanted to call you and let you know that I'll be going to the police station tomorrow to give them the information on your brother." My lip wobbles as tears form in my eyes again. "This is so hard for me and I know how hard it must be for you. Just know that whatever you decide, I don't blame you for anything. I could never ask you to choose between the two of us and I understand your loyalty to him. If I don't hear from you again, I want you to know that I love you and I'm so grateful for the time we had together. You taught me to trust and love again and you're always going to hold a special place in my heart. I hope, one day, you can find happiness because that's what I truly want for you, Lucas. I just want you to be happy and get the life you deserve." I bite my lip to hold back the sob that desperately wants to break free. "Good-bye."

Chapter Twenty
Quinn

"Are you sure you don't want me to go with you?" Alice asks, bouncing Brooklyn on her hip and I shake my head, forcing a smile to my face. My stomach feels uneasy but I know that this has to be done. Even if a part of me still doesn't want to.

"No. I don't know how long it will take and I don't want her there."

She sighs, glancing toward the front door. "I'm not happy that you're going alone. You should have someone there with you."

"I'll be okay, Al," I whisper, thinking back to the message I left for Lucas yesterday as I fight back tears. When I called him, I truly meant what I said. I had no expectations but I can't deny that not hearing from him hurts. I guess it's time to come to terms with the fact that things are truly over between us.

"Maybe Willa could go with you or something. Or I could ask her to babysit Brooklyn and I'll go with you."

I shake my head and force a smile to my face. "I need to do this alone, Sis, but I appreciate the thought."

"Well… if you're sure."

"I am," I answer, nodding as I grab my purse and turn toward the front door, sucking in a breath.

"You've got this," Alice calls as I grab the doorknob. "And call me if you need anything."

I nod in response as I pull the door open and step outside.

"Quinn."

I gasp as his voice melts over me like chocolate and tingles race up my spine. I turn to the swing on the other end of the porch where he's sitting with his elbows propped on his knees with a ball cap on his head. My stomach rolls. My heart skips a beat.

Oh, God, he's here to end it.

"Lucas," I breathe, blinking back tears. He looks up and as soon as our eyes meet, it punches me in the gut, stealing the air from my lungs as my heart thunders against my ribs. "What are you doing here?"

He stands. "I'm here for you."

"I don't understand," I whisper, my mind completely blank as he walks toward me, looking just as fine as he did the first time I met him. Gripping the railing, I suck in a breath and fight the urge to close my eyes just to breathe in his familiar scent.

"I got your message last night and I'm going to the police station with you."

"But what about your brother?"

He shakes his head. "What about him?"

"Are you really just going to turn your back on him? Just like that?"

"No," he snaps, closing the distance between us and pulling me into his arms. "Not just like that. I've killed myself for years, trying to help him and now, to know that he was out there hurting people, hurting you." He reaches up and brushes his thumb over my cheek. "The woman that I know with every ounce of my soul was made for me - it makes me sick to my stomach. I can't protect him anymore."

"Lucas," I gasp, shaking my head. "I can't ask you to do that to him. He's your brother."

"I'm not doing anything *to* him, Quinn. I'm just not cleaning up his messes anymore. This is one mistake that he's going to have to own."

I shake my head, staring down at the boards of the porch. "I don't know what to say. Your support is exactly what I had hoped for but I can't get rid of this guilt I feel for what I'm doing to you."

"No," he growls and my gaze flicks up to his. "I don't ever want to hear you talk like that again. You're not doing anything to me. You're not doing anything to Clay. You are the victim here and you deserve to get justice for what was done to you."

"I can't ask you to do this to him. He's your brother, Lucas."

"Baby," he urges, cupping both sides of my face in his hands as he forces my gaze to his. "Listen to me. You're not asking anything of me. I'm choosing to do this. I love my brother but he needs to face the consequences this time and I would be turning him in whether we were together or not."

My eyes widen. "You would?"

"Yes."

"And where does that leave us?"

He pulls me closer and I melt into his body as the ache that's been plaguing me for the past three days slips away. "I can't lose you, Quinn. Or Brooklyn. I've spent the last three days drunk off my ass, trying to find a way around all of this but it just keeps coming back to one simple truth and that is - I'm not strong enough to walk away from you."

"I love you," I whisper. He smiles.

"I love you, baby."

He dips down and seals his lips over mine. My eyes flutter closed and my heart pounds like crazy in my chest as I reach up and wrap my arms around his neck, pulling him even closer. A deep rumble sounds in his chest as he grips my hips and flicks his tongue against my lips. They part for him. Groaning, he pushes my back up against one of the columns and slips a hand into my hair.

Someone clears their throat and we break apart, turning toward the front door as we both gasp for air.

"Nice to see you again, Lucas," Alice says with a shit eating grin on her face. Brooklyn squeals and reaches for Lucas from Alice's arms.

"Dada!"

He beams, pressing a kiss against my forehead before he releases me and bounds toward the door. She squeals again as he scoops her out of Alice's arms and tears well up in my eyes.

"There's my girl. Did you miss me?" he asks, digging his fingers into her belly and she giggles before cuddling into his neck.

"Dada."

A tear slips down my face and my cheeks ache from my smile as I wipe it away. There's something so damn special about seeing Lucas and my daughter together. It hits me right in the chest every time.

"So I take it this means y'all are good?" Alice asks and I turn to Lucas with an expectant expression. He saunters back over to me with Brooklyn still in his arm and reaches into his pocket. I gasp as he pulls out a large diamond ring and holds it up in front of me.

"I'm not asking you right now because you deserve a whole hell of a lot better than this but I just need you to know how serious I am, Quinn. I love you and I love your daughter like she is my own. There's no future for me that doesn't involve the two of you. You feel me, baby?"

I nod, beaming up at him. "Yeah, I feel you."

"Shit," Alice hisses, turning away from us as she wipes at her eyes and I laugh.

"Got something in your eye, Sis?"

She nods. "Yeah, fucking bug, I think."

Lucas and I laugh and Brooklyn joins in as we watch Alice flip us the bird and disappear into the house for a second. When she comes back out, any sign of her tears are gone and she reaches for Brooklyn.

"Let me take her. Y'all should probably get going."

My stomach flips as I glance up at Lucas. His face falls and I grab his hand as Alice takes Brooklyn.

"You okay?"

He blows out a breath and nods. "Yeah. It's not easy but I know it has to be done."

"You don't have to come with me, you know. I can do this alone if that would be easier for you."

"Absolutely not," he snaps with a scowl. "I'm not letting you go there without me by your side. I'm good with my decision."

I nod. "Okay."

"Good luck," Alice calls as we walk down the stairs and I peek over my shoulder as she waves and disappears into the house. Lucas is jittery as we climb in the truck and I sigh, worry eating away at me as we pull onto the street. He said he was good with this but I know it has to be hard. This is his brother we're turning in and despite what he said, I can see the hesitance in his eyes.

"Lucas."

He glances over at me. "Yeah?"

"Thank you for doing this."

"Of course, gorgeous," he answers, reaching across the seat and grabbing my hand. I want to tell him that he doesn't have to again but the closer we get to the police station, the more my nerves kick in and I'm thankful that he's here with me.

I just hope he doesn't come to regret it.

We park in front of the station and climb out of the truck before meeting on the sidewalk and he takes my hand, giving it a squeeze as we walk up the front steps. A young officer looks up from the front desk as we walk in.

"Can I help you?"

Lucas nods. "We need to speak to Detective Rodriguez."

"Have a seat and I'll let him know you're here."

He leads me over to the waiting area and I turn to him as he sits down next to me. "Who is Detective Rodriguez?"

"Someone the club works with. I called him earlier and he'll take good care of you."

"Okay," I whisper, my heart pounding as memories of that night flick through my mind. Reaching over, I grab his hand and he slips his arm around my back.

"You okay?"

I nod. "Yeah. Just remembering that night a lot since

the baby shower."

"I'm so sorry, baby," he says, kissing the side of my head and squeezing my hand. Just like the moment we first met, his touch sends a feeling of peace washing over me and I close my eyes to just soak it in.

"Smith," a gruff voice calls. My eyes snap open and I turn to look at the man standing in a doorway off to the side of the front desk. Lucas stands up and pulls me with him as he flashes me a reassuring smile. We walk across the lobby and Lucas shakes the detective's hand.

"Diego, this is my girl, Quinn. Quinn, this is Detective Diego Rodriguez."

I smile and extend my hand. "It's nice to meet you."

"You, too," he answers with a nod before gesturing for us to follow him. "Right this way."

He leads us back to a large room filled with rows of desks and stops at the first desk in the first row, grabbing a file off the top.

"Let's go talk in a private room."

I nod and we follow him down a hallway lined with doors. He opens the last one on the left and holds it open for us as Lucas and I file into the small interview room. As Detective Rodriguez sits across from us and opens the file, I suck in a breath and Lucas squeezes my hand again.

"Okay, Miss Dawson, when Smith called, he told me there was an update to your case but why don't you tell me what brings you in today?"

I nod. "The man who raped me... I know who he is now."

"I see," Rodriguez says, jotting down something on a notepad before glancing up at me. "And how did you find out who he is?"

I glance over at Lucas and he nods. "Lucas took me to a baby shower at the clubhouse and I saw him there."

Rodriguez's gaze flicks to Lucas before turning back to me.

"Who was it?"

I open my mouth to tell him but no words come out so I snap it shut again as I suck in a breath.

"It's my brother, Diego," Lucas tells him and both of the detective's eyebrows shoot up toward his hairline.

"Come again."

"Clay is the man who raped her."

"Is this true?" Rodriguez asks, turning to me and I nod with tears in my eyes as images of that night flick through my mind.

"Yes."

Rodriguez drops his pen on the table and blows out a breath. "Shit... I'm, uh..." he sighs. "I'm going to need you to go over the statement you gave two years ago again and then we'll get him in here for a formal line-up."

I nod. "Okay."

"You can take my DNA, too. For a familial match," Lucas adds and I gasp as my gaze flicks between the detective and the man I love. Rodriguez stares at him for a second before shaking his head.

"Are you sure about that, man? Are you sure about all of this?"

He nods. "Yeah, I am. All this time, I've been trying to save my brother and turns out, I've just been enabling him. And now he's not just hurting himself but hurting other people as well. This is what has to be done. Who the hell knows, maybe going to jail will be just the thing he needs to turn his life around."

A feeling of unease settles over me as Rodriguez nods but I push it down, focused on finally getting justice after all this time. Rodriguez nods.

"All right, then. Let's do this."

*   *   *   *

"You okay?" Lucas asks as we pull into the driveway and I nod, avoiding his gaze. I've been quiet ever since we left the station because I know as soon as I open my mouth, the floodgates are going to burst free. All through the interview, as I told my story again and answered all the detective's questions, my heart felt heavy for reasons that I couldn't understand and as Lucas offered up his

DNA to match the sample in my rape kit, my stomach was uneasy but it wasn't until we were leaving and Lucas told Rodriguez that he hoped his brother would get the help he needed that I realized why. Lucas may have decided to turn his brother in and accompany me to the police station but our problems are far from solved and it hit me that, as much as I wish it wasn't, this relationship may be past saving. Which is especially hard since neither one of us did anything to deserve this.

Things would be so much easier if either one of us was to blame for our demise.

"Where's Alice and Brooklyn?" Lucas asks as we climb out of the truck and he scans the driveway.

"Alice took her to the park."

On our way home, I texted Alice and told her I needed the house to myself for a little while. She was all too eager to comply. No doubt, her mind went right to the gutter. God, I wish that were the case instead of the conversation I have to initiate right now.

"What's going on with you, Quinn? You've been weird since we left the station."

I glance up at him. "We should talk inside."

"Hey," he urges, pulling me into his body at the base of the stairs. Just like every other time, his touch makes me melt but I have to fight it. "Just tell me what's going on? Is it just going over everything again that's got you so upset?"

Tears fill my eyes as I look up at him and shake my

head. "Can we please go inside?"

He nods and wraps his arm around my shoulders as we walk up the steps. I soak up his touch. I wish I could bottle the feeling so that, after today, when he's gone and the nights feel impossibly long, I can open it up and let my heart not feel so damn broken for a moment.

"All right, we're inside now. Tell me what's going on," he says as he closes the door behind us and I shake my head, butterflies flapping around in my belly.

"We should go sit down."

He pulls me into his arms, a scowl twisting his handsome face. "I don't want to sit down, Quinn. I want to know what's going on with you."

"Please," I plead, barely holding the tears at bay. He searches my eyes for a second before he sighs and nods. Releasing me, he follows me as I walk into the kitchen. Glancing at the barstools, I know I'm too antsy to sit so I position myself on one side of the island and suck in a breath.

"I… don't think this is going to work," I whisper, my chest aching like nothing I've ever felt before and my eyes burn with tears. He stops in his tracks, studying my face.

"What the hell are you talking about?"

A tear falls down my cheek and I quickly wipe it away. "I think the…issues with your brother are too big for us to overcome."

"No, they're fucking not. Do you not remember me

standing out on that porch only a few hours ago and telling you that I have no future without you?"

"I wish that was enough, Lucas."

His brows furrow. "What do you mean it's not enough? It's everything."

"How do you see this working out?" I ask and he shakes his head.

"What do you mean?"

My throat burns and my chest aches as my entire body screams for him to charge across the room and wrap his arms around me but if he did that, I know I would crumble.

"Obviously, your brother is going to jail for a while but what do you see for us after that? Do I have to endure family dinners with my rapist? Are you going to sneak around to see him and lie to me about it? Or will you resent me for taking him away from you?"

He shakes his head, dropping his gaze to the floor for a second. "I hadn't thought about it all that much."

"Well, I have."

"What are you saying?" he asks, meeting my gaze again, and I wipe away a few more tears as they streak down my face.

"I'm saying that as much as we want this to work, I don't see how it can." The words taste like vinegar on my tongue and my body feels cold as I think about the obstacles in front of us. There are no good choices here. Every road I gaze down just leads to more heartbreak and it kills me. He shakes his head and rounds the island, pulling me into his arms.

"Don't talk like that, baby. We'll figure something out. I love you."

Yanking myself out of his grip, I back up and shake my head. Why does he have to keep saying the things that will make this hurt more? The tears are falling faster now but I don't care. "No, we won't just figure it out, Lucas. You came here this morning and said you couldn't walk away from me but I don't think you can walk away from your brother either and I can't live my life knowing the monster who tore my whole world apart could pop up at any moment. It would be hell."

"He's not a monster, baby. I know what he did to you was disgusting and horrific but that's not who he is."

A sob slips past my lips and I cover my mouth, trying desperately to regain some control over my emotions. I meet his eyes. "To me, he is always going to be a monster."

"Stop calling him that," he growls, shaking his head as he backs away from me.

"I can't!" I yell through my tears. "He's a monster in my eyes and I'm the bitch tearing two brothers apart. Those are our roles. Why can't you see that?"

He blows out a breath and begins pacing back and forth across the floor, running his hand through his hair. "What the hell do you want me to do?"

"Nothing," I whisper, my heart shattering into a

million pieces. "There's nothing you can do."

His blue gaze snaps to mine and he shakes his head. "No, don't you dare say that. I love you, Quinn."

Goddamn it.

"And I love you," I mumble, fighting back another sob. "But it's not enough."

"Shut up!" he shouts, crossing his arms over his chest as he resumes his pacing. "Don't say that. I've never fucking felt this way about anyone before so it means everything. We'll figure this out. Just don't give up on us, baby."

"Nobody wins here, Lucas. No matter what we do, we all lose."

"Okay," he breathes, stopping next to the island and bracing his hands on the top. I can see the indecision tearing him apart. "I'll cut him out of my life. For good."

Tears pour down my face and I shake my head. "I can't let you do that. He's your brother and the only family you have left. What kind of person would I be to claim to love you one moment and then demand you kick your only brother to the curb in the next?"

"What the fuck do you want me to do then?" he yells, his eyes locking with mine, desperate. It breaks another piece of me. "Just tell me what to do, Quinn, and I'll fucking do it. But don't tell me that I have to lose you because I can't fucking do that!"

"I'm so sorry, Lucas."

Fire lights up his gaze and he shakes his head as he

closes the distance between us and grabs my arms, pulling me into his body. "No! This is not over."

"I don't see any other way," I whisper, my body feeling weak as my chin trembles. I don't have much strength left. He shakes his head again. "Please don't make this harder than it has to be."

"Are you insane? I'm being fucking ripped in half by my love for you and my loyalty to my brother," he seethes, taking a step back as he grips his t-shirt and pulls it away from his body like he might rip it off. "It literally feels like the two of you are tearing me apart and I don't know what to do. If I choose you, I lose the only family I have left and if I choose him, I lose the only woman I've ever loved."

I nod, another sob slipping past my lips. "Which is why I'm choosing for you. I love you enough to let you go and I meant everything I said in that message yesterday. I don't blame you for any of this. I'm so grateful that I met you."

"Don't you dare say good-bye to me," he growls, yanking me back into his body. "I told you, I can't walk away from you. I don't know how."

"You are the most incredible man I've ever met," I continue, brushing my fingers over his cheek and his eyes plead with me to stop. "And I am always going to love you but there is no future for us."

He stares at me for a second before releasing me and taking a step back. It feels like the world just dropped out from underneath me and even though I'm the one ending things, it still kills me. His eyes narrow into a glare and he opens his mouth like he might say something else before turning and storming out of the house. As the front door slams shut, I collapse into a heap on the kitchen floor and sob, my whole body shuddering as my cries echo through the empty house - reminding me of how alone I truly am.

Guess I'd better get used to it.

A.M. Myers

It Ends Tonight

Chapter Twenty-One
Lucas

"Smith?" Fuzz asks, flipping on the light over the bar and I squint as I glance over my shoulder at him. "It's two in the morning. What the hell are you doing, man?"

I shake my head. "Nothing."

"You drinking?" His gaze falls to the full glass of whiskey on the bar in front of me and I shake my head.

"Thought about it but no."

He sits on the stool next to me and claps my shoulder. "What's going on, brother?"

"Oh, you know, just my whole world falling apart."

"Quinn?" he asks and I nod. "What happened at the station?"

"She went over her statement from two years ago and I gave them my DNA to match my brother's in the rape kit and then we left."

His eyes narrow, years of being a cop engrained in everything he does. "Okay, what happened after that?"

"I drove her home and she decided to try and break up with me."

"Why?"

I throw my hands up in the air. "Fuck if I know. Something about how there being no future for us because of my brother."

"Shit, man. I'm sorry."

Shaking my head, I turn to him. "No. Don't do that. She may think this is over but it isn't. I just gotta figure out a way to fix things."

"Dude, I know you care about her but you have to see things from her perspective. This whole situation is beyond fucked up. What is she supposed to do?"

"Are you on her side?" I snarl and he sighs.

"Do you plan on cutting your brother out of your life entirely?"

"Maybe."

He scoffs. "Don't give me that shit. We've all watched you rip yourself apart for the last few years for him and now you're just going to walk away? I don't think so."

"See, that's what I've been thinking about all night long. Yeah, Clay is my brother but besides a shared past, what do I get out of our relationship? What would my life look like if he was clean and is it enough to make giving up the only woman I've ever loved worth it? I don't know... but I can see my future without her and it looks like fucking shit."

"So," he muses. "That's it, then."

I blow out a breath. "No, that's not fucking it because I still feel guilty as hell for even thinking about turning my back on him."

"Look, I will say that if you decide to cut ties with your brother, you never once turned your back on him. In fact, you've taken metaphorical beating after beating from him for years but the simple truth is this - you have to choose. It's either Quinn or Clay. You can't have both."

"Yeah," I mutter as my phone rings and I pull it out of my pocket. "I know."

Quinn's name flashes on the screen and my heart jumps into my throat as I answer it.

"Babe?"

"Lucas, it's Alice..."

My gaze flicks to Fuzz's as my stomach sinks. "Alice, why do you have Quinn's phone?"

"Uh... Quinn and Brooklyn are missing. I know something happened between the two of you yesterday but I thought you'd want to know."

"I'm on my way," I snap into the phone before hanging up and Fuzz stands as I grab my bike keys off the bar.

"What's going on?"

"That was Quinn's sister Alice. Quinn and her

daughter are missing and I've got to get over there."

He nods and stands. "I'm coming with you. Lead the way."

We rush out of the clubhouse and jump on our bikes before peeling out of the parking lot. As I fly through the streets of Baton Rouge, my heart hammers in my chest and my mind races with scenarios. What the hell happened after I left earlier? I wish I had asked Alice before hanging up the phone but I'll find out soon enough.

Red and blue lights blind me as I pull up to Quinn's house and I barely get the kickstand down before I'm jumping off my bike and running up the front steps.

"Lucas," Alice calls as I reach the front door and I turn to the swing where she's sitting with tears running down her face. Fuzz joins me on the porch and we walk over to her.

"What happened, Alice?"

She sucks in a stuttered breath. "I'm so sorry, Lucas. I shouldn't have left her."

"What do you mean?" I ask, sitting next to her on the swing and she wipes away a few tears.

"When I got home from the park with Brooklyn earlier, I found Quinn crying on the kitchen floor but she wouldn't tell me what happened. She just said that she wanted to be alone."

Fuck. I never should have left her.

What the hell was I thinking?

"What happened after that?" Fuzz asks and Alice glances up at him before turning to me. I nod to let her know he's okay and she sighs.

"She somehow convinced me to go out to dinner and a movie with my friends so she could be alone with Brooklyn. When I got home an hour ago, the front door was wide open and they were just gone. Her purse and her phone were still sitting on the island and she was just...gone."

"Jesus," I breathe, dropping my head into my shaking hands as my heart thunders in my chest. Fuck. Where could she be? I think back over the past few weeks, searching for clues or signs that she was in danger but nothing stands out to me.

"There's one more thing," Alice whispers and I meet her gaze as fresh tears drip down her cheeks.

"When I called the police, they found blood in the entry and the kitchen. They said whatever happened here, she put up one hell of a fight."

"Smith. Fuzz," someone says and I glance up as Rodriguez walks toward us, his face somber.

"Please tell me you've got something."

He presses his lips into a thin line. "I have a theory but you're not going to like it."

"What?" I ask, scowling when it dawns on me. I shake my head. "You mean my brother? No... Why would he do this?"

He arches a brow. "You mean besides the fact that

she identified him as her rapist only hours ago? How about the fact that the results from the DNA test came back? It was a match, Smith. I was going to send some deputies out to pick him up in the morning."

I shake my head. "He didn't know about that yet, though, did he? It has to be something or someone else."

"Well, did you see anything when you were watching the house?" Alice asks and I turn to look at her.

"What?"

"When you and Quinn weren't talking and you were sitting out front in your truck, did you see anything weird?"

I shake my head, trying to piece together what she's saying to me but it doesn't make sense. For the most part of those three days, I was drunk off my ass but was I really stupid enough to drive over here and sit out in front of Quinn's house? No, I wouldn't do that. I glance up at Fuzz for confirmation and he shrugs.

"Oh my god," Alice whispers. "It wasn't you, was it?"

Shit.

"Clay," I murmur, shaking my head again before dropping it into my hands. I shouldn't be surprised that he stole my truck since this isn't the first time but it still knocks the wind out of me. What kind of fucking game is my brother playing right now?

"Where would he go, Smith?" Rodriguez asks. "Where would he take them?"

I shake my head. "He's got his usual hangouts but I don't know where he would take them if he wanted privacy."

"Well, give me a list and I'll send guys to check each one."

I nod and start listing places Clay likes to hang out at when the boxcar we lived in as kids pops into my head. No, he wouldn't take her there… would he? Right? Blowing out a breath, I stare down at the boards of the porch. At this point, I think it's safe to say that I have absolutely no idea what my brother would or wouldn't do but if he is there, I need to find him first.

As Rodriguez and his men leave to start searching, I stand and grab my keys from my pocket.

"Lucas?" Alice asks and I turn back to her. Worry streaks across her face and I force a reassuring smile to my face.

"I'm going to go look, too. Don't worry, Alice. We'll find them."

Fuzz steps forward. "You want company, brother?"

"Naw, you stay here and keep an eye on her." I motion to Alice and he nods, leaning back against the house as he crosses his arms over his chest, scanning the yard in front of the house.

"Call if you need anything. I'll let Blaze know what's going on."

I nod and jog down the stairs to my bike with a pit in my stomach. As much as I don't want to believe it, I know that Clay's got them. I can't explain it but somehow, I know. I just hope I can get there before he does something that will destroy us all.

The roar of the bike does nothing to drown out my thoughts as I fly toward Iris's house and I can't get rid of the awful sinking feeling in my stomach every time I think about Clay taking Quinn and Brooklyn. It doesn't make any sense. Why the hell would he take them? If he found out about Quinn turning him into the cops, his best bet would be to run or hide out, not kidnap the two of them. Then again, maybe nothing makes sense in his head anymore. Maybe he's done so many drugs that they've just eaten away at his brain. If that's true though, there's no telling how far he'll take this or what he'll do to my girls.

Please let them be all right, a little voice in my head whispers.

I speed up but it still doesn't feel fast enough and I'm praying with each breath I pull into my lungs that I get there before Clay does something else that he can't take back.

When I get close to Iris's house, I park along the road and cut the engine. With any luck, I'll be able to sneak up on them and keep Clay from overreacting. Shit, what if he's not even here? Where else would he go? Sending up a prayer to a God I haven't believed in since the night Mom died, I hope my brother still has a piece of the old Clay left inside him.

It Ends Tonight

The crickets and frogs greet me as I jog through the trees and as soon as the outline of the boxcar comes into view, it takes me back to all those years ago when I saw it for the first time. Clay and I had been walking all night and he was getting upset, asking questions that I couldn't answer yet, when he spotted it and begged me to stay there. That first night, neither one of us slept all that well but I felt safe for the first time in a long time and that meant everything. And then for weeks afterward, we did whatever it took to survive because that was all that mattered back then.

Fuck, how the hell did everything go so wrong?

As soon as I get close, I hear Brooklyn crying. My chest tightens and fear races up my spine as I creep along, making as little noise as possible in an attempt to catch him off guard.

"You don't have to do this," Quinn pleads, tears in her voice. The sound clouds my vision as my heartbeat thunders in my ears. I'm not above knocking my brother on his ass. In fact, after everything he's done, it's the very least that he deserves. Shit, if he was anyone else, I would have put a bullet in his skull a long damn time ago.

"Just shut up!" Clay screams and Brooklyn's cries grow louder, triggering something inside me. All I can think about is protecting her as I burst through the trees and jump into the boxcar, surprising all three of them. Quinn lets out a shriek. Her hands are tied together in front of her and she has a cut across her cheek and a swollen lip that makes me see red as I turn to my brother. Clay turns to me with Brooklyn in one arm as he points a gun at me with his other hand.

"Lower the gun, Clay."

His face drops and the gun falls to his side but his finger stays on the trigger as I slowly step toward him.

"Why are you doing this?" I ask and he shakes his head.

"I can't believe it. The proof, Luke. The proof!"

I nod, my gaze flicking to Quinn's tear stained face for a second before turning back to my brother. "What proof, Clay?"

"The proof!" he screams, waving the gun in the air as he meets my eyes. I suck in a breath. His gaze is glassy and vacant as he stares at me and I shake my head.

"You don't look so good, brother. How much did you take this time?"

He shakes his head and begins pacing as Brooklyn reaches for me.

"Dada!" she wails. Her wobbly lip and terrified eyes rip my heart right from my chest and I'd do anything to get her away from Clay right now. Taking a deep breath, I remind myself to take it slow and steady so no one gets hurt even though every cell in my body is screaming at me to act now.

"It's okay, baby girl," I whisper to her, offering her a smile, but she just cries harder. "Clay, let me have the baby."

He glances down in his arms like he's just realizing that she's there and stares at her for a second before he shakes his head and looks back up at me.

"She's mine."

"No," I answer, shaking my head slowly as I struggle to keep my voice calm. As soon as I met Quinn and Brooklyn, I felt something settle inside me, like this little girl and her mama were always meant to be mine and it doesn't sit well to hear my brother claim her. "She's not."

His brows furrow. "Yes, she is! She's my daughter."

"She'll never be yours!" Quinn yells, struggling against the rope tied around her wrists and I flash her a pleading look as Clay turns to look at her. He lets out an animalistic yell before marching across the boxcar and pointing the gun against her temple.

"Shut up, bitch!"

"Clay," I snap, my heart jumping into my throat as my thoughts screech to a halt.

No.

No.

No.

"Don't you dare hurt her, you hear me?"

His arm goes slack at my tense tone and he nods, taking a few steps back as he whispers, "Everything is wrong, Luke."

"How is it wrong?"

"Dada!" Brooklyn wails again and I can see Clay's patience wearing thin as he turns to look at the little girl in his arms with a scowl. I have to get her away from him. Once I do that, we can talk and I can calm him down but as long as she's crying, he's going to be impossible to reach.

"Hey, Clay," I say, talking softly as I take a tentative step forward. "Why don't you let me hold Brooklyn so she'll stop crying and we can talk? Okay?"

He studies me for a second before nodding and handing Brooklyn over to me. As soon as she's in my arms, her cries quiet and relief washes through me. I nod in encouragement.

"Okay, now tell me what's wrong."

He runs a hand through his long greasy hair as he blows out a breath. "He lied to me, Luke. He told me he was innocent but when I got my hands on the files, all the evidence…."

He gestures wildly to the corner of the boxcar and I spot an open file. Photos of our mother are splayed across the floor and I suck in a breath.

Oh, shit.

"Where did you get those?"

He shakes his head. "This officer at the station. She was nice to me whenever I was locked up and I asked her for help."

What the fuck?

Why would anyone, knowing how unstable my

brother is, give him that file?

"Clay," I whisper, taking another cautious step toward him. "It's okay. I know this isn't what you wanted but it's not the end of the world."

He meets my eyes and a single tear slips down his cheek. "I just want a family, Luke. Why can't I ever have a family?"

"You have me. I'm your family."

"No," he seethes, his gaze dropping to Brooklyn as she cuddles into my neck before he turns to look at Quinn. "You went and made yourself a new family to replace me. And you did it with my kid." He gestures to Brooklyn with the gun and I wrap my arm around her to shield her. "She's mine."

I shake my head. "You don't get to claim her. Not after what you did to her mama."

"What did I do to her?" he asks, turning to look at Quinn as she struggles to free her hands from the ropes. She freezes and meets my gaze as tears pour down her face. The pleading in her eyes pulls at my heart and it takes all my strength to keep my feet rooted to the ground. I have no clue how far Clay is willing to take this and I would never forgive myself if she got hurt because I didn't have the patience to handle this situation correctly. Turning back to my brother, I release a breath.

"You raped her, Clay. Don't you remember that?"

He jerks back with a scowl, studying me before he turns to look at her. "No...I didn't do that."

"Yes," she breathes and his gaze drifts back to her. "You did."

"I…" He turns to look at me, bewildered. "I wouldn't…"

"I was out with my friends," Quinn says, her voice hoarse as she meets Clay's eyes and holds steady. Goddamn, she's so strong. "And I went outside to get some fresh air when you pulled me into the side alley. You pushed my dress up and cut my panties off before forcing yourself inside me. When you were done, you smiled at me and left me lying on the ground, bleeding."

"No," he mutters, stumbling away from her before turning to me with a look of horror in his eyes. "No. I wouldn't… I didn't…"

"You did, Clay. I offered up my DNA to the police and it was a familial match to her rape kit."

He takes another step back like if he can just get far enough away from me, it will protect him from the truth and I sigh. Running his hands through his greasy hair, he shakes his head and starts muttering to himself.

"Oh my god, I'm him. I'm just like him. What have I done? What have I done?"

Fuck.

This is falling apart, fast.

I glance down at the little girl in my arms before running across the boxcar and placing Brooklyn in Quinn's lap. I make sure she gets her arms over her before marching back over to my brother and grabbing his arms.

"Hey, look at me."

His vacant gaze flicks to mine. It's like I'm staring at a ghost as he stares at me and I wonder if I'm already too damn late to save him.

"It's going to be okay," I whisper. "We need to go to the police but you can get through this."

He shakes his head, ripping free of my grip and taking a few steps backward. "I read all the police reports. Mom… she had bruises all over her body. Dad had been beating her for months and then, that night, he just lost it. I remember the yelling. I remember listening to him scream at her that night. And the photos… oh, God, the photos. Mom… she looked so broken and he did that to her. Dad killed her and I…" His voice cracks as he glances over at Quinn and Brooklyn. "I'm a monster, just like him."

"No," I force out through the tears building in my eyes. "You're not just like him. Listen to me, Clay. It's the drugs. This isn't who you are."

He nods, glancing back at Quinn before meeting my eyes again. "I hurt people… just like him. I don't deserve a second chance."

"Don't say that," I whisper, gritting my teeth. "I know who you are, deep down under all the drugs and pain, I know the kind of person you are and you're not a monster."

"I think she would have a different opinion," he

whispers, nodding to Quinn and my chest tightens. "I don't want to hurt anyone again, Luke. I don't want to be this person anymore."

"And you won't once we get you clean. You'll do your time and you'll get clean and you can start a new life that's better than all this."

He stares down at the floor for a long second before meeting my eyes and the certainty staring back at me scares the hell out of me. "No second chance, Luke. I'm already dead."

My world spins as he lifts the gun to his head and I freeze, unable to propel myself forward like my mind is screaming to and he smiles at me.

"I love you, big brother," he whispers and my heart hammers against my rib cage as tears well up in my eyes. I shake my head, taking a step forward but he pulls the trigger before I can reach him.

"No!" I scream, my voice echoing through the trees around us as Quinn's screams and Brooklyn's cries join my own.

His body slumps to the floor of the boxcar, his lifeless eyes staring back at me and I fall to my knees, gasping for air as the world spins and my stomach rolls.

No.

This can't be happening.

Not again.

It Ends Tonight

Chapter Twenty-Two
Quinn

Sighing, I wring my hands together and stare at myself in the mirror in front of me as I wait for Detective Rodriguez to come interview me. After Clay shot himself, I finally managed to get my hands free of the ropes. With Brooklyn in my arms, I had to crawl across the floor, careful to avoid Clay's blood, to a damn near comatose Lucas and pull his phone out of his pocket to call the police. Once they arrived, Brooklyn and I were loaded into an ambulance and checked over by the paramedics. By the time they were done, Lucas was gone and we were carted to the station to give our statements. They let me call Alice so Brooklyn didn't have to spend anymore time here, which is good since I've been waiting here for a couple hours, at least.

My heart aches as I remember the look on Lucas's

face while we waited for the police to show up and tears well up in my eyes. God, I can't imagine what he's going through right now and all I want to do is pull him into my arms.

The door to the room swings open and a haggard looking Detective Rodriguez walks in with several files in his hand. I quickly wipe away my tears and sit up straight as he sinks into the chair across from me.

"I'm so sorry to keep you waiting, Miss Dawson," he says, setting a notepad down on the table in front of him as he places the files off to the side.

"It's okay."

He nods with a heavy sigh. "Before we go over what happened last night, let me just ask... are you okay?"

"Uh... I don't even know what that word means at the moment," I admit and he nods, rubbing his hand over his face before he flips open the notepad.

"Right. Well, can you go over what happened from the time Mr. Julette showed up at your house?"

"Sure," I breathe, nodding. "I was sitting on the couch and Brooklyn was asleep in my arms when someone knocked on the door. I laid her in her playpen and answered the door. I didn't even see him at first because as soon as the door was open, he shoved the gun in my face and pushed into the house."

He nods, scribbling notes on the notepad. "And what time was this?"

"Around midnight."

"What happened after Mr. Julette pushed his way inside your residence?"

I suck in a breath. "I could tell pretty quickly that he was highly impaired…"

"You mean drugs?" he asks, interrupting me, and I nod.

"Yes."

Jotting down more notes, he nods. "Continue."

"Since he was so high, I thought I might be able to get the upper hand. I didn't want him anywhere near Brooklyn so I grabbed my sister's backpack from the foyer and swung it at him."

"Did it hit him?" he asks, glancing up at me in surprise. I nod.

"Yes. He yelled and stumbled back but he recovered faster than I expected him to and he charged me. He tackled me to the floor and hit me with the butt of the gun."

He flips through the notebook, reading some other notes before meeting my gaze. "How did you end up in the kitchen?"

"When he hit me," I mutter, wrapping my arms around myself as I relive the fear I felt in that moment, "I screamed and Brooklyn started to cry, which got his attention immediately. I didn't want him anywhere near her and we fought some more but I somehow managed to break free and run into the living room. I grabbed her from the playpen before moving to the kitchen."

"And he followed you?"

I nod. "Yes."

"What happened there?"

"He cornered us behind the island and demanded that I give him the baby. When I refused, he lifted the gun and fired at me."

He points to the bandage on my arm. "Is that how you got that?"

"Yeah, he just grazed me."

"What happened after that?"

I suck in a breath. "After he fired the gun, I was too scared to fight him anymore and I let him lead Brooklyn and me out to his car. From there, he drove us to the boxcar."

"Were your hands tied in the car or once you got to the woods?"

"In the car."

"Did he say anything to you on the way there?" he asks, not even glancing up as he writes and I shake my head.

"Just fragments of thoughts. He kept talking about the overwhelming evidence and how his father was a liar. He even started crying over his mom at one point."

"Did you know what he was referring to?"

I nod. "Yes, Lucas told me about what happened to their mother."

"At any point, did you try to reason with him?"

"Not really," I answer, shaking my head. "I did try at

one point but he just yelled at me to shut the fuck up and I was too worried about Brooklyn to press any further."

He looks up. "And once he got you to the boxcar, what happened?"

"He took Brooklyn," I whisper, my hands shaking as I remember watching Clay take my daughter from me. "And he left me on the floor while he kept ranting about evidence and his father lying to him."

"And how long were you there before Luke showed up?"

"I'm not sure. We drove around aimlessly for a while but an hour, maybe more… like I said, I'm really not sure."

"Did he say anything else during that time?"

I shrug. "Just more of the same."

"What about when Smith got there? Did they talk about anything?"

My mind drifts back to just a few hours ago and the fear is as real now as it was when I was sitting on the floor of that boxcar, watching Lucas try to talk Clay down. "Clay started talking about evidence again and how their father claimed he was innocent but that he'd seen the photos. Then, Lucas told him we had to go to the police because he'd raped me."

"How did he react to that?"

"He seemed like he had no idea what Lucas was talking about and after I told him what happened that night, he looked horrified. He called himself a monster and said he didn't deserve a second chance before shooting himself."

He sighs and tosses his pen down on the desk before rubbing his hand over his face and crossing his arms over his chest. "After Clay shot himself, what happened?"

"Lucas was… empty… He just kept staring at Clay's body with this blank look on his face." Just thinking about it breaks my heart. "I knew that we needed to call the police but no matter how much I tried to get his attention, Lucas was lost so after I freed my hands, I crawled over to him and dug his phone out of his pocket to call y'all."

"Okay," he breathes, nodding. "I think that's all we need for now. The doctor at the hospital sent along his report and it all matches up with your story."

I nod, my hands shaking. It has to be past six by now and I need to crawl into my bed and sleep for the next twenty-four hours.

"You're free to go. If I have any more questions, I'll call or stop by your house."

"Wait," I call as he stands. "I actually have a question."

He nods. "What is it?"

"How did Clay get the file on his mom's murder?"

Rodriguez lets out another heavy sigh and shakes his head. "Apparently, one of the officers took pity on Clay and thought if he knew the truth, he'd be able to finally move on and get clean. She gave him everything –

photos, statements from neighbors, forensic reports, court transcripts."

"I see," I whisper, my hands shaking from anger this time. Clay may have seen Brooklyn and me at the baby shower but learning what his father did is what pushed him over the edge. My daughter and I were in danger all because of this misguided officer.

"She's been put on leave while we sort this all out and I promise, it will be dealt with, Miss Dawson."

I nod and he turns to leave. Reaching out, I grab his arm. "Wait. Have you see Lucas?"

His face falls as he nods.

"How is he?" I ask, my stomach flipping and my heart racing. He opens his mouth to answer before snapping it shut again and shaking his head. Taking a deep breath, he flashes me a sympathetic look.

"Just give him time. He's still in shock."

"Could I see him?"

"He left already. Storm, Chance, and Moose picked him up an hour ago."

I nod. "Oh, okay."

"Listen, I don't know if this is any consolation given everything that's happened, but I know that he loves you. Like I said, just give him a little time."

*　　*　　*　　*

381

Frogs croak from the yard, joining the chirp of the crickets and I shudder, pulling the blanket tighter around me. I used to love that sound but I don't know if I'll ever be able to hear it again without picturing everything that happened in that boxcar four days ago.

"Quinn?" Alice calls from the front door and I glance up. "You okay?"

I force a smile to my face and nod. "Yeah. Is Brooklyn asleep?"

"I think so. She fussed for a while but that's just cause she's missing Lucas so much." She walks out onto the porch and sits down next to me on the swing. "Have you heard from him?"

"No. And I don't expect to."

She wraps her arm around me and pulls me into a hug. "I wouldn't give up on him just yet."

"Not if I have anything to say about it," a voice calls and I glance up as Tate walks up the front steps.

"Tate," I say, forcing yet another smile. "What brings you by?"

"Well, if you wipe that fake ass smile off your face, I'll tell you."

My face falls and relief washes through me as she leans back against the house and sinks to her butt.

"That's better. How are you feeling?"

I shrug. "Numb."

The truth is, I've felt so many different emotions since that night that it's just easier to say numb than to describe my ever changing mood. On the one hand, my heart is breaking for not only myself but for Lucas, too, and on the other, I'm so goddamn angry at him. When we were in the boxcar, after he got Brooklyn away from Clay, I might as well have been invisible. Although, I don't know what else I expected. I always knew that he'd never be able to walk away from his brother and that night proved just that but it still hurt to watch as his only focus became Clay.

"Sounds like BS to me. How are you really feeling?"

"Anyone ever told you that you're pushy?" I grumble, pulling the blanket tighter around my body. She grins.

"Every day of my life. Now answer the question."

I sigh, dropping my gaze to the boards on the porch as I force back tears. "If you can name it, I've probably felt it in the last few days."

She nods in understanding. "That's better."

"Have you seen Lucas?" I ask, hope filling my chest as I glance up at her and she nods.

"He's a goddamn mess but I also think he's a little relieved - not that he'd ever admit that to anyone. As long as I've known him, he's always been worried about his brother and although he loved him and he's sad, I think he feels free, too."

"Which means he feels guilty," I supply and she nods.

"That, too. I've been trying to knock some sense into

him but the man is stubborn. You're the only one who has ever been able to get through to him."

Memories from just a few short weeks ago pop into my mind and I fight back tears. Maybe I was able to get through to him before but at this point, I doubt he'll ever want to see me again. Too much has happened.

"I hope he'll be able to find a way to be happy again…someday."

Tate arches a brow. "Why the hell are you talking like it has nothing to do with you?"

"Yeah," Alice adds, scowling. "Lucas is crazy in love with you, Quinn."

"Look at everything that has happened, you guys. It's too much for any relationship to survive, let alone one that was just starting."

"No, you're wrong," Tate urges, shaking her head. "He fucking loves you, even if he does have his head up his own ass right now."

I sigh and close my eyes. "Look, I'm not expecting anything from him, okay? He just watched his brother die in front of him and it was all my fault. I can't blame him for wanting nothing to do with me."

"Hold the fuck up," Tate growls. "Why the hell do you think this is your fault?"

"What she said," Alice adds, pointing to Tate as she glares at me. Memories from that night flash through my mind and tears well up in my eyes.

"Clay didn't know what he had done to me. He had

no idea that he had raped me and when we told him, he was horrified. He called himself a monster and said he didn't deserve a second chance."

"Shit," Tate breathes, shaking her head. "Despite that, Clay had so many issues and you were not the cause of his death. If you want to blame someone, blame their good for nothing daddy. Bastard is going to rot in hell for what he put Clay and Lucas through."

"Maybe I shouldn't have told him about the night he raped me… Maybe I should have just kept my mouth shut."

"Listen to me," Alice snaps, grabbing my face and directing my gaze toward her. "None of this was your fault. You were just another victim in a tornado of destruction that started damn near twenty years ago. I don't want you blaming yourself."

"Doesn't really matter if I blame myself if Lucas does."

Tate shakes her head. "No. He's going through a whole heap of shit right now but there's no way in hell that he blames you."

"Exactly."

"Then where is he, you two? He once said that being around me was the only thing that ever gave him any peace but now that he needs peace more than he ever has before, he's not here. What does that tell you?"

"That he's an idiot," Tate argues, rolling her eyes. "All men are when it comes to serious shit like this. He doesn't know how to fucking deal so he's hiding out at the clubhouse and drinking himself into a stupor. Give him a few more days and he'll realize that the thing he needs to ease some of his pain is the woman he loves and he'll come running home."

"I really wish I could believe that," I whisper, gazing out at the front yard as tears well up in my eyes again. "But this feels like the end for us."

Tate scoffs as she jumps up. "You know what, I'm going back to the clubhouse now to kick his ass some more and I'm going to remind you of this conversation on y'all's wedding day. In fact, I might even do a whole speech about it."

"I'll help you write it," Alice adds and Tate grins.

"Perfect. See y'all later."

We watch her leave and as she car pulls out of the driveway, I sigh.

"You want to try watching a movie or something?" Alice asks and I shake my head, pulling the blanket tighter around me.

"No. I'm just going to sit out here a while longer."

She sighs as she stands. "Tate's right, you know. Lucas is coming back and you're going to have to eat your words."

"I admire your optimism."

"Fine," she grumbles. "Keep being stubborn but we're right. You and Lucas have the kind of love that doesn't die. I know it."

"Anyone ever told you that love sometimes isn't enough?" I ask, arching a brow in annoyance and she shakes her head.

"No. Love is everything, Quinn. And it's going to bring Lucas back to you. Mark my word."

I shake my head, tears welling up in my eyes again as I try to ignore the tiny little spark of hope in my heart. It's dangerous and I can't possibly afford to embrace it. Not when there's still a huge possibility that I could lose everything.

A.M. Myers

It Ends Tonight

Chapter Twenty-Three
Quinn

Alice eyes me skeptically as I stand up from the couch and toss the blanket back down on the cushion. "Are you sure you want to go into work again?"

"Yeah," I answer with a sigh. "I can't keep sitting around here, thinking about everything that happened. It will drive me crazy. Besides, Willa said that we've had a lot of interest after the charity gala so I'll have plenty of work to keep me busy."

"You don't have to act so strong, Quinn. I know this is killing you."

I shrug, tears welling up in my eyes. Turning away from her, I fight them back, unwilling to cry over this any more. "What other choice do I have? My daughter needs me and I have a business to run. It's time to get back to real life."

"So that's it? You're just giving up?"

"It's been a week since Clay died, Al. How long am I supposed to wait?"

She scowls. "Just because you're going back to work and getting back to your life doesn't mean you have to give up on him. Give him more time."

"It hurts too much. Each morning, I hope that today will be the day he shows up and then each night, I feel heartbroken all over again when he doesn't show."

"Have you thought about going to see him?"

I nod. "I have."

"Then why haven't you? For all we know, he's sitting at the clubhouse thinking that you don't want anything to do with him."

I press my lips into a thin line and shake my head. "He knows."

"How?"

"I've sent him a few messages, letting him know I was here if he wanted to talk."

She smiles, hope filling her eyes. "And? Did he ever text you back?"

"No. Like I said, it's time to move on."

"Quinn," she calls as I walk out of the room and I shake my head.

"Enough, Alice."

She steps into the foyer, calling my name but I ignore her as I start up the stairs to shower and get ready for work. God, I don't want to do this but I'm just hoping that if I force myself to go, it will slowly start to get better.

"Quinn!" Alice yells and my gaze jerks to her in the middle of the foyer. She's staring out of the front window and I turn, gasping at the sight of Lucas standing in front of the stairs, looking up at the house. There are dark circles under his eyes and his t-shirt is wrinkled like he's spent the last couple days in it, at least, but even in his sadness, he looks so damn handsome I could cry.

"What do you think he wants?" I ask and Alice scoffs.

"Only one way to find out."

My heart thunders in my chest as I stare out the window and shake my head. "No, I can't."

"You have to," Alice hisses. "This is what you've been waiting for."

She runs into the living room and I suck in a breath as I watch him. He hasn't moved from his place at the base of the stairs and it scares me that he hasn't moved. Shit, what if he's here to end things? Alice walks back in with the blanket I discarded on the couch and tosses it to me. I catch it, glancing down at my tank top and sleep shorts.

"Go talk to him."

My belly flips as I nod and walk back down the stairs before throwing the blanket around my body. My heart races and my palms sweat as I stop in front of the door and suck in a breath.

"Whatever happens, Sis, it's going to be okay."

I nod, despite the pit in my stomach. "Right."

"You can do this," she whispers and I nod again, gripping both edges of the blanket in one hand as I take a deep breath and open the door.

Lucas's gaze flicks to mine and my knees almost buckle as I step out onto the porch, closing the door behind me.

"Hi, Lucas," I whisper, my hands trembling violently.

"Hey, baby," he answers, a hint of a smile teasing his lips and I swallow a little bit of my fear as I take another step toward him.

"What are you doing here?"

He drops his head. "I suppose I deserve that."

"No, you don't…I just… I don't know what else to say…"

He nods in understanding as he slowly walks up the three steps between us. When he stops in front of me and meets my gaze, I gasp at the tears shining in his eyes. "This past week has been one of the absolute worst of my life. I've been drunk off my ass, fighting with anyone who tried to help me, and angry at the whole damn world. It wasn't until last night that I realized the thing I needed the most to make me feel better was the one thing I was avoiding."

"Which is?"

"You, sweetheart," he whispers, reaching up and brushing his thumb over my cheek. His touch sends goose bumps racing across my skin and my eyes drift closed as I let it sink in. "It's always been you."

"I don't know how you can even look at me."

"Quinn," he chastises. "I love you. Looking at you is one of my favorite damn things. Why would that be any different now?"

I grab his hand and press it against my cheek as I look up at him. "You know why."

"Tate mentioned something about you thinking that I blamed you but I had hoped that she was wrong."

"It's just..." I start, my lip wobbling. "If I hadn't confronted him about what he did to me... maybe he wouldn't have..."

"Stop right now," he snaps, his gaze hard as he stares down at me. "This is the very last time I want to hear you say anything like this. You had every right to confront him. Every. Fucking. Right. And what he did, the turmoil that drove him to end his life... that was there long before either one of us ever laid eyes on you. This is *not* your fault."

"How are you so put together right now?" I ask, watching him in awe. Yes, he's sad - that's clear to anyone that looks at him but seeing him now, I have no doubt that he's going to be okay. He smiles and pulls me closer, wrapping his arms around me.

"Well, for starters, I'm holding you and like I told you when we first met, you make everything else melt away. Also because I know he's in a better place now. He's free of the drugs and the pain that weighed him down his entire life and I have to believe that Mom was waiting for him with open arms."

"I thought you would be…"

He lets out a humorless laugh. "Baby, there's a reason you haven't seen me all week. I've been to hell and back over everything that happened but I know I did everything I could for my brother. I have no regrets and like I said, he's at peace now. And, for what it's worth, so I am."

"I'm so sorry, Lucas. I never wanted this for you."

He smiles, pulling me closer and pressing a kiss against my forehead. "I know you didn't, baby, but like I said, I really am okay."

"I don't see how…"

"Look, it's sad and I'm going to miss him but I've been missing my brother for a very long time. The drugs ate away at so much of him that he hasn't been my brother for years and the worry I always carried around with me is gone now. As shitty as it sounds, I'm free now, too, and I think Clay would want that for me. There will probably be a piece of me missing for the rest of my life but that's been the case since the moment we met. I was just hanging on to the hope that I might get him back someday."

"And where does that leave us?"

"In exactly the same spot we were in the morning we went to the police. I love you, Quinn Dawson, and I'll tell you again, there is no future for me without you or

Brooklyn."

I shake my head and take a step back. "Everything is so complicated now."

"Really? Because I'd say things are less complicated now than they were before. I've lost my brother and I've got to learn to live with that but I can't lose you, too. You are everything to me, baby. You and that little girl inside."

I shake my head. "You really don't blame me?"

"The thought never even once crossed my mind, sweetheart."

"And you love me?" I ask, my hands shaking and my heart racing for a whole new reason now. He smiles.

"With every broken, twisted piece of my heart and soul."

I nod, studying him as I hold back a grin. "I guess there's only one thing left to do then."

"Yeah?" he asks, arching a brow. "What's that?"

"Kiss me."

He grins and pulls me closer. "Yes, ma'am."

A.M. Myers

It Ends Tonight

Epilogue
Quinn
Three Months Later

"Babe," Lucas drawls as he rounds the front of the truck and takes my outstretched hand. "You really don't have to do this with me. I don't want to upset you."

I glance up at the gravestones and turn back to him with a smile. "It's not upsetting me, Lucas. I'm here for you. Always."

"But after everything he put you through..." His voice trails off as his gaze flicks to Clay's grave. "I don't expect you to come with me."

Rolling my eyes, I grab the bouquet of flowers from the seat and close the door to the truck before turning toward the grave with his hand in mine. It won't do me any good to continue arguing with him - something I've learned countless times over the past three months. He's so careful not to say or do anything that might trigger memories in me that I have to show him that I really am okay before he will actually believe it.

"Let's go," I urge, stretching my arm out in front of us and he sighs. As we walks across the grass with the early morning dew still clinging to its blades, my mind drifts back to Clay's funeral. It was another instance where Lucas tried to keep me from going in an effort to protect me but I refused. Part of loving this man is standing by his side even when it's uncomfortable for me. Not that I didn't get anything from the service. As I listened to Lucas and Iris tell stories from Clay's childhood, something happened inside me - almost like he became two different people. The first, Lucas's little brother - a sweet, funny, charismatic boy who had been hurt more than any person ever should and the second, the man who was being eaten alive by that pain until he had no other choice but to lash out to free himself from some of it.

If I learned anything that night in the boxcar, it was that what Clay did to me was never about power or malice. It wasn't even all that sexual. He was just someone in a tremendous amount of pain and when he couldn't take it any more, he tried to find some comfort in something other than the drugs he had relied on for years but because of the drugs, he did something he never would have done sober. As the man I love said good-bye to his brother, I was able to forgive him - not only for myself but for Clay, too. I sincerely hope that Lucas was right. I hope Clay is free and finally at peace now somewhere beyond the clouds with their mother by his side.

Besides, in a weird turn of events, I suppose I'm even thankful for what he did.

Yes, it was horrific and the single worst thing I've ever experienced but through that night, I gained Brooklyn and no matter how she was conceived, she's been one of the biggest blessings in my life. Glancing over at the other biggest blessing I've found, I squeeze his hand and smile. I went through hell when Clay raped me but it led me here - to the family that I've always wanted and I couldn't be happier.

A.M. Myers

It Ends Tonight

Epilogue
Part Two
Lucas
One Month Later

"Shit," I whisper, my heart thudding in my chest as I wipe my sweaty hands on my jeans and stare down at the engagement ring I've been carrying around since before my brother died. I think I knew from the moment I met her that Quinn was the *One* but after everything that happened with my brother, I didn't want to rush anything. We both needed time to just settle into our new normal and damn, I'm so glad that I did.

About a week after Clay's funeral, Alice moved into her own apartment a few blocks away and I moved in with my girls. There's something to be said about the feeling of coming home to them after a long day with the club and for the life of me, I can't understand why I was so quick to laugh it off whenever Storm, Chance, or Kodiak talked about it before I met her. Hand to God, there is nothing better than the smile that spreads across my woman's face when she first sees me at the end of the day. It makes me feel like a goddamn king and that's why I know it's time to lock it down.

Well, that and the not so subtle hints that Alice has been dropping about Christmas being Quinn's favorite holiday and how perfect it would be if I proposed now.

I roll my eyes.

My new almost sister-in-law is about as subtle as a brick to the face. Actually, she reminds me a lot of Tate in that way.

"You ready?" Alice asks, poking her head into the room with Brooklyn in her arms.

"Dada!" she squeals, reaching for me and I grin as I strut across the room and scoop her out of Alice's arms. She's decked out in a red and white dress that makes her look like a little angel.

"Hey, gorgeous girl. You ready to surprise your mama?"

This morning, Brooke and I woke Quinn up with breakfast in bed before we all got dressed and did a little Christmas shopping downtown. When we just so happened to stumble upon the horse drawn carriage I had hired for the afternoon, I talked her into going for a ride around the city and I reveled in the look of complete joy on her face as we all cuddled together in the carriage.

Once we got home, I sent her off to have some "me time" and get her nails done as Alice instructed because apparently, it's a must that her nails be nice if I'm going to pop the question.

Whatever.

It gave me the perfect amount of time to set up my surprise in the garden but she's due back soon and we need to get out there.

"Nervous?" Alice asks with a grin and I shake my head.

"Naw. Your sister was made for me."

She laughs out loud and pats my cheek before turning away from me. "Oh, Lukie. I had you pegged from the start."

"What the hell is that supposed to mean?" I yell after her but she just laughs again and I sigh as I swipe the ring off the dresser and slip it into my pocket. Once we get outside, I set Brooklyn in the wagon Alice and I decorated to look like Santa's sleigh and I suck in a breath as I tuck the ring into the special ornament I had made to hold it. Alice lets out a whistle just as I'm hanging it on a nearby tree and my heart hammers against my chest as I wipe my hands again and turns toward the direction of the driveway.

"Alice?" Quinn says, her voice drifting from the front of the house and I hit the button for the first set of lights to come on. She gasps and I can't help but grin. "What the hell is going on here?"

"There's a surprise for you."

"Where's Lucas?" she asks and her sister laughs.

"So impatient," Alice teases. "Just follow the path."

I press the second button and the little candy canes light up on either side of the path as Quinn gasps again.

"What in the world are the three of you up to?" she asks as her voice grows closer and I lean down, scooping Brooklyn out of the wagon as I hit the last button and the entire garden springs to life - thousands of white twinkling lights casting a glow over the house and yard.

"Lucas," Quinn breathes as she rounds the back of the house and even in the dim light, I can see the tears in her eyes. "What is this?"

"Welcome home, baby," I call, smiling and she shakes her head as she closes the distance between us and glances down at Brooklyn's dress.

"What are you all dressed up for, baby girl?"

I laugh. "We have a surprise for you, Mama."

"You mean besides all this?" She motions to the lights hanging off the trees above us and I nod as I set Brooklyn on her feet and hold her little hand in mine. Quinn's gaze rakes down my chest before meeting my eyes with heat in her own. "You look real good, baby."

"Well, thank you, but that's not the surprise."

She wiggles in front of me, flashing me an impatient look that I know all too well. "Well, get to it, Smith. It's cold out here."

"Alice," I say and she steps out of the shadows to

take Brooklyn's hand with a smile on her face. She winks at me and I nod. Turning toward the tree next to me, I grab the ornate silver ornament I had designed and hold it up for Quinn to see. "This is for you."

Grinning, she takes a step toward me and reaches up, gently running her fingers across the surface of it. "It's gorgeous."

I can barely hear her over the rushing in my ears as I suck in a breath and meet her gaze. "You should open it."

"Open it?" she asks, scowling at me and I nod as I extend my hand. With her brows furrowed, she takes the ornament from my hand and inspects it for a second before gently lifting it open to reveal the ring I showed her months ago. Her shocked gaze flies to me and I smile. "Lucas?"

"Four months ago, I stood on our front porch and showed you that very same ring. Do you remember?"

"Of course," she breathes, her eyes watering at she watches me.

"I told you then that there was no future for me that didn't involve you and that little girl back there," I say, pointing to Alice and Brooklyn. "And it still holds true today. You and I… we've been through so much, baby, and we've managed to come out on the other side stronger than ever. Each day, you inspire me to be a better man, the kind of man you deserve to have by your side, the kind of man that little girl deserves to have for a daddy, and I'm so in awe of your strength and your incredible, beautiful heart. Just when I think I've got you all figured out, you do something that surprises the shit out of me and makes me love you even more." I step forward and take the ring out of the ornament as I grab her trembling hand. "I never would have gotten through the last few months if it hadn't been for you and your unconditional love, Quinn. You build me back up when I am weak and you make me believe in happy endings when the world has done all it can to break my faith." Smiling, I drop down to my knee and hold the ring up as tears run down her face. "I love you with every fucking piece of me, Quinn Evelyn Dawson. Please tell me you'll make me the happiest, luckiest son of a bitch alive and agree to be my wife?"

"God, yes," she whispers, holding her hand out to me and I slip the ring on her finger before standing and pulling her into a kiss so powerful it could keep these lights blazing all night long. Laughter and clapping greet us from Alice and Brooklyn and Quinn laughs as she pulls back, meeting my eyes. "I love you, you sweet, beautiful man."

"No more than I love you."

She's about to protest when I see Alice hand my second surprise off to Brooklyn and I press my finger to her lips.

"There's one more thing."

She quirks a brow. "Yeah? What's that?"

I turn her around and point to Brooklyn as she tottles

over to us with the envelope in her hands and Quinn peeks over her shoulder at me with a questioning expression.

"Is that for me, baby girl?" she asks, crouching down in front of Brooklyn, who squeals and hands her mama her second surprise. Quinn's gaze flicks from the envelope to me and back again as she peels it open and pulls the papers out, gasping.

"What?"

Holding my hand out, I wait until Brooklyn grabs it before lifting her into my arms. "If we're going to do this, we're going to do it right. Biologically, she may not be mine but in my heart, this little girl belongs to me. I love her almost as much as you do and I would be honored to adopt her as my own."

"Lucas," she gasps, crying as she covers her mouth with her hand. "Are you sure? You can't take this back. This is forever."

"Baby," I breathe, shaking my head. "When are you ever gonna learn…"

She smiles and pulls me closer. "You never say things you don't mean."

"So believe me when I say that this is what I want. Forever. And on my death bed, when I look back at my life and all the memories and love the three of us will share, I'll smile and tell anyone who'll listen that I lived a damn good life."

"Okay," she muses, smiling at her daughter before

her gaze flicks back to me. Heat dances in her eyes and my heart kicks in my chest. "Do you know what I'm going to say next, then?"

Grinning, I hook my arm around her waist and pull her into my body until my lips brush against hers. "Kiss you?"

"Get to it then, handsome. Now and for the rest of forever."

"Shit. You don't have to tell me twice, woman." I seal my lips over hers and she melts into me as she grips the lapels on my jacket and moans.

Fuck.

Yeah, if I get to spend the next seventy years doing this right here, I'll have absolutely no regrets.

The End

Follow Me:

Want to make sure you can stay up to date with me and never miss a new release again?? Follow me at any of the links below!

NEWSLETTER SIGNUP:

http://eepurl.com/cANpav

BOOKBUB:

https://www.bookbub.com/authors/a-m-myers

AMAZON:

https://www.amazon.com/A.M.-Myers/e/B00OPLCL20/ref=sr_tc_2_0?qid=1495847384&sr=8-2-ent

GOODREADS:

https://www.goodreads.com/author/show/3975855.A_M_Myers

FACEBOOK:

https://www.facebook.com/authorammyers/

TWITTER:

https://twitter.com/authorammyers

READER GROUP:

https://www.facebook.com/groups/585884704893900/

A.M. Myers

It Ends Tonight

Other Books by A.M. Myers

The Hidden Scars Series

- Hidden Scars:
https://www.amazon.com/dp/B014B6KFJE
- Collateral Damage:
https://www.amazon.com/gp/product/B01G9FOS20
- Evading Fate:
https://www.amazon.com/gp/product/B01L0GKMU0

Bayou Devils MC

- Hopelessly Devoted:
  https://www.amazon.com/dp/B01MY5XQFW
- Addicted to Love:
  https://www.amazon.com/dp/B07B6RPPPV
- Every Breath You Take:
  https://www.amazon.com/dp/B07DPNTV2G
- Little Do You Know: TBR February 2019
- Don't Let Me Down: TBR May 2019
- Every Little Thing: TBR: August 2019
- Wicked Games: February 2020

A.M. Myers

About the Author

A.M. Myers currently lives in beautiful Charleston, South Carolina with her husband and their two children. She has been writing since the moment she learned how to and even had a poem published in the sixth grade but the idea of writing an entire book always seemed like a daunting task until a certain story got stuck in her head and just wouldn't leave her alone. And now, she can't imagine ever stopping. A.M. writes gripping romantic suspense novels that will have you on the edge of your seat until the end.

When she's not writing, you can find her hanging out with her kids or pursuing other artistic ventures, such as photography or painting.

Made in the USA
San Bernardino, CA
10 November 2019

59713594R00231